PRAISE FOR THE DEBUT
MISS MORTON MYSTERY!

MISS MORTON AND THE ENGLISH HOUSE PARTY MURDER

"Smart and colorful sleuthing trio."
—*Publishers Weekly*

"A charming cross between a Regency romance and a well-constructed detective story with a surprising denouement."
—*Kirkus Reviews*

"An intriguing new series. . . . Caroline is an absolute gem of a heroine whom readers will surely come to love. Fans of historical mysteries and uncompromising women protagonists will find *Miss Morton and the English House Party Murder* impossible to put down."
—*Mystery Scene*

"An enjoyable read. If you're looking for a fun historical mystery, definitely give this a try."
—*Historical Novel Society*

Books by Catherine Lloyd

Kurland St. Mary Mysteries

DEATH COMES TO THE VILLAGE

DEATH COMES TO LONDON

DEATH COMES TO KURLAND HALL

DEATH COMES TO THE FAIR

DEATH COMES TO THE SCHOOL

DEATH COMES TO BATH

DEATH COMES TO THE NURSERY

DEATH COMES TO THE RECTORY

Miss Morton Mysteries

MISS MORTON AND THE ENGLISH HOUSE
PARTY MURDER

MISS MORTON AND THE SPIRITS OF THE
UNDERWORLD

MISS MORTON AND THE DEADLY
INHERITANCE

Published by Kensington Publishing Corp.

Miss Morton
and the
Spirits
of the
Underworld

CATHERINE LLOYD

KENSINGTON
PUBLISHING CORP.

www.kensingtonbooks.com

KENSINGTON BOOKS are published by

Kensington Publishing Corp.
900 Third Avenue
New York, NY 10022

All Kensington titles, imprints, and distributed lines are available at special quantity discounts for bulk purchases for sales promotion, premiums, fund-raising, educational, or institutional use.

Special book excerpts or customized printings can also be created to fit specific needs. For details, write or phone the office of the Kensington Sales Manager: Attn.: Sales Department. Kensington Publishing Corp., 900 Third Avenue, New York, NY 10022. Phone: 1-800-221-2647.

KENSINGTON and the K with book logo Reg. US Pat. & TM Off.

First Kensington Hardcover Edition: September 2023

ISBN: 978-1-4967-4063-2 (ebook)

ISBN: 978-1-4967-4062-5

First Kensington Trade Edition: August 2024

10 9 8 7 6 5 4 3 2 1

Printed in the United States of America

Miss Morton
and the
Spirits
of the
Underworld

Chapter 1

London 1838

Caroline Morton paused at the doorway to allow her employer's three small dogs to rush past her and claim their favorite spots on the hearthrug. Their owner followed them in, beaming as her favorite pug, Max, snuffled at her skirts.

"Shall I order some tea, ma'am?" Caroline inquired as she adjusted the curtains to prevent the afternoon sun from shining into Mrs. Frogerton's face.

"Yes, please." Mrs. Frogerton sat in her favorite chair and fanned herself vigorously. "It was rather warm out there, today, but I'm glad we went. Dotty enjoyed herself immensely."

Caroline rang the bell and went to sit opposite her employer. "She was acknowledged by several eminent ladies in their carriages and Mrs. DeBloom actually paused to speak to her."

"Is that good?" Mrs. Frogerton perked up. "Because from what I could see it backed the other carriages halfway up the park."

"That is to be expected during the fashionable hours to

promenade," Caroline said. "And being noticed by a society hostess like Mrs. DeBloom who has a very eligible son to marry off with an obscenely large fortune is very good news indeed."

"My girl doesn't need his money." Mrs. Frogerton waved off the DeBloom diamond mines with a flick of her hand. "And I can't say that I appreciate her condescending attitude. She makes me feel like a parlor maid who's dropped the china."

"She is rather overbearing," Caroline conceded. "But Dorothy is hard to intimidate."

Mrs. Frogerton laughed heartily. "Aye, that she is. I raised her to stand up for herself." She shook her head. "How she finds the stamina to attend all these events I don't know. I'm already exhausted and she barely sleeps in her bed."

"The Season can be quite crowded if one is invited to all the best events," Caroline acknowledged. "And Dorothy has certainly been a success."

"That's my Dotty." Mrs. Frogerton smiled fondly. "She'll snare a duke before the end of the summer."

Having gotten to know Dorothy well over the past months, Caroline thought Mrs. Frogerton might be right. Despite being only a generation removed from industrial money, Dorothy's refusal to be ignored had been taken well by the leaders of the *ton* and she'd been declared an "original" rather than a moneygrubbing industrialist's daughter tolerated only because of her fortune.

With Caroline's gentle guidance, as she didn't take well to being told anything, Dorothy was beginning to find her feet and was tolerated far more than her mother, who luckily didn't give a hoot about who approved of her or not.

"Where is Dotty?" Mrs. Frogerton asked.

"She went up to her room to change her dress for our afternoon callers."

"Of course she did."

Caroline looked down at her own serviceable gown. To

her surprise she didn't miss the constant need to keep up with society as much as she had feared and almost enjoyed her quieter role where her conduct wasn't scrutinized. The two years since her father's untimely death had lessened her resentment and given her the ability to move on in a new world where she proudly earned her own living and didn't have to rely on her relatives.

Mrs. Frogerton chuckled. "She doesn't want anyone to see her in the same outfit twice in one day."

The butler came in carrying the tea tray and was followed by the parlor maid with a tray of cakes and pastries.

"There is a Dr. Harris in the entrance hall, ma'am. He claims to know you."

"Then let him in immediately!" Mrs. Frogerton clapped her hands. "Did you know the dear doctor was coming to visit us, Caroline?"

"I did not," Caroline replied. "I only correspond with Rose Harris about my sister Susan's educational needs. I have no contact with the doctor himself."

Mrs. Frogerton had offered to help pay Susan's fees at the boarding school in Norwich for which Caroline was immensely grateful. She'd been unhappy about leaving Susan with their invalid aunt and the Greenwood family after such a series of tragedies. Mrs. Frogerton had insisted that she bore some responsibility for the dire situation Susan found herself in and had refused to take no for an answer.

Dr. Harris came in looking his usual forbidding self. His dark hair needed cutting, but at least his linens were well starched, and his coat was free of darns. He bowed to his hostess and Caroline.

"Mrs. Frogerton, Miss Morton! What a pleasure to see you both again."

Caroline raised an eyebrow at his pleasant tone. Last time they'd spoken he'd been less than communicative, which had been rather frustrating. The camaraderie they'd shared while solving the murders at her aunt's house party had disappeared and she wasn't sure whether to be pleased or vexed about it.

"Dr. Harris! What brings you to London?"

He smiled at Mrs. Frogerton. "I have taken a position at St. Thomas's Hospital, ma'am. I will be teaching new students and attending patients on the wards."

"How wonderful." Mrs. Frogerton smiled warmly at him. "Then I hope you will be a frequent visitor to my door, sir. Caroline and I always enjoy your company."

Dr. Harris's skeptical gaze flicked toward Caroline, who tried to look as if the matter had never occurred to her.

"Have you secured yourself adequate lodgings?" Mrs. Frogerton asked.

"I have, ma'am. The boardinghouse is quite close to the hospital grounds. I can walk to work in five minutes and the rent is reasonable."

"This is good news." Mrs. Frogerton winked at Caroline. "I thought we might be offering the good doctor one of our attics."

"I'm sure Dr. Harris wouldn't mind the one with the hole in the roof and the rain coming through it," Caroline said sweetly. "He is very resilient."

Dr. Harris looked revolted. "I am well situated, thank you, Miss Morton. I do not require charity."

"Oh, I'm sure Mrs. Frogerton would insist that you pay rent, sir. She doesn't approve of hangers-on, do you, ma'am?"

"I do not. Even my son knows that," Mrs. Frogerton said firmly. "Learning to pay your own way builds character. Now, would you like some tea, Dr. Harris?"

"Thank you, ma'am." Dr. Harris went over to collect his cup and sat beside Caroline as his hostess helped herself to the tiny cakes. "I hear from my sister that Susan has adapted well to her new environment."

"She has indeed," Caroline placed a plateful of cakes at Dr. Harris's elbow. "Rose has been immensely kind to her."

"I understand that Susan still believes her cousin Mabel

will come and fetch her." Dr. Harris drank most of his cup of tea in one swallow. "Has there been any more news of her whereabouts?"

"All I know is that she succeeded in leaving England and is somewhere in Europe, presumably with Harry," Caroline said. "I must confess that I try not to involve myself in the Greenwood family's affairs."

"Understandably." Dr. Harris frowned at the cake selection. "Why are they so small?"

"Because they are meant to look decorative for afternoon tea and for callers who rarely bother to eat them," Caroline explained.

"Typical," Dr. Harris snorted as he picked up a delicate meringue and popped it into his mouth. "I'll need at least a dozen to make up for one currant bun for a penny from the baker's shop."

Dorothy came into the drawing room and Dr. Harris rose to his feet.

"Good afternoon, Miss Frogerton."

Dorothy looked him up and down. She wore a dress in her favorite pink with a triple flounce of lace at the hem and her hair was elaborately coiffed. "Why are you here? Has someone died?"

Her mother shuddered. "I do hope not. We had enough of that at Greenwood Hall to last a lifetime."

"I merely came to pay my respects to your good selves, Miss Frogerton. I have taken a job at one of the London hospitals."

"Then you'd better get back to it. I don't want you cluttering up my mother's drawing room when our afternoon callers arrive," Dorothy said briskly as Caroline concealed a smile.

"I have no intention of overstaying my welcome, Miss Frogerton." Dr. Harris wasn't quite as easy to intimidate as a member of the *ton*. "The last thing I want is to be stuck making conversation with a bunch of vapid society women."

"Some of those women support the charities your hospital is involved in," Caroline couldn't help but point out. "In truth, being charming to those ladies is expected of you."

"I thought I'd left all the bowing and scraping nonsense in the countryside," Dr. Harris muttered. "All I want to do is treat my patients, educate my students, and be left alone."

"Then please don't let us keep you from your worthy goals." Dorothy raised her eyebrows. "The first carriage has drawn up outside and I'd prefer it if you were gone."

Dr. Harris finished his tea in one gulp. He scooped his plate of cakes into his large handkerchief, put it in his coat pocket, and bowed to his hostess.

"I'll be off then." He handed Mrs. Frogerton his card. "My address is on here if you should need me."

"Thank you, Dr. Harris. I will be inviting you to dine with us in the very near future."

Dorothy's expression said otherwise, and Caroline again fought a desire to laugh. She rose to her feet.

"Goodbye, Doctor."

"Miss Morton." He nodded to her and then to Dorothy. "Miss Frogerton."

Dorothy barely waited until he'd crossed the threshold before speaking. "Mother, you simply cannot let him sit at our dinner table."

"Why not, my love? He's always amusing company."

"Because his contempt for society is palpable and he has no desire to amend his behavior!"

"Six months ago, you would have agreed with every word he said," Mrs. Frogerton noted. "Be careful that you don't turn into the worst kind of snob, Dotty my girl. I won't stand for it."

The butler came in and bowed.

"Mrs. DeBloom, Mr. Philip DeBloom, and Miss De-Bloom."

With a sigh, Mrs. Frogerton rose to her feet as Dorothy's expression grew triumphant.

"Mrs. DeBloom." Mrs. Frogerton stepped forward, her hand extended. "What an unexpected pleasure . . ."

Caroline curtsied and was ignored by the DeBloom females as she quietly got them tea and offered cakes. Her position as a companion was often awkward as she existed in a netherworld—neither a servant nor a worthy guest.

"Thank you." Mr. DeBloom smiled at her as she set the cup of tea at his elbow. "I saw you in the park earlier with Miss Frogerton and her mother, but I didn't catch your name."

"I'm Miss Morton, sir. Mrs. Frogerton's companion."

She waited for the expected rebuff and was surprised when he chuckled. "I should imagine that keeping an eye on Miss Frogerton and her mother is something of a trial at times."

"It can be, sir." Caroline found herself smiling in return. "But they are well worth the effort."

"I'd say." His gaze moved to Dorothy, who was talking to his mother. "I like a woman who knows her own mind."

"Then you will certainly appreciate Miss Frogerton," Caroline said. "And she appreciates an honest and forthright man."

She reclaimed her seat on the couch and found herself being stared at by Mrs. DeBloom.

"And who are you, dear?"

"Miss Morton, ma'am." Caroline kept her head high and met Mrs. DeBloom's gaze straight on.

"Lady Caroline Morton, if you wish to use her correct title, which she says isn't important, or necessary," Mrs. Frogerton added with a fond smile.

"Morton?" Mrs. DeBloom frowned. "I believe I met your father out in Africa."

"That's very possible," Caroline said lightly. "He did like to travel."

"A most charming man," Mrs. DeBloom continued. "And how is he?"

"He died a few years ago, ma'am, leaving his children penniless and dispossessed of their home."

Mr. DeBloom choked on his tea and turned it into a cough.

"Oh." Mrs. DeBloom turned back to Dorothy. "I do hope your mother will allow you to accompany us to the theater tonight. We have hired a box and will be serving an intimate supper during the interval." She smiled graciously at Mrs. Frogerton. "I will, of course, chaperone the party and make sure your daughter is safe at all times."

Dorothy looked pleadingly over at her mother. "I would very much like to go, and it would mean that you and Caroline could have an evening to yourselves for a change."

"I am quite happy to relinquish you into Mrs. DeBloom's care," Mrs. Frogerton answered.

"Excellent. We will pick her up in our carriage at seven." Mrs. DeBloom rose to her feet, her tea untouched at her side. "Come along Philip, Clarissa."

She swept out, bringing her daughter, who hadn't spoken a word in her wake. Mr. DeBloom took a moment to say his goodbyes to Dorothy and Mrs. Frogerton before turning to Caroline.

"A pleasure, Miss Morton. I always appreciate someone who can stop my mother midflow." He winked and turned to the door. "Enjoy your evening off."

Several hours later, Caroline, who was avidly reading one of her employer's favorite gothic novels by the fire, heard the door open, and hastily closed the book. Mrs. Frogerton came in, her expression aglow.

"Caroline! Oh, my goodness, you should have come with me tonight." She patted the dogs, who had gathered in a disconsolate pile around Caroline during their owner's absence, and sat in her favorite chair. "It was quite incredible!"

"I thought you said it was a scientific lecture?" Caroline wedged the book down the side of a cushion and sat up straight.

"Not quite. It was more in the way of an . . . intimate meeting of like-minded people open to the possibilities beyond this mortal realm."

"I beg your pardon?" Caroline regarded Mrs. Frogerton's flushed features more closely. "Are you feeling quite well, ma'am? Did you drink rather too much sherry?"

Her employer flapped her hand in front of her face. "I am most invigorated, lass. The lady who ran the séance was French. She spoke in tongues!" She shuddered. "I had chills down my spine."

Caroline frowned. "Have you been attempting to contact the dead, Mrs. Frogerton?"

"Not only attempting but succeeding. Madam Lavinia had a message for me from Septimus in the beyond!"

"And what exactly did your departed husband have to say for himself, ma'am?" Caroline tried hard not to let her skepticism leak into her voice. For such a shrewd woman, her employer did tend to be a little too credulous sometimes.

"That he was fine where he was and very proud of me for expanding the business." Mrs. Frogerton smiled. "Which is exactly what I'd expect him to say. He was never one for being overly dramatic and he was always impressed by an increase in profit."

"With all due respect, such a comment is rather general," Caroline said. "It could apply to many in your particular situation."

"I am well aware of that. It was what she said next that caught my attention." Mrs. Frogerton paused impressively. "Madam Lavinia knew his pet name for me!"

"Matty?"

"No, that's what my father called me, much better than Matilda." Mrs. Frogerton lowered her voice. "Septimus used to call me his little pug."

Caroline blinked hard. "Pug?"

"Yes, indeed. It is not something generally known, because Septimus was not a demonstrative man in public. It was his private name for me because of my round face, short stature, and brown eyes." She chuckled. "How Madam knew that nickname is a mystery unless she really can speak to those behind the veil."

"That is certainly remarkable," Caroline acknowledged. "Perhaps I should visit this mysterious marvel for myself?"

She had a shrewd suspicion that Madam Lavinia, whoever she was, would soon be expecting a financial return for her "prophecies." Caroline was determined that Mrs. Frogerton would not end up being one of her victims. She had lived in society long enough to know there were always gifted flimflammers trying to relieve the rich of their money and Mrs. Frogerton's enthusiasm might lead her astray.

"I was just about to suggest the same thing, my dear." Mrs. Frogerton beamed at her approvingly. "The next night Dotty is busy with her new friends, we'll go together. I cannot wait for you to be as enthralled as I was!"

Chapter 2

Two weeks later, Caroline followed Mrs. Frogerton up the steps of a narrow town house in St. John's Wood. The door was opened by an elderly man in an old-fashioned white wig and faded livery.

"Good evening, ma'am."

"Good evening, Mr. Murphy. Madam Lavinia is expecting us."

Mrs. Frogerton swept into the black-and-white-tiled hall, which was dark and rather pokey. The main staircase ran up the left-hand wall and a series of rooms opened off a long corridor to the right. Although the place was clean, it was obvious to Caroline that it was rented rather than owned. The furniture was from the previous century and the shutters and drapes needed either a coat of paint or replacing.

The butler took their cloaks. He had a pleasing Irish accent, which was very soothing. "Please follow me. Madam is in the back parlor."

"Thank you."

Caroline's suspicions as to the ownership of the house were confirmed as she noted the lighter squares on the walls where previous artwork had been removed and not

replaced by the new occupant. Before accepting employment with Mrs. Frogerton, she had lived in such a building
in an attic room containing all her worldly goods and she
would never forget it.

"Has Madam lived here long?" Caroline inquired to the
butler's back.

"She settled here last year from Brighton, miss, where she
was a great success with the patrons of the Royal Pavilion."
He paused to open the door. "Your visitors, Madam."

Caroline stepped back so that Mrs. Frogerton could go
ahead of her and took a moment to review the interior. A
large circular table set with numerous nonmatching chairs
took up almost all the space in the square, paneled room.
A candelabra draped in black gauze sat in the center along
with a bell and a tarnished silver bowl containing what
looked like water. At the end of the table farthest away
from Caroline sat Madam Lavinia Dubois.

She wore a white wig in the style of Marie Antoinette
with a black veil draped over it. Her gown was gray satin
with silver thread that caught the candlelight, and she had
long lace ruffles at her cuffs and throat.

"Mrs. Frogerton. How delightful to see you again."

"Madam!" Mrs. Frogerton gestured proudly at Caroline. "I have brought my little doubting Thomas to meet
you as well."

Madam turned her head to look at Caroline, who advanced toward her. She had luminous dark brown eyes, a
small painted mouth like a doll, and rouge spots high on
her cheeks.

"Miss Morton, ma'am." Caroline curtsied.

A slight smile curved Madam's lip. "You are most welcome, *ma cherie*. Please take a seat beside your companion
and we will await the arrival of the others."

"*Merci, de m'avoir chez vous, Madam,*" Caroline
replied.

She wasn't surprised when Madam didn't reply to her
fluent French and instead turned to the door to extend a

welcome to a new arrival. If she was the kind of lady with the funds to risk a wager, she would bet that Madam Lavinia didn't have a French bone in her body.

Mrs. Frogerton nudged her as the butler served them tea. "I didn't know you spoke French!"

Caroline shrugged. "My mother spoke it very well and taught us from the time we were born, so it comes quite naturally to me."

"I must remember to take you with me next time I negotiate with my French suppliers whom I suspect are fleecing me."

"I'd be delighted to sit in with you on such a meeting, ma'am," Caroline said.

"I wish I'd thought to have someone teach Dotty and Simon to speak another language." Mrs. Frogerton sipped her tea. "But it never occurred to me that my business would start exporting across the Continent."

"I could try and teach Dorothy, ma'am," Caroline offered tentatively. "But I'm not sure she'd have the time."

"Or the patience to learn unless she thought it might snare her that duke."

"Most peers do speak French, so it might help."

"I'll ask her what she thinks. She's rather caught up with the DeBlooms now. Not that I think anything will come of that, but Mr. DeBloom is nice enough."

"He seems very taken with her."

Mrs. Frogerton raised her eyebrows. "I think he's very taken with you, lass, and if you had a fortune to match your beauty, he'd be down on one knee popping the question right now."

"Hardly. He, unlike many of Dorothy's suitors, simply has good enough manners to be pleasant to everyone around her who might influence his suit."

"As long as he doesn't offer you carte blanche, then you can protest as much as you like, miss, but don't let him fool you into anything other than a legal marriage." Mrs. Frogerton waggled her finger in Caroline's direction. "And now I know you understand French, I don't need to tell you what that means."

"I would never accept such an offer, ma'am," Caroline hastened to reassure her employer. "And Mr. DeBloom is far too intelligent to upset his mother and risk his inheritance."

"Men don't always use their intelligence when it comes to women, lass," Mrs. Frogerton said briskly. "They think with other parts of their anatomy."

Caroline looked up as a gentleman took the seat beside her.

"Good evening, ma'am," he said politely. He had a slight Irish accent. "I don't believe I have the pleasure of your acquaintance."

Mrs. Frogerton leaned past Caroline to smile at the man.

"Good evening, Professor Brown. This is Miss Morton, my companion."

"Miss Morton." He inclined his head. "I am delighted to meet you. Mrs. Frogerton was very impressed with Madam's . . . outpourings the other night." He smiled and indicated the notepad and pencil he'd placed on the table in front of him. "I try and keep a more open mind perhaps than most."

"The professor is conducting a scientific study of Madam's work," Mrs. Frogerton said as another couple came into the room and took their places beside a middle-aged woman swathed in black and two elderly ladies who looked like sisters. "He is very interested in mesmerism and spiritualism."

Caroline's opinion of Professor Brown went up a notch.

"I confess that I am quite skeptical myself, sir."

"As you should be, Miss Morton." He bowed to her. "There is no harm in using one's intelligence to draw one's own conclusions."

There was a slight stir as a young woman joined the group around the table, filling all the chairs. She had blond hair and wore a mask that concealed most of her face. The butler closed the door into the parlor and Madam rose to her feet.

"Good evening, everyone." She smiled as she reached forward to light the black candles in front of her. "I hope the spirits that speak through me tonight bring you all happiness and hope."

Caroline almost jumped as the new-fangled gaslights on the wall hissed as they were extinguished, plunging the room into half-darkness. Madam's face remained lit by the candles reflected in the bowl of water in front of her making it appear as if her skin was rippling.

"First, we must search out the energy around us so that the spirits know that it is safe to come through the barrier and speak to us. Please take off your gloves and join hands with your neighbor to allow the flow of animal magnetism to pass amongst us."

Caroline reluctantly placed her left hand in Professor Brown's as Mrs. Frogerton grabbed her right.

"Close your eyes and feel the strength of our purpose flooding through you."

A jolt of something slightly painful shot through Caroline's hand and Professor Brown murmured in her ear. "It's electricity, Miss Morton. We are the conductors. There is nothing to be concerned about, it's a party trick."

"Do not let go of each other in your thoughts," Madam implored. "We form a vital link against the forces of evil."

Mrs. Frogerton gripped Caroline's hand. To Caroline's surprise, Madam's voice did have a strange element of compulsion within it that made her want to obey her.

"Yes, your eyes feel heavy, don't they?" Madam continued. "The curtain between the two worlds is dissolving now and those behind it—those you love, and miss, are reaching out to you."

There was a loud bang on the table, and everyone jumped.

"Do not be afraid," Madam intoned. "They are just impatient to reunite with you." A moan echoed down the chimney and Mrs. Frogerton squeezed Caroline's hand even harder.

Caroline opened her eyes to see whether someone else had entered the room, but there was no one visible except the guests seated around the table. The random knocking noises continued along with echoing sighs causing more than one stifled shriek from the ladies.

A sudden draft of air blasted down the chimney, blowing out most of the candles, and Madam took a deep and audible breath as someone muttered a prayer.

"They are with us!"

Her voice was lower but still echoed through the room. Madam raised her face to the ceiling, her expression intent.

"Yes, yes, I will inquire. . . . Is there someone here with a loved one with a name beginning with E?"

"Is it my Edward?" a quavering voice inquired.

"Yes." Madam nodded. "It is he. He wants to know whether you still have his favorite gown of yours?"

"I do! He loved my blue dress with the gray lace ruffles."

"That is exactly how he is describing it." Madam smiled blissfully. "He says that you must wear it for him on his birthday next month and that he will be with you in spirit."

"How like him," The woman pressed her hand to her bosom. "I miss him so badly."

"He knows that, my dear." Madam paused and her voice deepened even further. "He also says you should speak to your land agent without delay."

"About what?"

Madam shuddered and dropped her gaze to the table, her shoulders bowed. "He has gone, others want to be heard."

Caroline turned her head very slightly and saw the professor was taking rapid notes as Madam drew herself upright again, her hands reaching to cradle the silver bowl as she called on another spirit. Smoke curled up from the surface of the water and the bell tinkled, making Caroline startle again despite herself.

Not everyone around the table was called out, but Madam's accuracy seemed remarkable. Caroline remained unmoved even as Mrs. Frogerton vibrated with excitement over every dire prediction and touching moment. The young blond woman broke down in tears when Madam spoke of her dearly departed uncle and looked set to leave the room until she was warned not to break the connection of the circle.

Caroline wasn't sure if it was because she had no particular desire to contact anyone who had passed away that she was resilient to Madam's powers or that since her father had died, she'd become more cynical. All the people around the table, apart from Mrs. Frogerton and Professor Brown, seemed desperate for reassurance. At some level it offended her to see Madam exploit such raw need, presumably for profit.

The clock on the mantelpiece wheezed to life and struck nine and Madam sat back.

"I can do no more tonight. The spirits have exhausted me." She raised a languid hand and rang the bell. "Please allow my butler to escort you out."

She slumped into her chair, one hand over her eyes as her guests rose to their feet and hurried toward the hall. Caroline was just about to leave when Madam dropped something on the floor. Caroline instinctively bent to pick it up.

When Caroline went to return the balled-up piece of parchment to its owner, Madam shook her head. "It is meant for you, Miss Morton. Guard it well."

"I—" Caroline was just about to protest when Mrs. Frogerton called her name, and she turned toward her employer. "I'm just coming, ma'am."

"Be careful, Miss Morton," the whisper came from behind her. "I am relying on you."

Caroline hurried to join Mrs. Frogerton in the hallway, aware of a discreet bowl set out on the hallstand where the guests could leave a financial donation for Madam. The young woman who had tried to leave earlier was now lingering in the hall speaking in low, urgent tones to the butler. There was something familiar about her but as Caroline had not heard her speak and her face was still obscured by the mask, she couldn't quite place her.

"Did you enjoy that, Miss Morton?" Professor Brown asked.

"It was . . . interesting," Caroline said guardedly, one eye on Mrs. Frogerton, who was placing rather too much money for Caroline's liking in the bowl.

"But you remain unconvinced?"

"I fear so."

"Good for you." The professor's gaze swept the rapidly emptying hall. "There are too many who are so desperate to hear from their loved ones that they fall for every con in town."

"You believe Madam is a fake?"

He regarded her steadily, the hint of a twinkle in his blue eyes. "I've studied such people for years, Miss Morton, and I've rarely met one with even a remnant of true talent." He looked back down the corridor where the blond woman was being escorted back into the parlor by the butler. "But Madam has . . . some abilities. I'll give her that." He paused. "Still, there is nothing to worry about. She can do very little harm."

Caroline considered what she'd seen and reluctantly agreed. "There were a couple of moments when her voice dropped, and words came from her mouth that did not appear to be part of what she had said before."

"You noticed that?" He bowed. "You have a keen ear, Miss Morton."

He turned to Mrs. Frogerton, who had come up beside Caroline. "May I assist you with your cloak, ma'am?"

"Thank you." Mrs. Frogerton made sure her bonnet ribbons were tied tightly under her ear. "I enjoyed that immensely! I am disappointed that she didn't mention my husband again, but perhaps she will on my next visit!"

Over the top of Mrs. Frogerton's head, Professor Brown raised his eyebrows at Caroline.

"You will return, ma'am?"

"Why ever not?" Mrs. Frogerton said. "It's better than the theater!"

Caroline smiled at the professor. "Do not worry, sir. My employer has a very shrewd head on her shoulders, and I will certainly not allow her to significantly dissipate her fortune."

"I have no intention of doing any such thing," Mrs. Frogerton chuckled as they headed for the door. "I'm far too penny-pinching."

Caroline went down the steps, aware that she was glad to get out of the gloomy house with its oppressive atmosphere and the taste of the tangible fears and emotions of its visitors. She doubted she could persuade Mrs. Frogerton to stay away, but she was determined not to allow her to attend alone in case Madam found a way to extort money from her. Despite Professor Brown's reassurances to the contrary, Caroline was not convinced the woman was harmless.

Her fingers closed on the ball of paper Madam had insisted was for her. As Mrs. Frogerton dozed off to the sway of the carriage, Caroline took it out, and uncrumpled it. The lettering was in black and large enough to read easily in the interior light.

Tell Caroline I fixed Nelly and that everything will soon be better.

She set the paper on her knee and smoothed it with her fingers, trying hard not to wonder what on earth was going on. A memory flashed unbidden of her father wiping away her tears as he sat her on his desk and patiently reattached her doll's head to its body.

"There, there, sweetheart," she could hear his voice even now. "Papa will always fix everything for you."

Except he'd lied and left her and Susan destitute and at the mercy of their relatives' less than charitable inclinations. . . .

How had Madam known about such an intimate moment between her and her father? Caroline raised her head and looked blindly out of the window. Was Madam truly able to connect to the dead, and if she was, did Caroline want to know what else her father might have to say to her?

Her glance strayed to her employer, who was snoring slightly. If she confided in Mrs. Frogerton, she knew she would be believed and encouraged to find out more, but at what cost?

She'd learned over the years never to believe her father's promises and after her mother died had come to hate him for his careless and profligate ways. Could she risk testing her hard-won indifference against the faint hope that he might have something useful to say to her? Perhaps even an apology?

She shook off the notion as the carriage swayed to turn the corner into their street. Her priority was to make certain Mrs. Frogerton didn't get caught up in something that would drain her of funds. She would have to accompany her employer to Madam's if she chose to return, and even if Madam chose to single her out again she didn't have to listen.

Mrs. Frogerton stirred as the carriage drew to a stop in front of their rented house and smothered a yawn behind her hand.

"What an exciting evening!"

"Indeed, ma'am." Caroline leaned over to unlatch the carriage door. "Let me help you descend."

"Thank you, my dear." Mrs. Frogerton leaned heavily on her arm as she exited the carriage. "I admit that I am rather fatigued. There is something about Madam's that makes me feel anxious."

"I wonder if it is because everyone there desperately seeks reassurance from Madam Lavinia. It is a somewhat oppressive atmosphere."

"It must be hard for her, too, what with all those spirits demanding her attention." Mrs. Frogerton climbed the steps to the front door. "She looked quite worn out by the end."

"I can only imagine." Once inside, Caroline helped her employer take off her cloak and bonnet. "Do you wish to go straight to bed, ma'am? I can send your maid up and bring you something to drink—some chamomile tea, perhaps?"

"That would be lovely, my dear." Mrs. Frogerton patted her hand. "Thank you for accompanying me this evening."

"It was my pleasure."

Mrs. Frogerton paused, her expression hopeful. "Would you be willing to come back with me at least once more? I would love to hear more from my Septimus."

"Of course, ma'am." Caroline smiled.

She waited until Mrs. Frogerton started up the stairs before going to the kitchen to find her maid and make the promised tea. Lizzie offered to take it up with her. Caroline handed it over and asked the maid to tell Mrs. Frogerton she would be up to say good night, shortly.

She had just made sure that all the candles, lamps, and fires in the reception rooms had been dealt with when the front door opened, and Dorothy and Mr. DeBloom came in laughing together. Dorothy wore a cream silk gown suitable for the opera with matching pearls in her hair and around her throat. For a moment, Caroline remembered how it felt to have a handsome man dedicate his evening to amusing you. Mr. DeBloom smiled over at her and bowed.

"Miss Morton. I return my lovely charge into your capable hands."

Dorothy lightly swatted his shoulder with her fan. "I am not a sack of coal and Caroline has no authority over me."

Caroline smiled at Dorothy. "Did you have an enjoyable evening?"

"It was quite dull," Dorothy said. "But Mr. DeBloom made it more bearable."

"Miss Frogerton misspeaks. It improved immensely when she sang a duet with me. She has a remarkable singing voice."

"I was just trying to outdo you, and you know it, sir." Dorothy mock frowned at her companion. "Now, shouldn't you be going? Your mother will not appreciate being left in her carriage while you dally with me."

"Dally? Is that what I'm doing? I thought I was behaving like a perfect gentleman."

Dorothy snorted and waved him toward the door. "Good night, sir."

"And to you, Miss Frogerton." He bowed again and turned to Caroline. "Miss Morton."

Dorothy waited until he closed the door behind him before speaking.

"He is very pleasant. It's a shame he has no rank to speak of."

"Perhaps that won't matter if you begin to care about him?" Caroline suggested.

Dorothy snorted. "You know what I want, Caroline. I haven't changed my mind."

They ascended the stairs together, Dorothy holding up her abundant silk skirts in one hand.

"In truth, he asks me more questions about you than about myself."

Caroline frowned. "I have no idea why and I'm not sure I appreciate it."

"Maybe he wants to marry someone with a title, too." Dorothy winked at her. "Don't worry. I don't tell him anything that isn't already public knowledge."

"I appreciate that." Caroline paused on the landing. "May I offer you one piece of advice?"

"Of course."

"If you aren't serious about Mr. DeBloom, you might consider widening your social circle. If you are constantly seen in his company, people will draw their own conclusions, and you don't want to be seen as flighty if you suddenly veer off in another direction."

Dorothy frowned. She disliked being in the wrong and had a tendency to be stubborn.

"That's ridiculous."

"It is simply my experience of such matters in this particular society," Caroline persisted. Despite a somewhat rocky start, she and Dorothy had become allies if not best friends. "If you truly want a peer, you need to be mindful of the impression you give and the company you keep."

"The DeBlooms are rich."

"Yes, but not the right kind of rich," Caroline reminded her. "Although, it might be worth considering whether such a family, who also draw their money from trade, might suit you better."

Dorothy scowled. "I want a duke."

"Then think about what I have said and act accordingly." Caroline wasn't intimidated and held Dorothy's gaze. "Remember whom you need to impress."

Dorothy nodded and started walking again without wishing Caroline good night. She wasn't bothered by the omission, having learned early on that even though Dorothy would often reluctantly take her advice she very rarely thanked her for it.

Caroline knocked gently on Mrs. Frogerton's bedroom door before letting herself in. Her employer was already fast asleep, a single candle burning by her bed.

"She went out like a light, miss."

Caroline jumped as Lizzie whispered from across the room. An evening spent with a supposed spiritualist had obviously left her nerves in shreds.

"Then I'll leave her to her slumbers. Good night, Lizzie."

"Good night, miss."

Caroline walked back to her own room knowing that Mrs. Frogerton wanted to visit Madam Lavinia again and that she would accompany her. The thought filled her with a mixture of dread and unwanted anticipation. If Madam wasn't a fraud, could she truly help her understand what had happened to her father and could she finally forgive him?

Chapter 3

"Balderdash, ma'am," Dr. Harris said bluntly as Mrs. Frogerton poured him another cup of tea. "This woman is merely trying to part you from your money in the most unscrupulous way possible."

The good doctor had arrived after the usual hours for calling, which suited both him and Dorothy. He looked tired and two buttons on his coat were hanging by a thread, which for some unfathomable reason made Caroline itch to fix them for him.

"Then explain how she knew my husband's pet name for me then?" Mrs. Frogerton raised her eyebrows. "That was quite extraordinary."

Dr. Harris shrugged. "It was probably a lucky guess, or you inadvertently revealed it to her yourself." He turned to Caroline. "Were you there when this happened?"

"I was not," Caroline assured him. "But I did accompany Mrs. Frogerton on a different evening and Madam put on quite a performance."

Dr. Harris sat back and regarded her; his brow furrowed. "You weren't convinced of her authenticity, were you?"

"Not particularly." Caroline paused. "But she did have some interesting things to say."

Dorothy, who had been pacing the room, her attention on the street outside, suddenly spun around.

"The Lingard carriage is outside."

Caroline frowned. "The Dowager Viscountess Lingard?"

"Yes, and her son, Augustus, the new viscount."

Caroline went to join Dorothy and peered down at the street. "Well, they are terribly late to make a call. Do you really wish to receive them at this hour?"

"You were the one who told me to widen my social circle," Dorothy reminded her. "I danced with him twice at the ball last night. Didn't you notice?"

"I did not, but he is from a very good family. His father was a friend of my father's." Caroline turned to Mrs. Frogerton. "He isn't quite a duke, but he is far more presentable."

Dr. Harris snorted and Dorothy spun around to look at him.

"You cannot be here when they come in."

"I came late to avoid your snobbish acquaintances!" Dr. Harris protested. "It's hardly my fault they can't abide by the social norms."

Caroline stepped in between them. "I wish to speak to you on a private matter, Dr. Harris. Would you mind accompanying me to the kitchen?"

"If I must." Dr. Harris stood and dusted off the cake crumbs. "Thank you for the tea, ma'am."

He followed Caroline down into the hall where they narrowly missed colliding with the butler, who was just opening the front door. At four in the afternoon, the kitchen was relatively quiet as there was no company expected for dinner and Mrs. Frogerton preferred to dine simply. Cook had retired to her rooms and only a kitchen maid sat by the stove tending the pots of stock and vegetables.

Caroline pointed at the doctor. "Take off your coat."

Dr. Harris raised his eyebrows. "I beg your pardon?"

"I cannot bear to see the perilous state of your buttons any longer." She held out her hand. "I'll sew them back on for you."

He handed over the coat. "I'm quite capable of doing that for myself, you know."

"I'm sure you are."

She went into the scullery and helped herself to some of the housekeeper's strong thread and a needle. When she returned, Dr. Harris had seated himself at the table and was pouring them both tea from the large brown pot.

"Were you really that concerned about my buttons or were you simply trying to extract me from the drawing room?" Dr. Harris inquired as he added a large lump of sugar to his earthenware mug and stirred vigorously.

Caroline started on the first button. "A little of both, perhaps? But I did want to ask your opinion on something as well."

She concentrated on her task, which meant she didn't have to look at him. "At the end of the meeting I attended, Madam Lavinia gave me a note."

"And?"

She slowly let out her breath. "It was remarkably specific."

"About you?"

"Yes. It mentioned the name of a doll I used to have and . . . my father. I cannot imagine how Madam knew that information." She risked a glance at his skeptical face.

"What exactly did it say?"

She recited the words that she already knew by heart. "Tell Caroline I fixed Nelly and that everything will soon be better."

"How bizarre." Dr. Harris frowned as she moved her attention to the second button. "Who's Nelly?"

"A doll I had when I was small that my father fixed for me."

"Hmm . . . What exactly do you want me to do about it?"

"Nothing, sir. I merely wished to solicit your opinion on how I should proceed. It was a remarkably specific note about something that even I had forgotten." She paused to frame her next words. "Perhaps I want you to tell me it is ridiculous and that I shouldn't be giving it a moment's thought."

She wrapped the thread around the repaired button and gave it an experimental tug before cutting the thread and handing the coat back to Dr. Harris, who had remained remarkably quiet.

"Thank you." He stood to put the coat back on. "Perhaps you and I should attend one of Madam's events ourselves. Can you arrange such a thing?"

She looked up at him. "You are offering to accompany me?"

He frowned. "Yes. I can hardly advise you when I haven't met the woman or seen her perform. I am free for the next two evenings. Send a note to my lodgings and I'll meet you at Madam's." He bowed. "Now I must be off. I have work to do."

"Then I will contact you if I am able to arrange the meeting."

He nodded and departed, leaving Caroline staring after him. Vincent, the errand boy, came into the kitchen whistling and winked at Caroline.

"Afternoon, miss!"

Caroline smiled at him. "Do you have time to deliver a note for me and await a reply?"

He nodded. "Yes, of course, miss."

Caroline put the needle and thread back in the scullery and used the housekeeper's stationery to compose and seal her note, which she gave to Vince with a sixpence. The thought of the unsentimental and brutally honest Dr. Harris meeting Madam was unsettling, but she needed him there to help her decide exactly what was going on.

* * *

After the butler took their coats, Dr. Harris bent his head to murmur in Caroline's ear. "If this is the best Madam can afford then she can't be doing that well, can she?"

He ushered Caroline ahead of him down the corridor. She'd been lucky enough to secure an evening appointment when Dr. Harris was free less than two days later. She was surprisingly eager to hear his opinion on Madam so that she could lay her doubts to rest.

Madam looked up as they entered, her gaze fixed on Dr. Harris.

"Good evening, please take your places. We are ready to begin."

The room was already plunged into darkness, and it was difficult to see exactly who was sitting at the packed table. Dr. Harris kicked at least two chair legs and knocked over an umbrella before he finally managed to sit down with a muted apology. Caroline slipped into the seat beside him and recognized Professor Brown, who winked, to her left.

Madam began speaking and Dr. Harris reluctantly took Caroline's hand in his. He audibly snorted when the electrical current shot through him. She squeezed his hand hard to remind him to at least attempt to remain impartial as Madam proceeded to offer her proclamations to those around the table. It didn't help that on her other side, Professor Brown was also murmuring under his breath as he wrote his notes.

Suddenly, Dr. Harris leaned so close to her that she could smell his hair pomade.

"Who's that fellow beside you?"

Caroline waited until one of the ladies around the table started shrieking in response to Madam's dire prophecy and threatening to swoon, and replied, "Professor Brown."

He leaned even farther forward and looked past her. "*Brown?*"

"My esteemed new colleague, Dr. Harris!" Professor Brown raised his eyebrows. "What brings you here?"

Caroline cleared her throat. "Could you both wait until after the session has finished? You are providing a distraction and Madam is now glaring at you."

Dr. Harris looked inquiringly over at his hostess, who didn't look pleased by the interruption.

"Apologies, Madam, pray continue."

She fixed him with a piercing stare. "You should be more careful, Doctor. Your hands are covered in the blood of others."

He shrugged. "I'm a physician, ma'am."

"Some of your patients would beg to differ." She raised her gaze to the ceiling. "Does the name Amelia mean anything to you? She is most insistent that you know her."

Dr. Harris frowned. "I have no idea what—"

Before he could finish speaking the door into the parlor crashed open and a man came in and looked around.

"Where is my mother?" He cursed at the butler, who was trying to persuade him to leave. "I'm not going anywhere until I've extracted my mother from this den of iniquity!"

"Alfred!" An older lady rose to her feet. "How dare you!"

He turned toward her, his brows lowering. "You're coming with me. You've wasted far too much money on this ridiculousness already. Money we can't afford in the present circumstances."

"I am not leaving. Madam hasn't spoken of your father yet."

Her son gave an ugly laugh. "When you stop paying her, I'll guarantee you she'll shut up about him completely."

Madam rose to her feet and the room went quiet, all attention on her pale and perfectly composed face.

"You will leave this space now."

"Not without my mother," Alfred snapped. "And I'll thank you to keep your mouth shut."

Dr. Harris stirred. "There's no need to be disrespect-ful, sir."

"There is every need." He held out his hand to his mother. "Come, now, or else."

"Or else what?" His mother wasn't budging. "You'll drag me out?"

"If I have to." He moved a menacing step closer, and Madam held up her hand.

"Your mother is perfectly safe with me." She paused. "I fear more for her in your company."

"What the devil is that supposed to mean?" Alfred de-manded. "Are you threatening me?"

Madam's smile was distinctly unnerving. "You cannot threaten the dead, sir. You of all men should know that."

His hands fisted by his sides, his gaze on Madam. "You're planning to murder me, now?"

"Oh, I don't need to do that." Madam shrugged. "Jus-tice takes care of her own."

"You . . ." Alfred cursed loudly and lunged at Madam. It took the combined strength of the butler, Dr. Harris, and Professor Brown to drag him out of the room, his shouted threats still ringing down the hallway as he was thrown out.

"I do apologize." His mother sat back down. "I don't know what's wrong with him."

"All is well." Madam sank into her chair. "But I fear I must end our séance tonight. The spirits will not answer me now."

A disappointed sigh ran around the table, and everyone started to get up and leave, whispering to one another as they passed through the door. Caroline glanced over at Dr. Harris, but he was looking at Professor Brown.

"I wouldn't have thought this would be your cup of tea, Brown."

"Or yours, sir."

"I merely accompanied Miss Morton," Dr. Harris said

loftily. "She had some concerns about the authenticity of Madam Lavinia."

"Good for her." Professor Brown winked at Caroline. "I am here because I'm writing a paper about current practitioners in London for the Society for Psychical Research."

"I see." Dr. Harris found Caroline's pelisse and handed it over to her. "And what do you think of Madam?"

"I think she has some . . . interesting attributes," Professor Brown said slowly.

"Really." Dr. Harris jammed his hat on his head. "I think she's a complete fraud."

"We should sit down together at the hospital and discuss this further at some point." Professor Brown patted Dr. Harris on the shoulder. "But after all that excitement, I suspect Miss Morton would rather like you to escort her home."

Dr. Harris swung around and regarded Caroline as if he'd forgotten she was there. "Ah, yes, of course." He bowed and held out his arm. "Come along, Miss Morton."

"Perhaps we can share a hackney cab?" Professor Brown suggested. "We are all heading in the same direction."

"That's an excellent idea. I can drop Miss Morton off on the way."

Caroline murmured under her breath, "Like an unwanted parcel."

He patted her shoulder in an absent-minded fashion as he helped her into the cab and then proceeded to ignore her as he continued his discussion with Professor Brown.

It wasn't until he walked her to the front door leaving Professor Brown in the cab that he spoke directly to her again.

"Miss Morton, may I ask a favor?"

"Of course, sir."

"Can you find the time to accompany me back to Madam Lavinia's tomorrow afternoon at three?"

Caroline blinked at him. "I beg your pardon?"

"I . . . need to speak to her about something very specific and would prefer not to do it alone."

"Why not ask Professor Brown to accompany you? You seem to have a lot in common, and you do work at the same hospital," Caroline suggested.

"I'd rather it was you." He paused and cleared his throat. "I'd appreciate it."

She sighed. "As you wish."

He took her gloved hand and kissed it. "Thank you. And please don't mention it to Mrs. Frogerton."

"That's . . ." Caroline realized she was speaking to herself as Dr. Harris turned his back and marched away. "Probably impossible."

She knocked on the door and was admitted by the butler, who offered her a warm smile.

"Did you have a pleasant evening, Miss Morton?"

"It had its interesting moments," Caroline replied. "Is Mrs. Frogerton still up?"

"No, miss. She retired to her chamber about half an hour ago."

Relieved at having avoided her employer's remarkably keen eye, Caroline ascended the stairs. She still wasn't quite sure why Dr. Harris wanted her company on the morrow, but she couldn't wait to find out what he was up to.

To Caroline's relief, Mrs. Frogerton had accepted her explanation of having an appointment with Dr. Harris that afternoon without asking for further details. To be fair she was distracted by the delivery of the latest edition of *The Supernatural Magazine* and intended to spend the afternoon reading while Dorothy made her calls in the company of the Lingard family.

Dorothy had taken Caroline's remarks about widening her social circle seriously, which had culminated in Mr. DeBloom laughingly complaining that he was being slighted.

Caroline had listened to his pleas for her to intervene and reminded him that she had no influence on Dorothy at all. That wasn't quite correct, but Mr. DeBloom didn't need to know that.

Dr. Harris appeared promptly at a quarter to three and helped Caroline ascend into the waiting hackney cab. After years of being told that ladies could not go out alone or in the company of an unmarried gentleman without damaging their reputation it was remarkably freeing to go out and not be censured. She was no longer a valuable commodity to be bought or sold on the marriage mart. Earning her own living made her invisible to the society that had once governed her every move. She knew she was extremely fortunate in her employer, but the sense of freedom was undeniable.

"Good afternoon, Miss Morton." Dr. Harris tipped his hat to her. "Thank you for agreeing to accompany me."

Caroline sat back and regarded him from her seat opposite. He appeared rather agitated, which was quite unlike him.

"May I ask what this is all about?"

He frowned. "I am not at liberty to disclose that information at present."

"That is remarkably unhelpful, especially when I am doing you a favor," Caroline pointed out. "We are friends, are we not? I can assure you that anything you divulge to me in confidence will be kept private."

"I have complete faith in your ability to keep a secret, Miss Morton, but this is something that concerns others." He avoided her gaze and stared out of the grimy window.

"I assume it has something to do with what Madam said to you yesterday, otherwise we wouldn't be going to see her," Caroline prompted.

"She . . ." Dr. Harris paused. "Is a fraud and a charlatan."

"If that is your considered opinion, why do you care what she said about you?"

He turned to glare at her. "Did I say that I cared? I merely wish to have a conversation with her as to her sources."

"I see." Caroline held his gaze. "That makes perfect sense."

He snorted and turned his attention to the road outside. "We should be there in no time. The traffic is particularly light this afternoon."

Realizing that she was unlikely to get any more information from her unusually tight-lipped companion, Caroline stopped speaking and spent the remainder of the journey speculating to herself as to what Dr. Harris would ask Madam Lavinia. If Madam chose to be honest with him, she might learn all she needed to know without having to interrogate Dr. Harris any further.

When the cab pulled up outside Madam's dwelling, Dr. Harris paid the driver, and came around to help Caroline descend.

"Is Madam expecting us?" Caroline asked.

"I sent her a note so one would assume so." Dr. Harris knocked loudly on the door.

"Were you not concerned that she would abscond?"

"Hardly. I suspect she had much bigger fish to fry than me." He knocked again and the door opened a crack to reveal the butler.

"Madam is resting, sir. Please return at a more convenient time."

"She is expecting me." Dr. Harris somehow managed to get his foot in the door and kept inexorably pressing forward until the butler yielded his space. "It won't take more than a few minutes. Is she in the back parlor?"

"No, sir. She's in her study." The butler pointed at the middle door on the right.

Caroline smiled sympathetically at the butler as she followed Dr. Harris through the door and gave the man a coin for his trouble. She wasn't surprised when he stepped back, and disappeared in the direction of the kitchen. Dr. Harris was something of an irresistible force.

She went after him and almost bumped into his back as he opened the door and paused.

"Good Lord."

"What is it?" Caroline tried to peer around his large frame.

Dr. Harris didn't bother to answer her. Instead, he advanced slowly into the room where Madam was sitting in a chair behind a large desk, her tarot cards spread out in front of her, and a half-finished glass of wine at her right elbow. She didn't acknowledge their presence. There was something about her glassy-eyed stare that reminded Caroline of the unpleasant events at Greenwood Hall.

"She's dead, isn't she?" Caroline asked in a whisper.

"I believe so." Dr. Harris was staring at Madam.

"Shall I go for help?"

"No. Shut the door, will you? I don't want anyone coming in and finding us here."

"I beg your pardon?" Caroline squeaked. "She's dead!"

"As a qualified physician I am well aware of that, Miss Morton." He finally turned to look at her. "I thought we might take a moment to . . . investigate before we raise the alarm."

"Investigate what exactly?"

He shrugged. "The contents of her desk, perhaps?"

"I can't believe you are suggesting this!"

"This woman is not what she seems, and I think it behooves us to ascertain whether she has any damaging information in her possession before we alert the authorities."

"Damaging information about you?" Caroline asked. "I don't recall Madam threatening *me* with anything in particular."

Dr. Harris raised his eyebrow. "You sound slightly hysterical, Miss Morton."

"That's because I can't believe that you're more interested in delving into Madam's personal affairs than making sure that she truly is deceased!"

He sighed. "Fine." He approached Madam and gently held her wrist. "I can confirm that she is dead and has been for a while. She might have suffered heart failure or had a stroke. Can we proceed now? I don't want the butler coming in here when he thinks my fifteen minutes are up and discovering us with a dead woman. And don't you want to know whether Madam has any further information about your father?"

Caroline hadn't considered that.

When Dr. Harris turned his attention to the drawers of Madam's desk, she followed his example. None of the drawers were locked and they appeared to consist of appointment books and ledgers containing the names and addresses presumably of her clients.

"These could prove useful," Caroline admitted.

"In finding her murderer?" Dr. Harris was rapidly sorting through a pile of correspondence.

"You just said she died of heart failure or a stroke. Why would you think she was murdered?"

He shrugged as he continued his search and didn't reply to her question. "Can you fit those ledgers in your reticule?"

"Of course not! I can't steal her property, Dr. Harris. Do you have no scruples?"

"There's no need to take that self-righteous tone with me, Miss Morton. I'll ask the butler if we can borrow them, instead."

"As if he will lend them to you when he'll think you just murdered his employer."

Caroline wrenched open the central drawer and went still.

"Dr. Harris?"

"What is it now?"

She reached in, took out the two envelopes at the top of the pile, and showed them to him.

"How bizarre." He frowned. "They have our names on them."

Caroline's gaze went to Madam Lavinia's lifeless corpse, and she shuddered.

"It's almost as if she knew we'd be the ones to find her."

"Perhaps she did. Professor Brown insisted she had some latent psychic talent." Dr. Harris sorted through the pile, stuffed something into his pocket, replaced the rest of the contents, and shut the drawer. "Now, will you go and get the butler? And if he asks why it took so long, tell him I've been trying to revive Madam."

"Shall we take the letters with our names on or leave them here?" Caroline wasn't sure why she was asking the question or why she was playing along with the doctor's directives.

"Take them."

"And what of the items you just concealed in your pocket?"

"That doesn't need to worry you in the slightest, Miss Morton." He gestured toward the door. "The sooner you get the butler, the quicker we can be out of here."

"I don't like this, Dr. Harris." Caroline held his stare. "I have a lot of questions."

He inclined his head. "Which I will be delighted to answer once we're out of our current predicament of being arrested as possible murderers."

Caroline headed for the door. "I'll hold you accountable for that."

"Knowing you, I am quite certain you will. Now, please hurry."

After one last scathing backward glance, Caroline chose not to retaliate and went to fetch the butler, a queasy feeling in her stomach. She had no desire to become embroiled in another murder, but it seemed inevitable. She paused in the hallway to gather herself before she went to locate the kitchen. It was a good thing Dr. Harris had asked her to join him, or things might have turned out very differently.

She frowned as the silence of the house closed around her. Had he done so deliberately? And why had his thoughts immediately turned to murder? Was there far more to this situation than met the eye, and how had she ended up in the middle of it?

Chapter 4

Mrs. Frogerton looked up as Caroline came into the drawing room. "Did you have an enjoyable afternoon with Dr. Harris? It is nice to see the two of you getting along again."

Caroline sank into the chair opposite her employer. "May I trouble you for some tea, please, ma'am?"

"Of course, lass." Mrs. Frogerton studied her carefully as she poured her a cup. "You seem distraught."

"That's because . . ." Caroline waved a distracted hand. "I am."

"Did you have a disagreement with Dr. Harris?"

"You might say that was part of it."

Caroline gratefully sipped her tea. It had taken an hour to extract herself from Madam's house. The butler had required considerable attention, the rest of the female staff even more so, and Caroline's patience was wearing thin. Dr. Harris hadn't been much help as he'd quizzed the butler about Madam's visitors earlier that day and had somehow persuaded the man to part with a list of her clients and her daily caller logs.

"I don't even know where to start telling you what happened." Caroline smoothed down her navy skirt.

"At the beginning is generally recommended," Mrs. Frogerton said briskly. "And remember, I'm quite hard to shock, lass, and if there are wrongs to be righted, I'm more than willing to act in your defense."

"I appreciate that." Caroline drank the rest of her tea and made an effort to compose herself. "Dr. Harris asked me to accompany him to Madam Lavinia's house. When we got there, she was dead."

"No!" Mrs. Frogerton uttered a little shriek and pressed her hand to her rounded bosom. "I was planning on returning to see her at the end of the week. What did she die of?"

"Dr. Harris thought it could be heart failure or a stroke, but he said the coroner would discern the actual cause."

"She wasn't elderly," Mrs. Frogerton pointed out. "And she never appeared to be sickly."

"She did not," Caroline agreed.

"I can see why that might have upset you, lass, especially after the deaths at Greenwood Hall." Mrs. Frogerton poured her more tea.

"It wasn't just that." Caroline gratefully accepted her refilled cup. "It was Dr. Harris's behavior. He insisted that we search Madam's desk before we notified the butler or the authorities of her death."

Mrs. Frogerton frowned. "That is quite irregular. Did he say why he wished to do so?"

"When we attended Madam's meeting, she mentioned him in an unflattering manner. I suspect it had something to do with that, but he refused to be forthcoming."

"You think he was searching for evidence to refute her claims?"

"I think he was trying to ascertain where her information had come from." Caroline met her employer's interested gaze. "He was more insistent that we search her desk than in making certain that Madam was indeed dead."

"That seems very unlike Dr. Harris," Mrs. Frogerton agreed. "He is normally the first to insist that a person's well-being is more important than anything else. What did he say when you challenged him?"

"That I was being hysterical!" Caroline met her employer's gaze. "Which didn't endear him to me at all."

"Men . . ." Mrs. Frogerton shook her head. "I assume you eventually contacted the authorities?"

"Yes, but only after Dr. Harris had retrieved certain items from Madam's desk and concealed them in his pocket."

"That is most concerning." Mrs. Frogerton frowned. "I imagine he wouldn't tell you what he'd taken?"

"You are correct." Caroline hesitated. "There was one other strange occurrence, ma'am."

Mrs. Frogerton gasped. "Don't tell me that Madam's ghost appeared and denounced her murderer?"

"I almost wish she had," Caroline said as she opened her reticule she'd set beside her chair. "Because this feels much worse."

She extracted the letter she'd taken from the desk and held it up for Mrs. Frogerton's perusal.

"What is it?"

"A letter addressed to me."

"Good Lord, it's almost as if Madam knew you would be the person to find her!" Mrs. Frogerton took a shuddering breath. "What did she ask of you?"

"I don't know." Caroline grimaced. "I haven't had the courage to open it yet."

"Would you like me to do it for you?" Mrs. Frogerton held out her hand. "I am more than willing."

"I think I should do it myself." Caroline stared at Madam's unfamiliar writing.

Mrs. Frogerton uttered another cry and made the sign of the cross over her bosom. "Lord save us!"

Knowing her employer's intense interest in the supernatural, Caroline wasn't surprised that although sympathetic, Mrs. Frogerton appeared to be enjoying herself immensely.

Caroline broke the wax seal on the back of the note, unfolded the single sheet of paper, and began to read.

"Well, what does it say?" Mrs. Frogerton asked eagerly.

Caroline read it aloud. " 'If you are reading this note, Miss Morton, I have been murdered. I am relying on you to discover my killer and bring them to justice. When you accomplish this task, you will discover the riches you deserve.' "

Caroline raised her gaze to meet Mrs. Frogerton's enthralled expression.

"Then you must do as she asks."

"I'd much rather not," Caroline replied. "I've had enough of murderers to last me a lifetime."

"But how can you ignore a plea from beyond the grave?" Mrs. Frogerton asked. "I will assist you in your endeavors."

"That is very kind of you, ma'am, but we are both rather occupied in ensuring that Dorothy has a successful London Season."

"Dotty is perfectly capable of doing that for herself." Mrs. Frogerton waved away her daughter's claims to her attention with a flick of her fingers. "Madam Lavinia is *dead*, and we are the only ones who can help her receive justice in this world."

Caroline set her cup back on its saucer. "Perhaps it might be best to wait for the official coroner's verdict on the cause of her death before we rush into anything?"

"That is a good point," Mrs. Frogerton conceded. "But what if they find nothing suspicious? Is that not suspicious in itself?"

"We'd have to ask Dr. Harris. He was the one who found her after all."

"But he thinks Madam was murdered."

"He said he wouldn't be surprised if someone had killed her."

"Why is that?"

"From the little he told me he thinks Madam is a charlatan and a blackmailer," Caroline said. "He was intent on discovering where she got her information from."

"But Professor Brown thought she was a true psychic,"

Mrs. Frogerton said. "And he is an expert in such matters."

"Professor Brown suggested Madam had some talent, but he believed a lot of the questions she asked were designed to get her guests to provide information for her rather than vice versa."

Mrs. Frogerton frowned. "Then how did she know about Septimus's pet name for me?"

"That might have been genuine, ma'am, but you must admit that she also asked a lot of very general questions."

Mrs. Frogerton relapsed into deep thought and then shook her head. "I suppose we were all too eager to hear from our loved ones to notice if we were being manipulated."

"Exactly." Caroline was relieved that her employer's common sense was reasserting itself.

"But why would someone want to murder Madam because she tries to bring comfort to the grieving?"

"I suspect it has more to do with how she comes by such intimate information and what she does with it." Caroline frowned. "And perhaps people might hear things from their loved ones that contradict what they thought they knew."

"Indeed." Mrs. Frogerton nodded. "Messages from the dead are not always welcome and as Madam is the conduit for them, she might well be a target of resentment."

"I think that is highly likely." Caroline paused. "She might also have used that information to enhance her profits."

"Which is why Dr. Harris believes she was murdered."

"I did wonder . . ." Caroline stopped speaking.

Mrs. Frogerton raised her eyebrows. "Do go on."

"Exactly what Dr. Harris hoped to accomplish by visiting Madam today. He was not himself at all."

"Do you remember what Madam said to him at the séance?"

"Something about him having blood on his hands and a woman called Amelia."

"And he was upset by that?"

"He was very perturbed."

"I wonder who she was?" Mrs. Frogerton asked. "And he asked you to accompany him today to confront Madam."

"Yes, I did wonder about that as well." Caroline glanced uncertainly at her employer. "Did he want my support as a friend, or as a witness?"

Mrs. Frogerton snorted. "If he'd planned on murdering Madam, I doubt he would've taken you with him."

"I suppose that is true," Caroline conceded. "Perhaps he thought bringing a woman with him would reassure Madam that he had no intention of physically harming her."

"That sounds more like the Dr. Harris I know," Mrs. Frogerton agreed. "I will ask him to attend us here tomorrow and explain himself."

"That is a very good notion," Caroline said. "Whether he'll actually agree to turn up is another matter entirely."

"I'll send him a note right now before I forget." Mrs. Frogerton rose and went over to her writing desk. "He can join us for dinner while Dotty is out with the Lingards tomorrow night. I'll tell the boy to wait for a reply so Dr. Harris can't avoid answering me."

Caroline hadn't told Mrs. Frogerton that Dr. Harris had also received a note from Madam, but she fully intended to ask the doctor what it had said at the earliest opportunity. If he truly wanted her help with this matter, he'd have to speak to her at some point. Until then, she would keep her counsel and await further developments. She had a horrible feeling that the matter of Madam's death would not disappear without some controversy.

The last thing she wanted was to be involved in another murder inquiry. For some reason she was certain that her faint hope Madam had died of natural causes would be dashed by the coroner. If Madam could irritate a relatively ordinary man such as Dr. Harris with her prophecies, who else had she offended? From the size of her ledgers and client lists that could be a lot of people. It only took one of them to decide that Madam should be permanently stopped from speaking out.

The killer might have hoped Madam's death would be discovered later in the day and attributed to natural causes. Having Dr. Harris turn up and suggest otherwise might have interfered with their plans. Caroline wished she hadn't agreed to go with Dr. Harris, but it was too late for regrets. She could only hope that the matter would be solved easily and that the authorities would do their job before she had to take any part in the investigation.

Unfortunately, she'd learned at Greenfield Hall that those in authority often had their own ideas about whom and what should be prosecuted, and such a minor death might not interest them at all. Which meant that if she honored a dead woman's wishes and tried to find a murderer, she'd be involved whether she wanted to be or not.

Mrs. Frogerton looked over her shoulder. "Ring the bell for me, dear, would you? I'll get this note sent off to Dr. Harris and we will see him tomorrow night at dinner." She glanced up at the clock. "And now we should both go and change. Dorothy is expecting us to accompany her to the theater tonight."

"Yes, ma'am." Caroline rang the bell. "I am looking forward to it."

A night at the opera would provide the perfect escape from the image of glassy-eyed Madam Lavinia that refused to leave her head. Tomorrow would be soon enough to deal with the inevitable call from the authorities investigating Madam's death and to practice her careful replies to the questions they would ask her.

As the door opened to admit the butler, Caroline rose from her seat and left Mrs. Frogerton to deal with the delivery of the note. She climbed the stairs, suddenly weary after her far too exciting day. Women such as Madam Lavinia lived vulnerable lives without the protection of family or someone to speak up for them. Perhaps it was her duty to be the person who stood up for Madam when no one else would.

But maybe the authorities would surprise her and easily discern the murderer. If they arrived to question her on the morrow, she had a few suggestions about persons of interest for them to investigate, starting with the gentleman who had interrupted the last meeting and threatened Madam in front of a whole room of witnesses.

If she was able to help Madam without being more directly involved in the matter than that, she would consider herself lucky. Caroline went into her bedroom and rang the bell for the maid. After Mrs. Frogerton's nagging, she'd ordered a new evening dress in a dark navy silk and was looking forward to wearing it for the first time. It was plainer than she was used to and far less influenced by current fashion because she intended to make it last for several years. The color suited her admirably and it was very pleasant to own something new.

After some help with her hair and the fastenings of her dress from the maid, she went downstairs and found Dorothy and her mother awaiting her in the hallway of the house.

"You look beautiful," Dorothy pouted. "It's not fair."

"And you sound very petulant, Dotty," Mrs. Frogerton said reprovingly. "That isn't kind."

"Oh, Caroline knows what I mean." Dorothy pointed at her own lavishly ruffled yellow skirts. "If I wore anything that plain I'd look like a nun, yet it suits Caroline perfectly."

"You look very fashionable, Dorothy," Caroline said.

"Mutton dressed as lamb my mother will probably say, whereas you look like a veritable swan." Dorothy winked at her. "Please remember to seat yourself as far away from me in the box as possible."

"Naturally." Caroline was used to Dorothy's forthright sense of humor and didn't take offense. "Although I doubt anyone will get close to you because of your skirts."

"They are rather voluminous," Dorothy agreed. "But it is the fashion and I have to keep up." She sighed dramatically. "Shall we go, Mother? We don't want to keep the DeBlooms waiting."

"Of course, my dear." Mrs. Frogerton put on her cloak and went to the front door. "I only hope we'll all fit into the carriage with you in that dress. How many petticoats do you have underneath your skirt?"

Caroline smiled as she followed along behind the mildly bickering pair. She was determined to enjoy her evening, to sleep well, and to leave worrying about what tomorrow would bring until it was upon her.

Chapter 5

"Miss Morton?"

The two gentlemen the butler had ushered into the rarely used front parlor on the ground floor rose to their feet as Caroline and Mrs. Frogerton entered the room.

"I am Miss Morton, and this is Mrs. Frogerton, my employer," Caroline said. "How may we assist you on this fine morning?"

"Thank you for agreeing to see us. I'm Sergeant Dawson and this is Constable Rice. We represent the Metropolitan Police Force."

The sergeant had a flat London accent and an air of weariness that belied the sharpness of his brown eyes and his apparent youth. He carried his tall black hat in his hand and wore the distinctive dark blue long-tailed coat with brass buttons designed to make those enforcing the law more distinctive than the general population and the military.

"Peelers!" Mrs. Frogerton interjected brightly. "Isn't that what you're called?" She turned to Caroline and whispered loudly, "After Sir Robert Peel, their founder."

Sergeant Dawson bowed. "We prefer our official moniker, ma'am."

"I'm sure you do." Mrs. Frogerton twinkled at him. "Now, will you sit down and tell us why you are here?"

"Thank you, ma'am, I prefer to stand. We believe Miss Morton was at an address in St. John's Wood yesterday afternoon with a Dr. Harris?"

"If you mean that I accompanied Dr. Harris to Madam Lavinia's house yesterday, then you are correct," Caroline answered for herself as Mrs. Frogerton decided to ring for tea.

"Thank you, Miss Morton." The sergeant nodded. "Would you say that your visit went as expected?"

"Not at all. We discovered Madam was dead shortly after we entered the house," Caroline said. "It was something of a shock."

"I'm sure it was, miss." Sergeant Dawson gestured to his companion to open his notebook. "Can you remember what time it was when you first realized Madam was dead?"

"It was about a quarter past three. The clock on the mantelpiece rang the quarter hour while we were in the room," Caroline said. "As a physician, Dr. Harris was quick to notice something was wrong. He immediately checked Madam to see if she was still breathing."

In truth she'd had to remind him to do so, but she wasn't going to mention that to the police.

"And Dr. Harris confirmed that Madam was dead?"

"Yes, Sergeant."

"Did he comment on how he believed Madam had died?"

"He thought she might have suffered heart failure or had a stroke," Caroline said.

"And did you agree with him, miss?"

Caroline raised her eyebrows. "As I am not a trained physician, I deferred to Dr. Harris's superior knowledge in such matters."

"Dr. Harris is very skilled," Mrs. Frogerton interjected. "He trained in Edinburgh, you know."

"So I understand, ma'am."

Sergeant Dawson returned his attention to Caroline. She already had a sense that he would doggedly pursue his objectives and would not be led down any false trails.

"What were your own thoughts when you found Madam, Miss Morton?"

"I was quite shocked," Caroline said. "Although Madam was sitting upright in her chair and there was no sign of any disruption or violence, it was obvious that she was dead."

"You have encountered death before, miss?"

The sergeant's tone was decidedly skeptical.

"Yes, indeed." Caroline raised her chin. "I recently attended a house party with Mrs. Frogerton where a murderer ran riot."

Mrs. Frogerton nudged her. "Now, don't be saying that to a policeman, lass, or he'll think it's you."

Sergeant Dawson didn't smile. "From your observations, Miss Morton, was Madam dead before Dr. Harris approached her?"

"Yes, of course." Caroline frowned. "Are you trying to suggest I stood by and watched Dr. Harris murder her?"

"One has to investigate all possibilities, Miss Morton."

"You believe Dr. Harris and I are in cahoots? For what purpose?"

The sergeant shrugged. "If we do our jobs properly, such information will emerge during the investigation."

"Do you know how Madam died?" Caroline chose not to rise to the bait.

"Not yet, miss, but the coroner should have an answer on that tomorrow." He paused to glance at the constable, who was still writing his notes. "Is there anything else you'd like to tell me about your association with Dr. Harris or Madam Lavinia, Miss Morton?"

"I'd suggest that you talk to the people who attended her last séance and ask them about the gentleman who disrupted the meeting and threatened Madam for deceiving his mother."

"Which lady was that?" Mrs. Frogerton asked with great interest.

Caroline turned to her employer. "The widow who was present on the evening we went together, ma'am. Madam Lavinia spoke about her deceased husband's favorite dress of hers."

Sergeant Dawson looked mildly interested as Mrs. Frogerton frowned.

"Lady Fielding?"

"I don't know her name," Caroline replied.

"Dressed in unrelieved black with veils covering her face and hair? Cried into a black lace-edged handkerchief throughout the session?"

"I believe that was her."

"Then it *is* Lady Fielding." Mrs. Frogerton sat back. "She did mention that her son was vehemently opposed to her attending the meetings with Madam, but such an attitude wasn't uncommon amongst our nearest and dearest." Mrs. Frogerton appeared to have forgotten they were in the presence of the law as she chattered on to Caroline. "Did her son turn up and start a fight? What a shame I missed it!"

"I will tell you all the details after our visitors have departed, ma'am," Caroline promised before turning back to Sergeant Dawson, who was listening intently. "I should imagine Madam's butler has a list of her clients if you wish to investigate Lady Fielding and her family further."

"We have already acquired some of that information, Miss Morton." Sergeant Dawson bowed. "We will find the rest of it soon enough."

"I'm sure you will, Sergeant," Caroline agreed.

The constable finished writing, closed his notebook, and looked over at his superior.

"We have an appointment at the court on the hour, sir."

"Ah yes." Sergeant Dawson inclined his head and handed Caroline and Mrs. Frogerton his card before rising to his feet. "If you think of anything else you wish to tell me, Miss Morton, please send me a message at this address."

"I will certainly do that."

"And we would very much like to know how poor Madam Lavinia died," Mrs. Frogerton added. "If you would be so kind as to let us know."

"I'll see what I can do, ma'am."

The sergeant and constable exited the parlor, leaving Caroline and Mrs. Frogerton staring at each other.

Mrs. Frogerton was the first to speak. "Did you get the impression that Sergeant Dawson believes Dr. Harris murdered Madam?"

"Yes, and even worse he thinks I stood there and let him get away with it," Caroline replied. "What an unpleasant man."

"That's why I mentioned Lady Fielding," Mrs. Frogerton confided. "I had a sense that he needed a distraction."

"That was well done of you, ma'am. I wish I'd thought of it."

"I don't believe Dr. Harris murdered anyone." Mrs. Frogerton looked up as the butler brought in the tea tray. "Take that up to the drawing room, please. It's warmer in there."

"I don't understand why they think Dr. Harris is the murderer," Caroline commented as she followed her employer up the stairs.

"Perhaps they know more than they are letting on." Mrs. Frogerton went into the drawing room, where her dogs who had been sleeping by the fire greeted her with great enthusiasm. "That is a common theme in the books I like to read."

"Unless the butler actually witnessed Dr. Harris murdering his mistress earlier in the day." Caroline poured the tea. "In which case Dr. Harris is already in jail and won't be coming for dinner."

"Then why wouldn't they just say that?"

"Because they think I am his accomplice?" Caroline passed over a cup of tea. "Or they want me to turn on him and confess my part in it."

Mrs. Frogerton regarded her critically and then shook her head. "If they'd ever seen you and Dr. Harris converse, they would know you're incapable of getting along, let alone plotting a murder together."

"One might hope Dr. Harris would tell them that himself," Caroline said tartly. "But he hasn't *been* himself since Madam called him out the other evening."

"So, is it possible he *did* kill her after all?" Mrs. Frogerton asked.

Caroline sipped her tea and considered that audacious notion. "He has never struck me as the kind of gentleman who would murder anyone, ma'am, but we are barely acquainted. But I think Lady Fielding's son is a far more likely candidate, don't you?"

"Was he very angry?"

"Yes. It took the butler and Dr. Harris to remove him from the room."

Mrs. Frogerton's eyes widened, and she pressed her hand to her bosom. "How exciting! Did Lady Fielding leave with him?"

"No, she apologized for her son and stayed firmly in her chair," Caroline replied. "She was remarkably calm about the whole thing. But Madam was too overcome to continue so we all had to leave anyway."

"Poor Madam Lavinia must have been very disturbed by such threatening behavior." Mrs. Frogerton shook her head and tutted. "I would be mortified if my son behaved like that."

"He was very angry. I wouldn't be surprised if he killed Madam in a fit of temper."

"I will ask my maid to find out where Lady Fielding lives. She might need our support."

"Dr. Harris might have that information. He tried to get me to conceal Madam's ledgers in my reticule."

"Did he, now." Mrs. Frogerton looked thoughtful. "I must say that for a man who isn't a murderer, Dr. Harris is acting remarkably like one."

"If he remains a free man, we can ask him all these questions when he comes to dinner this evening." Caroline finished her tea and went to place her cup back on the tray. She glanced out of the window and paused. "There is a hackney cab outside."

"And?"

"Dr. Harris and Professor Brown are getting out of it and coming up the steps."

Mrs. Frogerton clapped her hands. "How wonderful! Ask the butler to show them up and order some substantial refreshments."

Rather than admit the men herself, Caroline went down the back stairs directly to the kitchen to ask Cook to send up extra cups and refreshments. After their recent difference of opinion, she was reluctant to see Dr. Harris and yet relieved that he hadn't been incarcerated. As she returned to the drawing room, she wondered whether he had any notion that the police considered him a suspect. By the time she reached the open door her employer was loudly telling Dr. Harris about Sergeant Dawson's visit and Caroline realized Dr. Harris would not remain ignorant of their suspicions about him for much longer.

"What?" Caroline winced as Dr. Harris replied to Mrs. Frogerton with some volume. "If I'd murdered her, I'd hardly be stupid enough to come back later that afternoon, would I?"

"Perhaps you might have wanted to make quite sure she was dead?" Mrs. Frogerton asked hopefully.

"Again, if I'd killed Madam, I'd do a good job of it, and I wouldn't need to come back and check my work." Dr. Harris glared at Caroline. "What on earth have you been telling Mrs. Frogerton and the police, Miss Morton?"

"Nothing to incriminate you, sir, I can assure you of that," Caroline snapped back. "In truth I was more concerned that Sergeant Dawson appeared to believe I was your accomplice."

Dr. Harris opened his mouth and for once obviously considered his words. "That is a ridiculous idea."

"We can at least agree on that," Caroline said.

"Sergeant Dawson isn't stupid," Mrs. Frogerton said. "He struck me as the kind of man who would pursue his goals regardless."

"Regardless of the facts?" Dr. Harris snorted and took a hasty turn around the room, his hands clasped around his back. "Typical. These new 'protection' officers only protect the wealthy and the powerful."

"They have done a great deal to bring order to the streets of our city, Harris." Professor Brown spoke for the first time. "I, for one am grateful for their existence. If they wish to talk to me about what transpired at Madam's I would be delighted to accommodate them."

"I suspect they will wish to speak to everyone who attended her sessions," Caroline said. "We did mention the behavior of Lady Fielding's son to the sergeant."

"The gentleman who interrupted the meeting and threatened Madam for fleecing credulous widows?" Dr. Harris asked.

"Yes."

"He does seem like an obvious suspect," Professor Brown agreed. "He was very angry."

"I do wish I'd been there," Mrs. Frogerton sighed. "It sounds very exciting."

"In truth, it was most unpleasant, ma'am," Caroline replied. "I was afraid Lady Fielding's son would physically harm Madam. He certainly threatened her."

Professor Brown cleared his throat. "For the sake of accuracy, Miss Morton, I must add that Madam Lavinia did sound as if she was threatening him *herself*."

"How so?" asked Mrs. Frogerton.

"I don't have my notes with me, ma'am, but I am fairly

certain Madam said Fielding couldn't threaten the dead and that he should know that all too well."

"That doesn't sound like a threat to me," Dr. Harris said.

"But it did to young Alfred, who I suspect took it to mean that she planned to murder *him*." Professor Brown frowned. "But, in retrospect, maybe she was referring to her own imminent death."

"At his hands . . ." Mrs. Frogerton shuddered. "How horrible."

Silence fell for a moment and Caroline took the opportunity to pour them all some tea while the butler delivered the additional refreshments.

"Has Sergeant Dawson interviewed you yet, Dr. Harris?" Caroline asked.

"I have an appointment with him later today." Dr. Harris turned to Mrs. Frogerton. "That is one of the reasons why I came around, ma'am. I suspect I won't have the time to come to dinner after he's finished with me as I'm due on the wards at ten."

"It sounds as if you should be wary, sir," Professor Brown said jovially. "I wouldn't want to see my esteemed colleague held on a murder charge. The hospital authorities would be most upset."

"As I didn't murder Madam, and I have nothing to hide, I'm not worried in the slightest, Professor." Dr. Harris helped himself to a large plateful of cake.

"Sergeant Dawson was very interested in recovering the records of Madam's clients," Caroline said. "I assume he wishes to interview as many of them as possible."

Dr. Harris looked right at her and raised his eyebrows. "I believe the butler has all that information in his possession, Miss Morton."

"Of course." She hoped he meant he'd returned all the books to Madam's house. "One would assume so."

"I will find out where Lady Fielding resides," Mrs. Frogerton spoke up. "Perhaps we should pay her a visit this afternoon, Caroline?"

"I think that would be an excellent idea." Caroline turned to Dr. Harris. "Would you care to accompany us, sir?"

"And meet the fool I had to help remove from Madam's parlor as he threatened to kill her? No, thank you." He finished his cake. "I hardly think I have anything of interest to ask him, and I'd be loath to incite his rage again. You and Mrs. Frogerton will handle the matter perfectly well."

"I'm sure we will," Caroline agreed. "Mrs. Frogerton has a unique ability to get people to talk to her." She paused. "Is there anything I should ask him in particular?"

"Nothing I can think of." Dr. Harris frowned. "Everything rather depends on the findings of the coroner, anyway. It might be a fuss about nothing."

"Do you truly believe that?" Professor Brown asked. "Because I don't."

"You think Madam was murdered?" Mrs. Frogerton shivered. "The poor woman."

"From my research into her background I suspect this isn't the first time she has come to the attention of the authorities." He paused. "It certainly explains why she has moved around the country so frequently."

"You believe she moved to avoid being prosecuted?" Caroline set the teapot down after refilling all the cups. "For what exactly?"

Professor Brown shrugged. "I'm sure Sergeant Dawson will have some theories on that, but my best guess would be blackmailing her clients."

Mrs. Frogerton gasped. "Surely not!"

"Madam certainly knew a lot about everyone," Caroline said slowly.

"Indeed." Professor Brown nodded. "The question is how did she obtain that information and what did she do with it?"

Chapter 6

Caroline was still pondering Professor Brown's words as she and Mrs. Frogerton headed for Lady Fielding's house later that afternoon. Had Madam met someone who knew Caroline's father well enough to remember not only his daughter's name, but also her favorite doll? It seemed unlikely. Caroline had never mentioned the incident to anyone, and she doubted her father had even remembered it.

And Madam hadn't tried to blackmail her. She'd offered to help her reclaim her father's fortune. Even as Caroline remembered Madam's promise, her recently acquired cynicism put a different interpretation on the words. If Caroline had been naïve enough to get involved, how much would it have cost her to find out she'd been fed a load of lies? Probably far more than she could afford. She'd been let down by her father all her life. Allowing it to happen again and to pay for the privilege would be madness.

And yet . . . Caroline sighed. There was some small part of her that yearned for something more, some sign that he had cared for her and Susan more than she'd thought and had somehow attempted to safeguard their futures.

"Are you fretting about Dr. Harris, lass?"

Caroline looked over at Mrs. Frogerton, who occupied the seat opposite. "Not at all, ma'am."

"Then why are you sighing like the wind has caught your sails?"

"I was thinking about my father."

"And what Madam Lavinia said about him?"

Caroline had told Mrs. Frogerton about Madam's strange message from her father after Dr. Harris and Professor Brown had left for the hospital.

"How could she have known that about him?" Caroline felt compelled to ask.

"Because she had a gift?" It was Mrs. Frogerton's turn to sigh. "And now she's dead because someone didn't like what she said to them."

"Or she was blackmailing them," Caroline reminded her employer. "Don't forget that possibility."

"It will be interesting to hear what Lady Fielding has to say on the matter." Mrs. Frogerton peered out of the window as they rounded the corner into a pleasant tree-lined square of terraced houses with a garden in the center. "Should we mention Madam is dead or wait for the police to inform her?"

"I suspect our conversation will be determined by whether Lady Fielding has heard that news or not." Caroline held on to the strap as the carriage swayed as it took the sharp corner and came to a stop. She waited until the coachman opened the door.

"Thank you, Giles." She accepted his hand to descend and waited for Mrs. Frogerton to join her.

She took a moment to look up at the Fielding house, which had a redbrick front, a black front door, and a well-polished knocker.

"Come along then, Caroline." Mrs. Frogerton hitched up her skirt and ascended the steps.

Somewhat to their surprise the door was opened immediately by the lady of the house. She wore her habitual black with a matching lace cap and a light shawl around her shoulders. Her face fell when she recognized them.

"Oh! I do apologize. I thought you were someone else."
She stepped back, her cheeks reddening. "Do come in."

Caroline's gaze took in the half-filled trunk that sat at
the bottom of the stairs, two pairs of dirty boots in the
fireplace, and a discarded cloak thrown over one of the
chairs.

"Is everything all right, Lady Fielding?" Mrs. Frogerton
asked. "You seem a little upset."

"I . . ." Lady Fielding pressed a visibly trembling hand
to her forehead. "Had something of a falling-out with
my son."

"Oh, dear." Mrs. Frogerton gently guided the distraught
widow toward the front parlor. "As a mother of a growing
lad myself, I can only sympathize. They can be quite difficult sometimes, can't they?"

Lady Fielding burst into tears.

"Alfred lost his temper because I refused to leave
Madam's with him the other evening."

Mrs. Frogerton guided the widow onto the couch and
sat beside her, gently patting her hand. Caroline extracted
a clean handkerchief from her reticule and offered it to
Lady Fielding.

"He's still angry about that?"

"Yes, because this morning he did the household accounts." Lady Fielding dabbed at her cheeks with the
handkerchief. "He wanted to know why the tradesmen
hadn't been paid and accused me of . . . giving his money
to Madam."

"Oh, dear."

"And that isn't fair when the vast majority of our income goes to his gambling and horses and . . . other things
leaving me in very straitened circumstances to begin with!"

"Men." Mrs. Frogerton shook her head.

Faced with such a sympathetic audience, Lady Fielding
began to regain her equilibrium. "I can barely afford to
pay my staff and put food on the table with the amount he

allows me. To suggest that I wasted those funds on Madam Lavinia was unfair."

"I quite agree." Mrs. Frogerton paused. "Did you tell your son that?"

"I did, and that's when he stormed out of the house in a rage." Lady Fielding blew her nose. "He started to pack and then said he'd send for his belongings when he had established himself in new lodgings. But how is he going to pay for them?" Her voice rose another octave. "And if he withdraws his support from this house, how can I survive?"

"Does Sir Alfred often lose his temper?" Mrs. Frogerton asked.

"Yes, he's just like his father. The two of them were always at loggerheads." Lady Fielding took a shaky breath. "Not that such ancient family history need concern you." She sat up straight. "I do apologize for my behavior."

"There is nothing to apologize for, my lady," Mrs. Frogerton said. "Please rest assured that nothing you have told us will go beyond your front door."

"Thank you." Lady Fielding tried to smile. "I'm sure this will all blow over and he'll be back demanding his dinner as usual at six. He's still young and losing his father has affected him greatly."

"When did your husband pass away?" Mrs. Frogerton asked.

"Almost a year ago. It was quite a shock as he appeared perfectly well."

Mrs. Frogerton nodded. "My Septimus had a heart attack and dropped dead right in front of me."

"How terrible." It was Lady Fielding's turn to pat her companion's hand. "Did visiting Madam Lavinia bring you comfort?"

"It certainly did. She told me Septimus was proud of how I was increasing the profits of his businesses."

Lady Fielding drew back. "You are in trade?"

"Yes, that's where the fortune my daughter needs to capture her peer of the realm comes from." Mrs. Frogerton beamed at her bemused hostess. "I won't deny it."

"And why should you, ma'am?" Caroline said bracingly. "You should be proud of your success." She glanced over at Lady Fielding. "Did Madam provide answers for you, too, my lady? She was remarkably perceptive."

"She . . . certainly helped me see certain things more clearly." Lady Fielding shot to her feet. "I fear I have been remiss in my duties as a hostess. May I offer you some refreshments?" She rushed toward the door. "Pray excuse me for a moment while I speak to my butler, whom I suspect is unaware that we have callers."

She left with some haste and Caroline looked over at Mrs. Frogerton. "I wonder which particular part of our conversation unsettled her?"

"Me being in trade, probably." Mrs. Frogerton chuckled. "She had no idea she was entertaining the working class in her front parlor."

"I suspect it has more to do with asking about Madam Lavinia."

"Then perhaps when she returns, we'll mention the true reason for our visit and see how she reacts to that," Mrs. Frogerton suggested.

"*If* she returns. For all we know she could have abandoned us and run off to join her son."

"You are remarkably cynical for a girl of your age, lass," Mrs. Frogerton said. "I always try and see the best in people."

"Whereas I tend to assume the worst."

The door opened and Mrs. Frogerton winked at Caroline. "See?"

The butler appeared with a silver tray of crystal decanters, a coffeepot, and a very small plate of biscuits.

"Lady Fielding will join you in a moment, ma'am. She is speaking to the coachman."

"Planning her escape," Caroline murmured to her employer as the butler set the tray down between them. "While we feast on coffee and hard ginger biscuits."

Mrs. Frogerton waited until the butler left before replying.

"She's probably trying to ascertain whether her son took a horse or his carriage, which might determine how far he's gone and how seriously she should take his threats."

Lady Fielding came back in looking marginally less worried. "It was very kind of you to call on me, Mrs. Frogerton." She looked over at Caroline. "I remember you from Madam's, but I don't believe we've been introduced."

"This is Miss Morton, my companion," Mrs. Frogerton said. "She has been an invaluable help to both me and Dorothy in navigating the London Season."

"Morton?" Lady Fielding frowned. "Wasn't there some scandal recently involving the Earl of Morton and the manner of his death? Are you connected to that family?"

"Yes. My father killed himself rather than deal with his mountain of debts and obligations to his family," Caroline said.

She'd recently decided she was tired of hiding the true consequences of her father's actions and was more than willing to own up to his past.

"Oh." Lady Fielding visibly swallowed. "I do beg your pardon."

"There is no need," Caroline said. "I suspect every family deals with such things. It is just that we rarely get to see them in the unflattering light of day."

"Caroline is right. I mean why else would all those people flock to Madam Lavinia's to ask their deceased relatives and friends to explain themselves?" Mrs. Frogerton asked. "We all have unanswered questions about our loved ones. I'll wager you gained great comfort from Madam's words yourself, my lady."

"I'm not so sure about that . . ." Lady Fielding sighed. "Madam could be rather . . . unclear in her meaning sometimes."

"Was there something in particular that bothered you?" Mrs. Frogerton asked.

"Not that I can recall right now." Lady Fielding held up the coffeepot. "May I offer you both some refreshment?"

Caroline was certain they would not be getting any further information from Lady Fielding, who had belatedly remembered that they were not her friends. She accepted her cup with thanks and turned the topic of conversation toward the inclement weather.

Her employer, who was far more tenacious than Caroline, was not deterred.

"Were you intending to return to Madam's, Lady Fielding?"

"I would like to." Lady Fielding glanced uncertainly back at the door as if still expecting her son to be listening in. "But it rather depends."

Caroline wondered if Lady Fielding knew Madam was dead—and if she did, how had she found out?

"We were hoping to go on Friday, but we had some distressing news today," Mrs. Frogerton said. "In fact, that's why I came—to find out if you had heard."

"Heard what?"

"That Madam Lavinia died quite unexpectedly." Mrs. Frogerton heaved a sigh.

"*Died?*" Lady Fielding's hand shook so hard that liquid flowed from the spout of the coffeepot onto the tray.

"Yes, the police came to see us this morning," Mrs. Frogerton continued as if unaware that her hostess looked like she'd suffered a terrible shock. "Miss Morton was unfortunate enough to be the one to discover Madam was dead."

"But she can't be dead! I was due to meet her later today, and—" Lady Fielding sucked in a breath and gazed at Mrs. Frogerton in horror. "That's impossible."

"It was a terrible shock to us, too, my lady," Mrs. Frogerton said. "At least Madam told me what I needed to know, but for those who were still trying to decipher her words or needed further clarity this will be a blow." She paused. "Were you hoping for more from her, Lady Fielding?"

"I'm not sure . . ."

"I only meant that if you intended to visit her today there was obviously something on your mind?" Mrs. Frogerton asked, her brown eyes as inquisitive as a bird's.

"Nothing in particular," Lady Fielding stuttered. "I . . . I simply wanted her opinion on something."

Caroline gently cleared her throat. "I suspect the police will be visiting all of Madam's clients, my lady."

Lady Fielding drew her shawl closely around her shoulders. "I suppose they will."

"We just wanted to make sure that you were prepared."

"Thank you." Their hostess made an effort to compose herself. "Did the police say how Madam died?"

"They said they were waiting on the coroner's report."

Caroline didn't want to alarm Lady Fielding. It was bad enough that she'd argued with her son, and he wasn't home. Suggesting that Madam had been murdered might make her remember her loyalties and urge her son never to return to face any questioning.

"You mentioned that you found her?" Lady Fielding fixed her gaze on Caroline. "Had she been robbed or . . . hurt?"

"There was no sign of violence, my lady," Caroline said. "She looked quite peaceful."

"That's reassuring." Lady Fielding managed a tremulous smile. "Perhaps she died of heart failure."

"That is quite possible," Caroline agreed.

Mrs. Frogerton caught her eye. "We should be going, my dear. Dorothy has a fitting at the dressmaker's."

"Of course, ma'am." Caroline set her cup back on its saucer and rose to her feet. "I do hope Sir Alfred returns home soon, my lady."

"I'm sure he will." Lady Fielding's expression was far less certain than her words. "He's a good boy, really."

"I'm sure he is." Mrs. Frogerton smiled and placed her card on the side table. "Thank you for receiving us, Lady Fielding, and please come and visit when you have a moment. We would be delighted to see you."

"Thank you, Mrs. Frogerton, Miss Morton."

Caroline followed her employer out into the entrance hall where the butler bowed them out of the front door. Mrs. Frogerton paused to speak to her coachman before getting into the carriage. To Caroline's surprise, after leaving the square the carriage pulled up behind a cartload of barrels in the shade of the trees on the main road.

Mrs. Frogerton lowered the window.

"What exactly are we doing, ma'am?" Caroline inquired.

"Watching to see what Lady Fielding does next."

"What do you think she will do?"

"Leave the house and try and find Sir Alfred." Mrs. Frogerton looked over her shoulder at Caroline. "That's what I would do if I thought my son was in danger."

"But she is at odds with him!"

"In this situation, blood is definitely thicker than water, lass. She's not stupid. She'll want to warn him."

"Because she thinks he might have been responsible for Madam's death," Caroline said slowly. "Of course. It was interesting that she asked if Madam had been harmed—almost as if she expected it."

"We already know Sir Alfred has a nasty temper and a tendency toward violent threats."

Caroline shivered as she remembered the man's red face and clenched fists as he shouted at his mother and Madam Lavinia.

"How long do we intend to wait here, ma'am?" Caroline asked. "Dorothy does have an appointment in less than an hour."

"I don't think we'll be here for very long," Mrs. Frogerton said. "In truth, I see Lady Fielding's carriage turning out of the square right in front of us."

"Do you intend to follow her?"

"Not this time." After a minute, Mrs. Frogerton tapped on the roof with her parasol, and their carriage moved off. "It doesn't matter whether she finds him or not because the police will."

"Then why did we stop?"

Mrs. Frogerton gave a satisfied smile as she settled her skirts around her. "Because I wished to see if I was right."

"Do you think she will tell the police that we visited her?"

"I have no idea."

Caroline frowned. "Don't you think it makes us look rather suspicious?"

"With all due respect, lass, Sergeant Dawson isn't interested in my doings."

"But he is interested in mine."

"Don't worry, once he meets Sir Alfred, he'll forget all about you," Mrs. Frogerton declared. "And, as Madam died well before you and Dr. Harris arrived at the house, he's probably already realized you can't be involved."

"And I have an alibi," Caroline reminded her. "The last two days were filled with social events I attended with you and Dorothy."

"Which we can thank Dotty for." Mrs. Frogerton chuckled. "I never imagined she would be so popular."

"She has a strong personality, ma'am."

"And a huge fortune." Mrs. Frogerton was no fool. "Let's not forget that."

Later that evening Caroline came down the stairs into the entrance hall just as the butler opened the front door. Sergeant Dawson stepped in and removed his distinctive black hat. Despite the relative lateness of the hour, he still wore his full uniform.

Caroline went toward him. "Good evening, Sergeant. How may I help you?"

Sergeant Dawson's slow gaze swept over her silk gown, fan, and shawl, and finally returned to her face.

"Evening, miss. I told Mrs. Frogerton I would keep her updated about our investigation into the death of Madam Lavinia."

"Then I will ask the butler to ascertain if she is able to receive you. We are on our way out to the theater, Sergeant." Caroline nodded to the butler, who headed up the stairs. "Would you care to accompany me to the front parlor while you wait?"

"Thank you." Sergeant Dawson followed her into the room. "I had the opportunity to speak to Dr. Harris."

"I'm glad to hear it." Caroline turned to look at him. "I do hope he set your mind at rest. Did you also speak to the Fieldings?"

Sergeant Dawson, who obviously didn't like to be told his business, frowned. "I am speaking to everyone who attended Madam's sessions in the last month."

Mrs. Frogerton entered the room at some speed, the voluminous petticoats under her olive-green gown rustling as she walked. Her emerald necklace and matching earrings gleamed in the candlelight.

"Sergeant Dawson! How kind of you to call." She beamed at the officer. "Did you come to tell us how poor Madam Lavinia died?"

"I do have that information, ma'am, yes, but I also have a few questions for you and Miss Morton."

"Ask away, Sergeant," Mrs. Frogerton said. "We have nothing to hide."

The sergeant's gaze flicked toward Caroline again and she felt a faint quiver of unease.

"Miss Morton, am I correct that your father was the late Earl of Morton?"

"Yes," Caroline replied.

"Then you are, in fact, Lady Caroline Morton?"

"It hardly matters, does it?"

"It would have been helpful if you had admitted it when we first met."

Caroline frowned. "I don't understand how it is relevant to the demise of Madam Lavinia."

"It isn't directly related, but perhaps one should not . . . obscure facts from the police."

"If I'd been speaking to you about a family matter, Sergeant, I would have disclosed that information to you immediately. As I said, I didn't consider it important in an investigation in which I play such an insignificant part."

"You discovered the body, my lady."

"And, as I'm sure Dr. Harris confirmed, Madam Lavinia died hours before we arrived at her abode." Despite her growing concern, Caroline kept her voice steady and her tone light.

Mrs. Frogerton set a comforting hand on Caroline's arm. "And I can confirm that Caroline was with me earlier that day, and the day before, as can half of London Society."

"I appreciate that, ma'am, but you mistake my intentions." Sergeant Dawson inclined his head. "The matter at hand is not Lady Caroline's whereabouts, but her ability to be truthful to the police. I would never have considered her as a potential suspect if I had known she was related to a peer of the realm."

"My rank has nothing to do with this. I have no need to lie, Sergeant." Caroline met his gaze straight on. "Ask me anything you want."

He looked briefly down at his well-polished boots before he spoke again.

"Do you consider Dr. Harris to be a truthful individual, my lady?"

"To a fault, Sergeant. He prides himself on his honesty," Caroline replied.

Mrs. Frogerton nodded vigorously. "I would agree. Dr. Harris is well known for speaking his mind even to his superiors."

"Is he a violent man?"

"Not to my knowledge when his main purpose in life is to heal the sick."

Sergeant Dawson cleared his throat. "Did you ever see him threaten Madam Lavinia?"

"The only person who did that was Sir Alfred Fielding, Sergeant," Mrs. Frogerton said strongly. "I do hope you are investigating him!"

"As I said, ma'am. We are investigating several avenues of interest. As both you and Lady Caroline have known Dr. Harris for some time, I am merely directing these particular queries to you."

"Do you really consider Dr. Harris to be one of your suspects?" Mrs. Frogerton pressed her hand to her bosom. "How ridiculous! He was the one who found Madam and realized she was dead."

"That doesn't mean he wasn't instrumental in her death, ma'am."

"Surely if Dr. Harris has been involved in her demise, he wouldn't have been foolish enough to return to her house?" Mrs. Frogerton turned to Caroline. "Does that not seem rather bizarre to you?"

"Indeed, ma'am."

"Does the coroner believe Madam's death wasn't from natural causes?" Mrs. Frogerton asked the police sergeant.

"Unfortunately, yes." Sergeant Dawson paused. "I regret to inform you that the coroner thinks she was poisoned."

Chapter 7

"Poisoned?" Dr. Harris frowned. "And that's why I'm under suspicion?"

After Sergeant Dawson's startling announcement on the previous evening, Mrs. Frogerton had asked Dr. Harris to visit them the very next day. He'd turned up just before they'd sat down to a quiet family dinner and had been invited to join them. Dorothy was attending an event with the DeBlooms and had not yet returned home.

"I assume Sergeant Dawson believes you might have access to the necessary chemicals," Caroline said.

"So does all of London!" Dr. Harris waved his fork in the air. "You can pick up rat poison and arsenic everywhere."

"That's true, Doctor." Mrs. Frogerton nodded as she ate her roast lamb. "My housekeeper's accounts always include such purchases. Although, personally I think that the introduction of a large cat has a far more detrimental effect on the rodent population. What I don't understand is why the police haven't arrested Sir Alfred Fielding."

"Perhaps it has to do with his rank," Caroline said.

"Why should that matter?" Dr. Harris asked. "He's far more likely to have murdered Madam than I am."

"Caroline is still annoyed that the good sergeant told her he never would've considered her party to any crime if he'd known her father was an earl." Mrs. Frogerton shook her head. "I wonder if that means you'd have to be tried by the House of Lords, lass?"

"I sincerely doubt it." Caroline set her fork down. "And I didn't appreciate being treated differently just because of my father's last name."

"One would think you would be grateful," Dr. Harris commented. "It means you are deemed innocent regardless."

"Whereas you have to prove your innocence." Caroline held his gaze. "Which seems somewhat unfair."

The doctor toasted her with his glass of wine. "Hear hear."

"I wonder whether Sergeant Dawson thinks that because Madam was killed in a less obvious way, then Sir Alfred Fielding can't be responsible." Mrs. Frogerton looked inquiringly around the table.

"He did ask if Dr. Harris was a violent man," Caroline said.

"Which we both insisted you were not, Doctor." Mrs. Frogerton patted Dr. Harris's sleeve.

"Thank you." Dr. Harris finished his glass of wine in one swallow. "I wish I could see a copy of the coroner's report."

"Why don't you ask Sergeant Dawson if you may view it?"

"Because, ma'am, if I am one of his suspects, I doubt he'll share the evidence against me." He grimaced. "He's asked to see me again tomorrow. I suppose I should be grateful that I've not been arrested and taken off to prison."

"We won't let that happen to you, Doctor," Mrs. Frogerton said. "And if he's still asking to speak to you, I doubt he has a very strong case."

"Let's hope that you are right, Mrs. Frogerton. Madam did have quite a lot of clients. I doubt I'm the only one who had suspicions about her integrity."

"What exactly did she say to you that was a lie?" Caroline asked innocently.

He frowned. "I don't care to discuss it, Miss Morton."

"But if it is patently untrue, why not tell us? You are among friends here."

"Because it is too absurd to even mention."

"You seemed quite upset at the time," Caroline pressed on.

His brows drew together. "That was only because I wasn't expecting to hear that particular name in that particular setting."

Caroline sipped her wine as she studied Dr. Harris, who was now fidgeting with his silverware. "I do hope you are more forthcoming with the police, Doctor, because taking such an obstinate stand is neither endearing nor helpful."

"I'll deal with the police in my own way, thank you, Miss Morton."

"I'm sure you will." Caroline offered him a sharp smile. "Have the police spoken to Professor Brown?"

"I believe so. He's taken lots of notes while attending Madam's events and was more than willing to hand them over as evidence."

"Then let's hope that helps your cause, sir."

"I'm sure it will. He has a theory that Madam was blackmailing some of her clients."

"Then I'm sure the police will be looking into that as well," Mrs. Frogerton said brightly. "Although, from reading the daily newspapers I do get the sense that they tend to arrest the first person they see and are quite often wrong."

"I'm sure Dr. Harris is aware of that and will be more than willing to assist the police with their inquiries rather than irritate them with his lack of cooperation." Caroline held the doctor's gaze. "Isn't that so, Dr. Harris?"

"I'd rather not be incarcerated if that's what you mean."

"Then your path is clear." She turned to Mrs. Frogerton. "Shall we repair to the drawing room for coffee, ma'am? Or do you wish to have it served at the table?"

"The drawing room is far more comfortable." Mrs. Frogerton rose from her chair. "Will you join us, Dr. Harris?"

"Unfortunately, I'm on night duty, and I must return to the hospital." He stood and bowed. "Thank you for an excellent and enjoyable dinner."

"You are most welcome." Mrs. Frogerton smiled up at him. "And if you find yourself in any difficulty with the police, please let me know, and I will do my best to aid you."

"That's very kind of you, ma'am." He took her hand, brought it to his lips, and kissed her fingers. "Although I don't think there is any real danger of the police coming after me when there are so many other candidates to consider."

He turned to Caroline and bowed. "Good evening, Miss Morton."

"Dr. Harris." She curtsied. "I hope your optimism is rewarded."

He left immediately and Caroline followed her employer through to the drawing room where a tray of coffee and tea awaited them.

"Does Dr. Harris appear somewhat naïve to you, Caroline?" Mrs. Frogerton asked as she settled herself beside the fire.

"I prefer the word 'arrogant' myself. He cannot believe that anyone would doubt his word." Caroline grimaced. "And, if anyone dares to do so he is rather too quick to take offense."

"Which is not ideal when dealing with the police," Mrs. Frogerton agreed. "I fear that he will lose his temper and accidentally incriminate himself."

"I agree." Caroline paused to pour the coffee. "I find it difficult to believe that Madam was poisoned."

"Why is that?" Her employer took the cup Caroline offered her.

"Because it doesn't sound like something Alfred Fielding would be involved in."

Mrs. Frogerton nodded. "Yes, I'd expect him to smash things and physically assault Madam rather than poison her."

Caroline pictured Madam's study on that fateful day. "There was a half-filled glass on her desk. I suppose someone could have put poison into that."

"Maybe her butler?" Mrs. Frogerton asked. "Has anyone thought to question him, I wonder?"

"I'm sure the police will do so. Despite what Dr. Harris thinks, Sergeant Dawson isn't stupid." Caroline turned as she heard voices coming up the stairs. "Is Dorothy bringing guests with her?"

"Not that I am aware of, but I always enjoy her friends." Mrs. Frogerton set her cup down and rose to her feet. "That sounds like Mr. DeBloom to me."

The door opened and Dorothy came in with not only Mr. DeBloom but his sister.

"I hope you don't mind us joining you for coffee." Dorothy came over to kiss her mother's cheek. "The play we went to see was simply dreadful."

"Is Mrs. DeBloom with you?"

"She had something of a headache and decided to go straight home. She'll send the carriage back for us." Mr. DeBloom bowed to Mrs. Frogerton and Caroline. "I hope you don't mind this intrusion."

"Not at all!"

Caroline was already ringing the bell to get the butler to bring more refreshments.

"How have you been, Miss Morton?"

She almost started as Mr. DeBloom spoke from directly behind her.

"Very well, sir."

"Busy?" He smiled at her and gestured at Dorothy. "I suspect you rarely get a moment's rest with this one."

Dorothy chose not to take offense at his teasing and instead wagged her finger at him before turning to his sister.

"I don't know how you put up with him, Miss De-Bloom."

"He is an excellent and considerate brother."

It was the first time Caroline had heard their guest speak above a whisper.

Mr. DeBloom took his sister's hand and kissed it, his affection for her plain to see on his face. "You flatter me, Clarissa, but feel free to say as much as you like about me in this particular company." He winked. "I need all the help I can get."

Miss DeBloom smiled at her brother and then turned to Caroline.

"I wonder if I might ask for your assistance, Miss Morton? I caught my heel in the hem of my skirt as I descended the stairs at the theater, and I need to repair it."

"Of course, Miss DeBloom." Caroline smiled at the young woman. "I'll take you upstairs and you can avail yourself of the contents of my sewing basket." She looked over at Mrs. Frogerton. "Will you excuse us, ma'am?"

"Of course." Her employer waved them away and resumed her conversation with Dorothy and Mr. DeBloom.

"Thank you for your help, Miss Morton," Miss DeBloom said as they ascended the stairs, her primrose yellow skirts held high. She was fair like her brother, but her features were far more delicate.

"You are most welcome." Caroline opened the door into her room and invited Miss DeBloom inside.

"You don't need to call for your maid. I think I can manage for myself." Miss DeBloom sat down and picked up the beribboned skirt of her evening gown as Caroline located her sewing basket and set it in front of her guest. "My mother insisted that I learned to sew."

"As did mine." Caroline moved the candles to the bedside table to illuminate Miss DeBloom's space more clearly. "I was grateful for that when I no longer had a maid."

Miss DeBloom looked up at her, her blue gaze serious. "My brother said that your father left you in somewhat precarious circumstances."

"He was correct." Caroline wasn't sure she appreciated Mr. DeBloom's interest in her, but she couldn't deny the truth. "My father died in debt and in disgrace and I was forced to earn my own living."

"You had no family to take you in?" Miss DeBloom threaded her needle and tied a knot in the end.

"I didn't wish to be beholden to them." Caroline had no intention of elaborating on the current tragic circumstances of her nearest relatives at Greenwood Hall. "And, I have a sister to provide for."

Miss DeBloom nodded; her head bent over her skirt as she searched for the beginning of the ripped hem. "My brother admires your independent spirit, Miss Morton." She hesitated. "May I ask you a somewhat personal question?"

Caroline stiffened. "If it relates to Mr. DeBloom, then—"

"Not at all! I would never presume to speak for him." Miss DeBloom rushed on. "It's just that I thought I saw you at a very particular place last week."

"Where was that?"

Miss DeBloom kept her gaze downward. "At Madam Lavinia's?"

Caroline suddenly remembered the blond woman who'd been speaking so urgently to the butler.

"Yes, I have been there on two occasions, Miss DeBloom."

Her companion finally looked up from her sewing. "I would prefer it if my mother and brother didn't know that I attended those meetings."

Caroline raised an eyebrow. "I am not on intimate

terms with your family, so I doubt they will ever ask me about the matter."

"I wouldn't want you accidentally saying anything to anyone that might get back to them."

"To be fair, I didn't even realize it was you at the séance, Miss DeBloom."

"Oh. Blast it." Miss DeBloom bit her lip. "And now you do."

Caroline waited until Miss DeBloom finished her repair, snipped the thread, and set the needle aside before she asked her next question.

"Do your family disapprove of your interest in spiritualism?"

"Philip would be intrigued, but he'd still want to know why I went." Miss DeBloom allowed her skirt to fall to the floor.

"Why did you go?"

Miss DeBloom shrugged, reminding Caroline of her brother. "Perhaps I am a seeker of truth."

"Madam Lavinia certainly liked to shock and amaze her audience."

"You don't believe she was truly gifted?"

"Not particularly." Caroline watched as Miss DeBloom went over to the full-length mirror to assess the success of her repair. "Did you?"

"Yes."

Caroline hoped her companion would say more but was disappointed as Miss DeBloom twirled in a circle and studied her hemline.

"That looks much better."

"Your mother taught you well," Caroline agreed as she placed the items back in her sewing basket.

"Thank my governess. My mother had very little to do with my raising. She was far too busy entertaining her houseguests." She paused to open the door. "Philip said that your father was one of them, but I don't remember him. Shall we go down?"

Caroline considered what to do as she went to join her companion.

"Were you planning on returning to Madam's?"

Miss DeBloom smiled. "If you don't believe she speaks the truth, why would it matter whether I go or not?"

Caroline paused as she opened the door. "Because Madam is dead."

"What?" Miss DeBloom gasped and pressed her hand to her cheek. "She *can't* be!"

Caroline lowered her voice. "I must warn you that the Metropolitan Police Force have all her records. You might receive a visit from the authorities, which means that unfortunately, your family will soon know all whether I say anything or not."

"How do I know you are speaking the truth?" Miss De-Bloom demanded.

"Because Dr. Harris and I were unfortunate enough to visit Madam and find her dead in her study. As a result, a Sergeant Dawson came to the house and insisted on interviewing Mrs. Frogerton and me."

Miss DeBloom shivered; her face waxen. "This is *terrible*."

"If there is anything I can do to help, please let me know." Caroline instinctively reached out a hand. "This has obviously come as something of a shock."

"I . . . will be fine." Miss DeBloom swallowed hard and pushed away from the wall and Caroline's touch. "Please don't say anything to anyone about this."

"I promise you I will not, but if you wish to speak to me about your concerns, I am more than willing to listen."

"Thank you."

Caroline sensed that Miss DeBloom just wanted to get away from her, which was quite understandable considering the shock she'd just had. She gestured toward the stairs.

"Shall we go down? I should imagine your brother will be impatient to return home."

"Yes, of course." Miss DeBloom started walking. "Do you really think I will be contacted by the police?"

"If your name appears in Madam's records, then it is quite possible," Caroline said gently.

Miss DeBloom nodded, her expression difficult to read. She stopped abruptly at the top of the stairs.

"You said that the sergeant visited you here?"

"Yes, he did."

"Would it be possible for you to arrange for me to meet him here rather than at my mother's house?"

"It's possible." Caroline studied her companion's flushed face. "But I would rather not be involved in anything underhand." She hesitated. "Wouldn't it be wiser for you to confide in your brother?"

Miss DeBloom looked away. "I was hoping to do that after I spoke to Madam again. She . . . promised me she had the answers to my questions and that she would divulge them at our next meeting."

Caroline had her doubts about that but was reluctant to share her suspicions when Miss DeBloom was so upset. "I suspect your brother would be more than willing to listen and offer support to you regardless."

"You might be right." Miss DeBloom straightened her spine. "I should go down. Philip will be wondering what on earth has become of me."

They descended the stairs together and headed toward the drawing room where Caroline recognized her employer's loud laugh and Dorothy's answering giggle. Just before they went in, Caroline touched Miss DeBloom's elbow.

"If you do have need of me, please send a message."

"Thank you." Miss DeBloom nodded. "I have much to think about."

Caroline let her guest enter ahead of her and wasn't surprised when Mr. DeBloom immediately came to his sister's side.

"Are you all right? I thought you'd fallen asleep."

"It was tempting." Miss DeBloom smiled up at him. "The tear to my gown was more substantial than I had anticipated."

"And your sister is an excellent seamstress who refused to be rushed," Caroline added, for once willing to engage Mr. DeBloom's attention if it meant his sister was spared from it. "One would never even know the hem had been damaged her stitches are so neat."

"Clarissa is good at everything she attempts," Mr. De-Bloom said fondly. "She puts me to shame."

Miss DeBloom took her brother's arm and patted his sleeve. "It is getting rather late, Philip, and Mama will be wondering where we are. She won't want the horses waiting in the cold."

"Then we should go." Mr. DeBloom bowed to Mrs. Frogerton, Dorothy, and Caroline. "Thank you for your hospitality."

"It was a pleasure." Mrs. Frogerton smiled affably at her guests as Miss DeBloom curtsied.

"I'll walk you down the stairs," Dorothy offered.

Caroline waited until the DeBlooms were out of earshot before sitting next to Mrs. Frogerton.

"Miss DeBloom visited Madam Lavinia's."

"Good Lord. Whatever for?"

"That I have yet to determine," Caroline said. "She recognized me at Madam's and asked me to keep her presence there a secret from her family."

Mrs. Frogerton frowned. "That might prove difficult now that Madam is the subject of a murder investigation by the Metropolitan Police Force."

"Miss DeBloom was unaware that Madam was dead. It came as something of a shock to her."

"Just like Lady Fielding." Mrs. Frogerton pursed her lips. "I wonder what Miss DeBloom was doing there?"

"She wouldn't say, and I can't remember whether Madam said anything specific to her that night."

"From what I recall she was also there when I attended Madam's sessions without you." Mrs. Frogerton tapped her fingers against the arm of her chair. "I wonder if Professor Brown wrote down anything useful that Madam said to her."

"I suppose we could ask him," Caroline said. "Although why he should agree to help us is somewhat debatable."

"He'll help us to aid Dr. Harris," Mrs. Frogerton said. "I'll write him a note."

She went over to her writing desk and sat down, leaving Caroline staring into the glowing depths of the coal fire as the pen scratched on the paper.

"I can't imagine Miss DeBloom murdering anyone," Caroline eventually remarked.

"Neither can I, but they do say poison is a woman's weapon."

"I wish I'd been able to persuade her to confide in me as to why she went to Madam in the first place."

"She has to learn to trust you, lass, and that will only come with time." Mrs. Frogerton sanded her paper, folded it in three, and set her seal on it. "I'll get one of the grooms to take this to Professor Brown's residence."

"Do you know where he lives?"

"He's in the same lodgings as Dr. Harris." Mrs. Frogerton went to ring the bell. "I believe he was the one who recommended the place to our friend."

Caroline stood up and hastily concealed a yawn behind her hand. "I wonder how many more of our acquaintances visited Madam Lavinia's house?"

"Let's hope Miss DeBloom's the last." Mrs. Frogerton handed the letter over to the butler with instructions to send it off immediately. "I suspect tomorrow will be a very interesting day."

Chapter 8

"Sergeant Dawson! What a nice surprise!" Mrs. Frogerton smiled as she came into the hall, Caroline behind her, and spotted the officer awaiting her. "We were taking advantage of the pleasant weather and strolling in the park."

Sergeant Dawson's expression made it clear that such frivolous pursuits were of no interest to him especially when they held up his investigation.

"Good morning, ma'am, Lady Caroline."

"Have you arrested Sir Alfred Fielding yet?" Mrs. Frogerton asked eagerly as she went into the small parlor.

"We have been unable to speak to Sir Alfred, who is not currently at home."

"He's probably bolted to the Continent," Mrs. Frogerton said. "That's what scoundrels generally do. Have you spoken to his mother?"

"You are acquainted with Lady Fielding, ma'am?" Sergeant Dawson asked.

"Of course! We met at Madam's."

"Lady Fielding says Sir Alfred might have returned to their house in the country. We have sent a message to him there."

"Which he will ignore," Mrs. Frogerton said. "Because he will not wish to be held accountable for his crimes."

"With all due respect, ma'am, we have no evidence that he committed a crime."

"Why else would he leave London in such haste?" Mrs. Frogerton asked. "Answer me that, Sergeant!"

Caroline almost felt sorry for the man as he struggled to answer Mrs. Frogerton's pointed questions.

"When I last spoke to Lady Fielding, she indicated that her son disliked the countryside and preferred to spend his time drinking, gambling, and whoring in London." Mrs. Frogerton wasn't shy about sharing her opinions with anyone, let alone the police. "Why would he leave unless forced?"

Noting the stubborn expression on Sergeant Dawson's face, Caroline hastened to intervene. "Debts, perhaps? Such . . . pursuits must be costly."

"Rest assured we are looking into Sir Alfred's affairs, ma'am," Sergeant Dawson said somewhat repressively. "Madam had many clients, and we are in the process of contacting all of them to further our investigation."

Before Mrs. Frogerton could launch another barrage of questions Caroline spoke up.

"Was there something in particular you came to ask us about, Sergeant?"

"Ah, yes." He took out his notebook and slowly turned the pages. "Dr. Harris gave us an account of his movements over the past week, and we are following up on that information."

"You still believe Dr. Harris might be a murderer?" Mrs. Frogerton obviously wasn't yet done with the sergeant.

"He is a doctor, ma'am, he has access to poison at the hospital, and he is currently refusing to cooperate with our investigation."

Mrs. Frogerton sighed. "He is such a silly, stubborn man."

"But that doesn't make him a murderer," Caroline added.

"Dr. Harris says he spent some hours at this house and

in your company." Sergeant Dawson read out a list and then looked up. "Can you confirm this information?"

"Yes, indeed." Mrs. Frogerton looked over at Caroline, who nodded. "We confirm anything Dr. Harris says."

"Thank you." Sergeant Dawson paused to write something in his notebook. "The hospital provided information as to Dr. Harris's shifts and his colleagues corroborated his appearances on the wards and in his office."

"Then I doubt the good doctor had much time to be out murdering anyone then, did he?" Mrs. Frogerton said pointedly.

"That remains to be seen, ma'am." Sergeant Dawson inclined his head. "I wish you both good day."

He bowed and headed toward the door.

"Sergeant?" Caroline called out to him. "Was the coroner able to identify the type of poison used to kill Madam?"

"Yes, my lady. He used the Marsh test to determine that it was arsenic."

"Which is commonly available on every street corner," Mrs. Frogerton commented.

Sergeant Dawson straightened his spine and opened the door. "Good day, ma'am."

Caroline watched the butler escort the sergeant from the house before turning to her companion.

"I'm not sure if you are helping Dr. Harris's cause by irritating Sergeant Dawson, ma'am."

"I am simply trying to make sure that he doesn't arrest the wrong man," Mrs. Frogerton said briskly. "Now, shall we pay a visit to Lady Fielding? She might be more willing to confide in us now that the authorities are breathing down her neck."

"Or even less likely," Caroline commented as her employer swept past her.

"You are far too pessimistic, lass. Now, come along."

The butler approached them in the hall. "Dr. Harris left something for you, Miss Morton."

"Did he drop it off himself?" Caroline asked as he handed her a well-wrapped brown paper parcel.

"No, miss."

"I wonder what he's sent me?" Caroline wondered.

"I doubt it's his confession—unless he wrote it in novel form," Mrs. Frogerton observed as they went back up to the drawing room. "We've got time for you to open it before we leave."

Caroline used the penknife from Mrs. Frogerton's desk to cut the string and unfold the paper to reveal the contents within.

"I believe it's a copy of Madam Lavinia's client list."

"Whenever did he have time to do that?" Mrs. Frogerton put on her spectacles and peered at the closely written pages. "His handwriting is appalling."

"But it might prove quite useful." Caroline considered the symbols next to every name. "I wish he'd provided a key to these notations."

"Perhaps he didn't know what they meant or didn't have the time."

"Which makes our task more difficult."

"I'm good at puzzles," Mrs. Frogerton said. "I'll sort it out. Shall we lock them in my desk and examine them more closely when we return?"

"Yes, ma'am." Caroline placed the closely written pages in the drawer, locked it, and offered Mrs. Frogerton the key. "We wouldn't want Sergeant Dawson to know that we are interfering in his investigation."

Somewhat to Caroline's surprise, after sending in their cards, Lady Fielding's butler admitted them into the inner recesses of the house. They followed him up the stairs to the drawing room that faced out over the tree-lined square to find their hostess sitting beside the fire. She wore her habitual black and despite the pleasant weather had a thick wool shawl around her shoulders.

"Mrs. Frogerton, Miss Morton. How kind of you to call again." She gestured for them to sit. "May I offer you some tea?"

As soon as the butler departed, Lady Fielding sat forward, her hands clasped together on her lap.

"I was intending to visit you today. An obnoxious young man called Sergeant Dawson came to the house and asked some very impertinent questions about my son."

"He came to see us as well." Mrs. Frogerton shook her head and tutted. "He seems to be taking this matter very seriously indeed."

"As he should—being a representative of the law," Caroline added.

"He insisted that I gave him the address to our place in Kent and said he would speak with Alfred if he was there." Lady Fielding continued as if they hadn't spoken. "I told him that Alfred had nothing to do with what had happened to Madam, but he said witnesses said otherwise." Her gaze shifted to Mrs. Frogerton's face. "Did you mention my son to the sergeant?"

"Yes, but only after Sergeant Dawson told me he already knew what had happened at the séance from others who were present. I did not feel it was right to lie to him."

Caroline was impressed by her employer's ability to breeze over the important fact that she had been the first person to draw Sergeant Dawson's attention to Sir Alfred's behavior and that she continued to do so.

"He *said* that someone had seen Alfred at Madam's house on the day she died. I told him he must have been mistaken. Why would Alfred go to Madam's without me?"

"Perhaps he wished to speak to her about getting your money back?" Mrs. Frogerton asked. "You indicated that he thought you had paid her too much."

"Even if he had done that, it doesn't mean that he is responsible for her death," Lady Fielding said.

"That is true." Mrs. Frogerton nodded. "It is perhaps

unfortunate that he chose to visit on the very day Madam died."

"And left London so precipitously," Caroline said. "Before he could clear his name."

"If Sir Alfred were my son, my lady, I would write to him posthaste and implore him to return so that he can speak to Sergeant Dawson and clear everything up," Mrs. Frogerton advised. "And then the authorities can get on with finding the *real* murderer."

"I have already done so—but I'm not even sure he has returned to Fielding Hall. He didn't come back or send a man to collect his belongings after our falling-out."

"I'm sure he'll turn up." Mrs. Frogerton smiled as the butler brought in the tea and Lady Fielding poured them all a cup. "Men can be very stubborn sometimes, but they usually come around."

"I did wish to ask you something, Mrs. Frogerton," Lady Fielding said. "Do you know the names of any of the others who attended our sessions? I thought it might be helpful to ascertain whether they too have been approached by the authorities."

"Sergeant Dawson said they intended to speak to all of Madam's clients."

"I'm sure he did, but can you remember any specific names?"

Caroline wondered why Lady Fielding was being so insistent. Did she want to stop anyone else from speaking ill of her son? It seemed likely.

"As you know, most people tended to keep to themselves at the séances, but I did make the acquaintance of a Professor Brown who works at St. Thomas's Hospital along with our Dr. Harris. I'm sure he'd be delighted to assist you," Mrs. Frogerton said. "He might even have the names of others in our group because he takes very detailed notes."

"That's an excellent suggestion." Lady Fielding visibly brightened. "I will send him a note this very day."

They were barely allowed to finish their tea before their hostess rose to her feet and politely indicated that she had better things to do than entertain them for a moment longer. Caroline could appreciate her haste and demurely accepted her dismissal along with her employer.

When they reached the carriage, Mrs. Frogerton called up to the coachman.

"Take us to Madam Lavinia's, please."

"Yes, ma'am."

Caroline assisted Mrs. Frogerton into the carriage and arranged herself on the opposite seat.

"Do you think that is wise, ma'am? To go to Madam's?"

"Why not? I can't think of anywhere else I'll get the information I require."

"What if Sergeant Dawson is there?"

"Then I'll ask him." Mrs. Frogerton winked at Caroline. "Don't look so worried, lass."

Caroline looked out of the window as the carriage turned out of the square. "The house might be deserted."

"Even better. Just because the mistress is no longer there doesn't mean there isn't a whole bevy of servants still running the place. At least until their quarterly wages are up."

"It is interesting that Sir Alfred was seen at the residence that day."

"Indeed."

"I assume that's what you want to find out about?" Caroline asked.

"That and a couple of other matters." Mrs. Frogerton delved into her reticule for her purse and jingled it at Caroline. "I have plenty of coin to grease a few palms."

"Then I can't wait to see what we learn, ma'am." Caroline sat back and smiled at her employer who nodded approvingly.

"That's my girl."

When they reached Madam's house, Mrs. Frogerton instructed the coachman to drive on past, drop them at the corner, and wait for them in the next street. It was a surprisingly warm day, and for once the lack of rain meant the pavements were dusty rather than muddy. Caroline put up Mrs. Frogerton's parasol to shield her from the worst of it as they walked toward the front door.

To her surprise, Mrs. Frogerton descended the iron stairs into the basement and Caroline followed her.

"Are you quite sure the servants will welcome our presence?" Caroline asked.

Mrs. Frogerton smiled. "Unlike most of Madam's clients, I tipped the butler very well. I doubt he'll throw me out on my ear."

After a brisk knock on the back door, she went in and made her way to the kitchen. "Good afternoon!"

The butler and a maid were sitting at the table sharing a pot of tea. There was no sign of a cook, or any other members of staff and the kitchen was unusually quiet.

"You've been here before," the butler remarked, his wary expression at odds with his soft Irish accent. "It's Mrs. Frogerton, isn't it?"

"What an excellent memory you have." Mrs. Frogerton smiled approvingly. "I was so sorry to hear about Madam's death."

"Not half as sorry as we were," the maid, who had a strong Cockney accent, chipped in. "The police have been all over the house, the rest of the staff have left, and who's going to be writing us a reference now?"

"I'd be happy to write you both a reference and employ a bright lass like yourself if that's something you'd consider." Mrs. Frogerton made herself at home at the table while Caroline remained standing. "I appreciate honesty and loyalty in my staff."

The butler's attention shifted to Caroline. "Miss Morton. You were here with that doctor when he found Madam dead in her study." He turned to Mrs. Frogerton. "She was a great help calming the female staff down."

"Caroline is always excellent in a crisis," Mrs. Frogerton agreed. "Have either of you encountered a Sergeant Dawson?"

"Yes, and his superior." The butler got up to fetch some more mugs and offered them some tea. "Right bunch of miserable bastards, excuse my language, ma'am. Asked me all kinds of insulting questions about Madam and the staff."

"Did they assume you were somehow implicated in her death?"

"Of course they did," the butler growled. "They didn't seem to care that Madam only moved here six months ago."

"I understand she came from Brighton." Caroline finally joined the group around the table.

"She did. I came with her," the maid said. "I acted as her dresser and other things."

"Yet you sound like a local girl," Mrs. Frogerton said.

"Yes, that's why I stayed on with Madam when she decided to come back to London. I wanted to come home."

"You have family here?"

"All over the city. Employed in some of the best houses." The maid nodded importantly.

"Sergeant Dawson came to see us, too," Mrs. Frogerton said. "He seemed to think Dr. Harris was the murderer."

"Which I told him was ridiculous," the butler said, "seeing as he didn't come to the house earlier that day—unlike some other folks."

"I suppose Madam had many people wanting her immediate attention," Mrs. Frogerton commented as she poured herself and Caroline some tea.

"Sometimes it was like being besieged—hysterical females begging to see her, angry gentlemen . . ." The butler shook his head. "I felt sorry for her."

"I can imagine," Mrs. Frogerton said. "Did you tell Sergeant Dawson who attempted to gain admission to the house on that particular day?"

"He didn't ask me about anyone except Dr. Harris."

"And you didn't volunteer any further information?"

The butler hesitated, his gaze shifting to the maid.

Mrs. Frogerton got out her purse. "I know this must be difficult for you both, but I am here with the best of intentions."

"How so?" The butler eyed the gold coins Mrs. Frogerton placed on the table.

"I liked Madam, and I want to see her murderer brought to justice. I have learned over the years that no one knows as much about what goes on in a household as the butler and his staff."

"I don't want to get caught up in any funny business, ma'am. I'm about to retire and go and live with my eldest down in Ramsgate." The butler didn't raise his gaze from the coins.

"Any risk will be entirely mine," Mrs. Frogerton said firmly. "Did you happen to mention the gentleman who caused the disturbance the other night?"

"Yes, ma'am, I did." The butler rubbed his fingers over his unshaven chin. "Sir Alfred Fielding turned up here around eleven."

"Did he speak with Madam?"

"Yes. I took in his card. I warned her it would be a mistake to let him in, but she overruled me. I offered to stay with her, but she said there was no point."

"Did you remain nearby regardless?"

"Of course I did." He looked insulted that Mrs. Frogerton had even asked.

"And did you hear anything of what passed between them?"

"There was no shouting or nothing." His brow crinkled. "He was only there a few minutes. When he came out his face was white as curdled milk, and he ran toward the door like the hounds of hell were pursuing him. I don't think he even saw me."

"Did you check if Madam was all right?" Caroline asked.

"I knocked on the door and went in. She was sitting at

her desk staring into space—which wasn't unusual for her. She said all was well and asked what was for lunch."

"Is it possible that Sir Alfred might have doubled back to the house later?"

"He might have done. I went out for an hour or two after I took Madam her lunch, but Letty was here, weren't you, girl?" The butler turned to the woman beside him. "Did you see any funny business?"

Letty sat up straight. She was a pretty girl with bright blue eyes and a pert smile. "I did admit a few people while you were out, Mr. Murphy. I took their cards in on a tray for Madam to decide whether she wanted to see them or not, just like you told me to do."

"Why didn't you ask their names?" Caroline asked.

"Wasn't my business." Letty folded her arms across her chest. "Mr. Murphy always says that the kind of people who want to see Madam don't necessarily want to be seen here—if you take my meaning, miss."

"Yes, indeed." Mrs. Frogerton nodded. "Can you remember if they were men or women?"

"Two of each I think." Letty pursed her lips. "Both gentlemen had beards and were middle-aged. One of the ladies was young, the other much older."

"Did they all come alone?"

"Yes, although the younger lady was accompanied by her maid, who waited in the hall."

"Do you think you would recognize them again?" Caroline asked.

"Maybe. But both ladies were heavily veiled." Letty's gaze drifted toward the coins. "My memory might get better after I think a bit more."

The butler snorted. "You're an ambitious one, aren't you, Letty? Didn't Madam pay you enough?"

"Not if I want to get out of service one day, Mr. Murphy, and open my own shop."

"What else did you do for Madam apart from acting as her dresser?" Mrs. Frogerton asked.

Letty grinned. "A lot of banging on the table and shrieking down the chimney to scare her guests. I'd do that for nothing. It's funny to see their faces."

"Then what *did* she pay you extra for?" Mrs. Frogerton asked.

Letty looked at the butler, who shrugged and said, "I'm retiring, lass. If you want to tell the ladies what Madam asked you to do, I can't stop you."

"Madam thought it important to know as much about the people who sought out her services as possible," Letty said carefully.

"So, you found out everything you could about them?" Mrs. Frogerton nodded. "As I always say, Caroline, servants know more about the families they serve than you'd ever believe."

"I never made anything up, ma'am," Letty said earnestly. "I just reported back what I heard, and she paid me for my trouble."

Mrs. Frogerton looked at the butler. "And what do you think Madam did with that information?"

He shrugged. "Wasn't anything to do with me, was it? She paid my wages, I opened her door, ran her household, and took care of her guests."

"Did she ever ask you to deliver notes from her to her guests?"

"All the time. People would write to her, and she would check her appointment book and see when she could make room for them."

"Did she just do the groups, or did she see clients privately as well?" Caroline asked.

"Private clients from one to four and groups in the evenings." He paused. "Except on Sundays when she went to church at St. Jude's down the road."

Mrs. Frogerton slid two of the gold coins over to the butler and one to Letty. "Thank you for your assistance in this matter."

"You're welcome, ma'am." Mr. Murphy pocketed the

coins. "Unlike a lot of Madam's clients, you was always kind and pleasant to me."

"I simply wish to find out who would want to murder Madam Lavinia." Mrs. Frogerton looked from the butler to the maid. "Do you have any suspicions as to who it might be yourselves?"

"It has to be one of the people who came to the house after lunch," Letty said slowly. "Because Mr. Murphy saw her alive and kicking before he went out."

"And by the time Dr. Harris and I arrived just after three she was already dead," Caroline said. "What time did Madam eat her lunch?"

"At noon, miss."

"Then she was killed in a relatively short period of time when four as yet unknown callers, plus Sir Alfred, visited her."

"I believe you are correct in your assumptions, Caroline." Mrs. Frogerton nodded. "Did Sergeant Dawson tell you how he thought Madam died, Mr. Murphy?"

"Poisoned he said. He took all the bloody decanters out of the house to examine the contents."

"Do you know whether any of the others contained arsenic yet?"

"No, because he still sees me as a suspect," Mr. Murphy said. "He told me not to leave town."

"Butlers *are* responsible for decanting the spirits into the decanters, Mr. Murphy," Letty observed. "It's quite understandable that he has his doubts about you."

"So much for loyalty, missy. How about you tell the ladies what else you and Madam got up to, eh?"

Caroline glanced at Mrs. Frogerton who was listening intently.

"I don't know what you're talking about, Mr. Murphy." Letty frowned at the butler.

"Let's just say that some of the people who turned up to see Madam were rather more worried than others." Mr. Murphy stared right back at her.

"Possibly because some gossip is more valuable to the receiver than other gossip?" Mrs. Frogerton asked delicately. "I can imagine that certain people would not want Madam to inquire too deeply into their affairs."

"Madam knew things. She had a real gift," Letty stated. "Sometimes people didn't like hearing the truth."

"Which is probably why she ended up being murdered," Mrs. Frogerton said briskly as she put her purse away in her reticule. "Would it be possible for us to view the rest of the house?"

"Why would you want to do that?" Letty asked. "Sergeant Dawson and his men took away everything they thought was valuable."

"Be my guest, Mrs. Frogerton," Mr. Murphy spoke over the maid. "I doubt you'll find anything useful, but as I'll be leaving as soon as Sergeant Dawson says I may, I don't have reason to object."

"I promise I won't steal anything," Mrs. Frogerton assured him as she rose to her feet and Caroline followed.

"As Madam arrived with very little luggage, ma'am, I doubt there is anything worth having." Mr. Murphy stood as well. "I'll put the kettle on."

Chapter 9

"What on earth are we supposed to be looking for?" Caroline asked as she and Mrs. Frogerton went into Madam's study. The stale scent of violet perfume and damp cinders still hung in the air. "I'm fairly certain Sergeant Dawson would be very thorough indeed."

"I'm not worried about what Sergeant Dawson took, lass. From what I can see he's already made up his mind that either the butler or Dr. Harris is guilty and will produce the evidence he needs to prove it."

"Then my money is on the butler." Caroline shut the door so that they would not be overheard. "He certainly had the best opportunity to tamper with the decanter."

Mrs. Frogerton sat herself in Madam's chair and frowned at the empty desktop in front of her.

"If Mr. Murphy were guilty, do you think he'd still be sitting here waiting for Sergeant Dawson to arrest him?"

"Perhaps he imagines he's too clever for that to happen."

"I think he simply wants to retire and live his life in peace and would not have risked that to murder his employer."

Mrs. Frogerton opened the first desk drawer.

"What would you like me to search for, ma'am?" Caroline asked, aware that she'd had almost an identical conversation with Dr. Harris in the very same room just days before.

"Anything that seems strange or out of place." Mrs. Frogerton looked up. "Where did you find the notes Madam wrote to you and Dr. Harris?"

"In the center drawer. I only took out the ones with our names on, but there were others." As Mrs. Frogerton searched the desk Caroline turned her attention to the ornaments on the mantelpiece and the pictures on the wall. From their decrepit appearance she suspected that most of them belonged to the house rather than Madam.

"There are none there now," Mrs. Frogerton observed. "I assume Sergeant Dawson has them."

"Or Dr. Harris. He did take several things when we were last here."

"Perhaps they are in that package he left you at home."

"It's possible." Caroline looked over her shoulder. "I still don't understand how Madam knew Dr. Harris and I would be the people to find her and that we would look in that particular drawer."

"Remember, she was expecting Dr. Harris to call on her that fateful day, and she knew he was a friend of yours," Mrs. Frogerton pointed out.

"But why would she imagine we'd go through her desk?"

Mrs. Frogerton looked thoughtful. "Has it occurred to you that Dr. Harris's letter wasn't in fact the same as yours?"

"He told me that it was."

"Did you believe him?"

Caroline hesitated. "Not particularly. He was behaving very strangely at the time."

"I wonder whether it was a blackmail note and that Madam knew Dr. Harris would take the time to search for any incriminating evidence she had on him?"

"It's possible," Caroline allowed. "He certainly wouldn't show me what she'd written."

Mrs. Frogerton folded her hands together on the desk.

"Then I suspect that's why Madam knew exactly where to leave the notes."

"She couldn't have known I'd be with him," Caroline objected.

"You don't know that, lass, and to be honest, if Dr. Harris had come alone and seen your name on that envelope, we both know he would've taken it with him." Mrs. Frogerton opened another drawer. "Now, just let me check the other drawers while you give the rest of the room a good look over."

"Yes, ma'am."

Even as Caroline obediently studied each book and ornament her mind was working furiously. If Dr. Harris wasn't careful, he might find himself being arrested for murder, and if he refused to be honest with her and Mrs. Frogerton, there was nothing they could do to save him.

"Have you found anything?" Mrs. Frogerton called out, making Caroline realize she'd been staring blankly at the furniture for far too long. Her gaze skimmed over a set of small portraits set on top of the bookcase and came back to look over the most prominent one.

"This looks like Madam when she was younger."

She took the picture over to Mrs. Frogerton, who put her spectacles on.

"Indeed, it does! I wonder who that handsome gentleman beside her is?"

"Maybe her husband?" Caroline wondered. "I must ask Letty if Madam was ever married."

"That's an excellent idea, and while you're off doing that, I'll finish here, and go and investigate Madam's bedroom." Mrs. Frogerton waved her away. "And, if the butler has made some more tea, perhaps you could bring me a cup?"

Later that evening, Caroline and her employer accompanied Dorothy to a musical evening at the Lingard house.

It was a small gathering by invitation only. Caroline was somewhat surprised they had been included until she saw how quickly the new Viscount Lingard came over to greet them. Dorothy had obviously made an excellent impression on him.

"Well done," she murmured to Dorothy as the viscount offered Mrs. Frogerton his arm and took them to meet his mother.

"I did nothing in particular to attach him to me," Dorothy replied with something of a smirk. "He is quite pleasant, and more of an age with me than most peers."

"His father died at a comparatively young age," Caroline agreed. "If you can keep his mother from meddling, you'd be in control of several estates in the countryside, a respectable fortune, and this town house."

Dorothy looked around the ornate drawing room. "It is all quite acceptable, and their main estate is in the north, so I'd still be near Mother."

Caroline doubted the Lingards would want anything to do with Mrs. Frogerton after they'd acquired her money through Dorothy's dowry, but she didn't mention it. Dorothy had a strong personality and Caroline would never wager against her getting her own way in the end.

"We share a lot of similar interests," Dorothy continued as they progressed through the open doors into the rear of the house where a stage had been set up for the performances. "He loves to be outdoors and hates to read."

"He sounds perfect for you." Caroline tried not to smile. "Why bother reading when you can mount a horse and be off into the countryside?"

"I know you are teasing me, Caroline, but not all of us are beautiful enough to be a bluestocking and still be considered marriageable."

"I am hardly that," Caroline said. "Nor do I want to be."

"Certain gentlemen might disagree with you." Dorothy nodded to her acquaintances as they walked past the other guests to where the dowager viscountess awaited them. "Mr. DeBloom for one."

"He is far more interested in you."

"No, he isn't."

Knowing how argumentative Dorothy could be, Caroline decided not to pursue the matter. The dowager viscountess was now speaking to Mrs. Frogerton. Dorothy lowered her voice as they approached.

"I don't think she likes me very much, but I suspect she'd be willing to hold her nose and accept me if I add to the family fortunes."

Dorothy sank into a graceful curtsy as they reached the viscountess and Caroline followed suit.

"Thank you for inviting us, my lady." Mrs. Frogerton was speaking. "Dorothy loves a musical evening."

The dowager inclined her head a reluctant inch. "Miss Frogerton, Lady Caroline. My son insisted that I issue you an invitation."

Mrs. Frogerton glanced up at the viscount, who was staring at Dorothy and grinning broadly.

"That was very kind of him. I understand that he and Dorothy have been practicing a duet? I can't wait to hear them perform." Mrs. Frogerton curtsied again. "Come along, Dorothy, let's find our seats."

One of the things Caroline had come to admire about her employer was her refusal to react to being condescended to. It was an attitude Caroline tried to emulate—not always successfully. Not only did Mrs. Frogerton ignore the deliberate attempts to undermine or ridicule her, but she did it with such calm good humor that the person offering the insult looked like an ungracious fool.

At first, Caroline had wondered whether Mrs. Frogerton simply didn't understand that she was being laughed at, but closer acquaintance had shown her that wasn't the case. Her employer's affable demeanor concealed a sharp and shrewd mind that noticed everything but rarely took offense. She was secure in her sense of self, knew her own worth, and was wealthy enough to ignore those foolish enough to look down on her.

"May I borrow Miss Frogerton for one last run-through of our duet, ma'am?" Viscount Lingard asked.

"Of course." Mrs. Frogerton smiled graciously.

After Caroline took her seat next to her employer, she was nudged in the ribs.

"What do you think of this one?"

"Viscount Lingard? He seems pleasant enough and Dorothy likes him," Caroline replied. "His family are financially stable and remarkably free of scandal, and, although an excellent dowry would no doubt be welcome, he is not a fortune hunter by any means."

"She does seem to like him," Mrs. Frogerton agreed. "Although his mother isn't quite so keen."

"Mothers rarely are," Caroline said.

"My son, Samuel, hasn't shown any interest in getting married yet, so I haven't met any potential daughters-in-law." Mrs. Frogerton chuckled. "I suspect I'll be just as hard to please as the dowager over there. Do you think it would be a good match for my girl?"

Caroline looked over to where the viscount and Dorothy were standing by the pianoforte, their heads together as they read through the musical score. Dorothy was laughing at something the viscount was saying and he looked absolutely besotted.

"Viscount Lingard has no need to marry in haste. If he is truly enamored of Dorothy, and I think he is, and he is prepared to override his mother's objections, then that is a point in his favor."

"I suppose so." Mrs. Frogerton fiddled with the fringe on her shawl. "How old is he exactly?"

"I believe he's twenty-eight, ma'am."

"Almost ten years older than Dotty, then." She sighed. "I was twenty years younger than my Septimus. I was his second wife. His first died in childbirth years before I met him."

"She is still quite young to consider marriage," Caroline said. "But she seems somewhat fixated on the notion that she has to marry during her first Season and take the cream of the crop."

"That's Dotty all over." Mrs. Frogerton shook her head. "She should've been the boy. She's far more ambitious than Samuel will ever be."

"I hesitate to offer advice in this matter, ma'am, but if I was counseling my own daughter, I'd make sure that her heart was engaged as well as her head and remind her that there are plenty more fish in the sea for those lucky enough to have a large dowry."

Mrs. Frogerton chuckled. "That is good advice, lass. I'd only add that I can refuse to pay her dowry if she chooses someone I don't like."

"There is that." Caroline smiled back at her employer. "Although whether Dorothy would care would be another matter."

"*She* might not care, but as she aspires to marry into the peerage her future husband would," Mrs. Frogerton said. "Maybe that would be a good indication as to whether the gentleman in question truly loved her or only wanted her fortune."

Caroline nodded as Dorothy came to sit beside them and the conversation moved on to other matters. The first half of the evening passed very pleasantly while they waited for Dorothy's performance, which was near the end because she was duetting with the host of the party. The guests were invited to partake of refreshments in the adjoining salon. Mrs. Frogerton and Dorothy had already moved toward the reception room where the dowager had provided a light supper while Caroline searched for her employer's lost glove.

"Miss Morton, what a pleasant surprise!"

She looked up to find Mr. DeBloom in the central aisle between the rapidly emptying chairs.

"Good evening." She smiled and held up the glove. "I was searching for Mrs. Frogerton's lost glove."

A slight frown passed over Mr. DeBloom's face. "You should have asked one of the staff to look for it."

"I *am* the staff," Caroline replied lightly as she put the glove in her reticule and went to step past Mr. DeBloom.

He placed his hand under her elbow. "May I speak privately to you for a moment?" Caroline hesitated and he continued. "It concerns my sister."

Caroline looked up at him. He was a very handsome man with his fair hair, light blue eyes, and firm mouth but she didn't personally find him attractive. "This isn't the ideal location for such a conversation."

"Then when may I speak to you?"

"You are welcome to visit me at home. Mrs. Frogerton wouldn't object."

"I'd rather we were alone."

"Dorothy might not appreciate that, sir," Caroline said. "And I'm not sure I would, either."

He smiled. "This isn't about anything improper, Miss Morton. Clarissa told me about her visits to Madam Lavinia."

Caroline raised her chin. "I assumed that was the case, sir. I suggested that she confide in you."

"That was good of you." He hesitated. "If I visit you at home, can you contrive to see me alone? If you wish to share what we discuss with the Frogertons after our discussion I will not object."

"That is certainly possible." Caroline considered their upcoming schedule of events. "Dorothy will be out in the park at eleven with the Lingards."

"Then I will present myself in Half Moon Street then." He bent to kiss her hand. "Thank you."

"You are most welcome, sir." Caroline disengaged her hand from his and glanced around the room, but no one was attending to them. "I do hope Miss DeBloom is well."

"She's feeling much better after confiding in me."

"I'm glad to hear it. No one enjoys being caught up in a murder investigation."

"*Murder?*" Mr. DeBloom blinked at her. "She didn't mention that. All the more reason to have a chat with you tomorrow."

He stepped back so that she could finally get out into the aisle between the chairs. She curtsied and was moving away when he spoke again.

"I forgot to mention that you look very beautiful this evening, Miss Morton. I sincerely hope that your days of serving others are soon over."

Caroline chose neither to turn around nor reply to his provocative comments. Safety lay in the reception room with Mrs. Frogerton and Dorothy, and she hurried to join them.

"Are you all right, lass?" Mrs. Frogerton handed her a glass of lemonade. She was seated by herself at a small table for two and there was no sign of Dorothy. "You look quite flushed."

"I was just speaking to Mr. DeBloom."

"And what was he saying to put such a blush on your cheeks?"

"He wants to speak to me about Miss DeBloom." Caroline sat down and used her fan vigorously. "I suggested he come to the house tomorrow to discuss the matter."

"I'll wager that isn't all he said, but I won't press you, dearie." Mrs. Frogerton winked at her. "Although I did tell you that he had his eye on you and not my Dotty."

"Miss DeBloom told him about her visits to Madam." Caroline steadfastly ignored Mrs. Frogerton's invitation to confide in her. "But she somehow failed to mention that Madam was probably murdered."

"Was she unaware of that?"

Caroline considered her previous conversation with Miss DeBloom. "I told her the Metropolitan Police Force were investigating Madam's death and to be on her guard. I assumed she would understand the implications of that."

"So, she did know." Mrs. Frogerton frowned. "I wonder why she didn't mention that to her brother? I suppose it is possible she didn't want to alarm him unnecessarily."

"We will find out tomorrow, ma'am." Caroline sipped her lemonade. "Now, can I get you something to eat? I noticed they had several desserts that you particularly enjoy."

Chapter 10

Finding herself unable to sleep after her encounter with Mr. DeBloom, Caroline wrapped a shawl around her shoulders and went down to the drawing room. She lit some candles from the embers of the fire and sat at Mrs. Frogerton's desk. If she had to be awake, she might as well make herself useful and review the papers Dr. Harris had left for her.

She squinted at his black-inked scrawl. His handwriting was atrocious even if she made allowances for the fact that he had probably written in haste to get the documents back to Madam's house at the earliest opportunity.

The first set of papers were a list of names and addresses of Madam's clients. As she read through them, Caroline was surprised to see some very familiar names. It seemed as if Madam's fame had spread widely through the upper classes, and many had flocked to meet her. Beside each name was a tally of the number of times they had visited Madam's establishment. It took Caroline a while to work out that the different designations meant whether they'd attended a group or as an individual or both.

There was another symbol she had yet to understand. She suspected it had something to do with the less well-known aspect of Madam's business—blackmail. She wished she'd paid more attention to the names on the other letters in the drawer at the time but had been too distracted by seeing her own.

She took a sheet of paper from the desk drawer and wrote her own list comprising of all the people who had the third symbol beside their names. It was interesting that the most influential and powerful families were not on it, which spoke to Madam's intelligence in selecting her victims. From what Caroline could see she deliberately chose widows, elderly spinsters, and those with wealth but not social class or power.

Caroline paused to dip her pen in the inkwell. It was somewhat surprising that Madam hadn't attempted to blackmail Mrs. Frogerton, who fitted most of her criteria. But if Madam's information came mainly from London, gossip about the Frogerton family was probably beyond her scope of influence.

She finished the list and set her pen down, her gaze fixed on the flickering candles. If she were honest with herself, her reasons for not sleeping went far beyond her worries for Madam Lavinia . . . her encounter with Mr. DeBloom had shaken her in other ways. His admiration and interest in her was not welcome, but was also a balm to her soul. She'd been told she was beautiful all her life but had decided she'd rather be known for her intelligence and good character.

But, as Mrs. Frogerton often reminded her, beauty was its own currency. Would she be willing to trade her prettiness for the status of marriage? Or in her present circumstances accept an offer from a gentleman to become his mistress? She shuddered at the thought. Becoming a man's mistress would be a betrayal of everything she'd tried to become, but a wife?

Since her father's demise she'd had to learn to count every penny and to obsess over her and her sister's futures. Mrs. Frogerton paid her handsomely but there was no denying that a marriage—any marriage—would improve both her status and her future financial security immeasurably. But was that what Mr. DeBloom was hinting at? He had no need to marry—especially to a lady like her, and his mother would be vehemently against such a match. It was far more likely he'd offer to become her protector, but that would cause other problems. Caroline didn't think Dorothy would marry any gentleman who had her as a mistress.

With a sigh, Caroline turned her attention to the second set of scribbled notes, parts of which were obviously in code. Mrs. Frogerton had been working on the document and had made a start on the translations, which proved helpful. Eventually, Caroline worked out that the numbers correlated to the client list, which helped a little. By using information she hoped was correct about Mrs. Frogerton, Clarissa DeBloom, and Dr. Harris, she was able to make further progress. She also noted that although her employer was present on the main client list there was no mention of herself or Mr. DeBloom, but both of them did appear in the accompanying notes.

Caroline sat back and considered the patterns that were beginning to emerge. Each paragraph appeared to be a summary of the client's financial status, personal information, and their vulnerability to blackmail, which was graded on a scale of one to five. Notes about family scandals, close associates, and status had also been added on different dates but in the same hand. She only wished there were notes as to which people *had* been blackmailed and the financial results, but they were not there. She had to assume Madam kept that information close and wondered if the butler even knew where it was secreted.

On a separate piece of paper, she wrote a few queries for herself. With Mrs. Frogerton's agreement they should return to Madam's and ask Mr. Murphy whether Madam had a safe box concealed somewhere on the premises. There had been no mention by Sergeant Dawson or the butler of Madam's money being discovered. Caroline was fairly certain Madam would have kept her coin close in case she needed to flee, rather than trust a bank.

The list Caroline had composed of those Madam had potentially blackmailed was relatively short and contained Lady Fielding and Miss DeBloom along with five other individuals. After double-checking all the lists, she noted there was no mention of Dr. Harris anywhere. He hadn't strictly been one of Madam's customers, but Madam had agreed to see him after mentioning him during the session, so there should be a record of him somewhere.

As Dr. Harris had transcribed the notes, it was possible he had simply erased his presence. . . .

"It would be just like him to think he could hide the evidence with a stroke of his pen," Caroline spoke into the silence. "But Sergeant Dawson will have the complete list and he isn't a fool."

Having completed her task, she locked all the items back in the drawer and rose to her feet. She blew out all the candles but one, and went to the door, pausing only long enough to make sure the fire was completely out. From below her came the sound of someone banging on the front door.

"Open up!"

She paused, caught between fear and curiosity, before she recognized the voice and hurried down the stairs, her light held high in her hand. It took quite a while to unbar the front door and open it to discover Dr. Harris on the doorstep.

"Why are you up at this time of night?" he inquired as he stepped inside, bringing a cold draft in with him.

"More to the point, what are you doing here?" Caroline countered.

"I saw the light from the drawing room and assumed someone was up."

"That doesn't answer my question." Caroline drew her

shawl more tightly around her shoulders and set the candle down on the table where it flicked uncertainly in the drafty air.

He stared down at her. "Your hair is much longer than I thought it would be."

"Dr. Harris . . ."

"I've often been impressed about how much hair a woman can conceal within a complicated hairstyle."

Caroline raised her eyebrows.

"I'm sorry, I'm avoiding the point, aren't I?" He seemed to gather himself. "I've been warned that Sergeant Dawson intends to arrest me tomorrow for the murder of Madam Lavinia."

Caroline's hand flew to her cheek. "Surely not."

"Apparently, someone wants this matter cleared up quickly and I'm the obvious suspect."

"But I've been making progress," Caroline said desperately. "I have compiled a list of names of people, who—"

He spoke over her. "It doesn't matter if they think they've found their man."

"It does matter." Caroline held his gaze. "Mrs. Frogerton and I will not allow an innocent man to be convicted of a crime he did not commit!"

"But what if I did murder someone?" His smile was twisted. "Shouldn't I pay for that?"

"Dr. Harris—I don't believe for a minute that you murdered Madam Lavinia."

"Your faith in me is both unexpected and definitely unwarranted." He held up a hand as she went to protest. "I didn't come here for sympathy. I came to deliver something."

He delved into the pocket of his greatcoat and brought out an envelope. "Perhaps you might keep this safe for me? I don't particularly want Sergeant Dawson to find any of these items on my person when he comes to arrest me."

"Of course." Caroline automatically held out her hand

and he placed the envelope in it. The contents were surprisingly heavy. "May I know what you're giving me?"

"It contains the key to Madam's strongbox, and a set of letters I removed from her correspondence."

"Stole."

He shrugged and offered her a challenging smile. "If you wish."

"Do you know where the strongbox is?"

"No. I didn't have time to discover it. I suspect that the contents might prove beneficial to my cause," Dr. Harris said.

"I had already come to the conclusion there was more to Madam's records than we had recovered and intended to ask Mrs. Frogerton to accompany me back to Madam's house."

"That's my girl."

"I am neither yours nor a girl," Caroline objected.

"Fair enough." He had the gall to lean down and kiss the top of her head. "Now, I must return to my lodgings and prepare to act in a surprised manner when Sergeant Dawson comes to arrest me."

She grabbed hold of his coat sleeve. "Don't do anything foolish, will you? Or deliberately provoke Sergeant Dawson with reckless and unnecessary remarks?"

"I'll do whatever it takes to survive, Miss Morton, even if it means I have to bite my tongue and be polite to the representative of a corrupt system of justice." He patted her shoulder. "Please don't worry. I fear the sergeant has overreached himself somewhat and I'll be out with an apology within a few hours."

"Somehow I doubt that."

Dr. Harris shrugged. "He doesn't have any real evidence and I'm not stupid enough to allow him to force me to incriminate myself."

"Good. Try and remember that." She gave him a gentle push in the direction of the door. "Now go before one of the servants comes to see what all the commotion is about."

"As you wish. Give my regards to Mrs. Frogerton." He set his hat back on his head and opened the front door. The gaslights in the street were still shining brightly against the dark, troubled sky. "Don't worry too much about me, Miss Morton. I'll come about."

"I'm sure you will, Doctor." Caroline tried to match his jaunty tone. "Please be careful on your return journey."

He went down the steps, gave her one last wave, and turned left. Caroline waited until he reached the end of the street before she went back inside. She spent several minutes locking the door so that the staff wouldn't realize it had been opened during the night. It was only when she went to pick up her guttering candle that she realized how badly her hands were shaking.

She sank down on the stairs, covered her face with her hands, and took several deep, restorative breaths. The last thing she needed was to swoon. Dr. Harris's lack of fear over his imminent arrest both infuriated and alarmed her. Was he really that confident he'd be vindicated, or had he been putting up a façade to stop her from worrying about him?

She slowly raised her head and stared at the well-barricaded front door. If he was so certain of success, why had he left her his possessions and somehow intimated that he might be a murderer after all?

"Did you ask Dr. Harris who alerted him to Sergeant Dawson's plans?"

Mrs. Frogerton paused as she buttered her toast to look across the table at Caroline, who was unsuccessfully trying to eat her own breakfast. Caroline had decided not to awaken her employer in the middle of the night with Dr. Harris's news and had told her what had happened when she'd come down in the morning.

"I didn't think to do so, ma'am," Caroline confessed. "I was rather more concerned at his belief that he'd be free by midday."

"He might be right," Mrs. Frogerton observed. "No one saw him entering the house before he arrived with you at three and the hospital confirmed he was active on the wards in the morning. When Sergeant Dawson thinks the good doctor had time to skip off and commit a murder I don't know. Even the butler didn't think it was Dr. Harris."

"Maybe Mr. Murphy was persuaded to change his mind when threatened with prosecution himself," Caroline suggested.

"That might be true." Mrs. Frogerton sighed. "He did say that all he wanted was a quiet life. But how Sergeant Dawson can believe it was Dr. Harris when Sir Alfred *threatened* Madam in front of us all I can't fathom."

"He must think he has the answers, or he'd never proceed."

"Having evidence has never stopped a prosecution." Mrs. Frogerton set her knife down. "When a starving child can be transported for stealing a handkerchief the law isn't doing right by the rest of us."

"I assume we should just wait to hear from Dr. Harris before we do anything further, ma'am?" Caroline asked.

"Not at all." Mrs. Frogerton set her napkin down and rose to her feet. "We're going to Madam's as soon as I can get my boots on, lass."

True to her word, Mrs. Frogerton ordered the carriage and within half an hour they were on their way to Madam Lavinia's house. Caroline hadn't slept well after Dr. Harris's unexpected visit and now had a terrible headache. She rested her chin on her hand and looked out at the crowded streets where no pedestrian was truly safe from the constant stream of heavy wagons, horses, and public conveyances.

She missed the simple pleasures of her father's country estate where she'd grown up while he roamed the world. He'd always been a restless presence in their lives, impatient with their attempts to engage his attention and visibly disinterested in both his wife and his estates. Yet, as children they'd all adored and accepted him just as he was, which had made his later betrayal even harder to bear.

"Here we are," Mrs. Frogerton said brightly. "I do hope Mr. Murphy is willing to answer some more questions."

"I suppose it depends on what he told Sergeant Dawson, ma'am." Caroline followed her employer down the steps to the basement entrance.

Mrs. Frogerton knocked and then tried the door, which opened with a creak.

"Mr. Murphy should look at oiling the door hinges," Mrs. Frogerton murmured as she preceded down the passageway toward the kitchen. "My housekeeper has an excellent concoction for that very thing."

They went into the kitchen to find Letty washing a plate in the scullery sink.

"Mrs. Frogerton, Miss Morton." Letty set the plate on the draining board and wiped her hands on her apron. "If you're wanting Mr. Murphy, he's not here."

"Will he return from his errand soon?" Mrs. Frogerton inquired.

"He's left, ma'am. Gone to his daughter in Ramsgate."

Caroline and Mrs. Frogerton shared a cautious look.

"I thought the authorities wanted him to stay in London until they completed their investigations," Caroline said.

Letty shrugged. "He said one of those peelers came round and told him he was free to leave whenever he wished."

"Did they say why?"

"Something about them finding their murderer, I think,"

Letty said. "It was hard to hear through the crack in the door."

Mrs. Frogerton concealed a smile. "I'm sure it was. I wonder who they believe the murderer to be?"

Letty glanced apologetically at Caroline. "That Dr. Harris you came with, miss. I heard that bit."

"Did Mr. Murphy agree with the police?"

"No, ma'am, he did not. But the fella told him not to argue or they'd clap him in irons as well."

"Did they ask you about any of this?"

"Not when they came the last time to tell Mr. Murphy he could leave. I would've told them they was wrong. I don't hold with no innocent gentleman ending up in prison just because no one spoke up for them."

Mrs. Frogerton patted Letty's shoulder. "You are to be congratulated for that."

"Still doesn't mean I've got a job though, does it?" Letty's gaze swept the deserted kitchen. "It's just me left here all alone with the ghosts."

"When are you expected to close up the house?" Mrs. Frogerton asked.

"I suppose when Madam's solicitor says so, or my employment runs out," Letty said.

Mrs. Frogerton held her gaze. "My offer still stands."

"I thought you was just saying that to get me to talk to you."

"No, I meant it." Mrs. Frogerton opened her reticule and gave Letty her card. "Your honesty speaks for itself."

Letty made a face. "Not when I was fooling all those people and finding out all their secrets."

"You were honest when it mattered most," Mrs. Frogerton said firmly. "And that's what's important."

"I will think on it, ma'am, and thank you." Letty put the card in her skirt pocket and curtsied. "Is there anything else I can help you with?"

"Well, there is the little matter of where your mistress kept her strongbox," Mrs. Frogerton said.

Letty smiled for the first time. "You're not the first person who's asked me that, ma'am. I wish I knew what she'd done with it."

"But she did bring such an item with her from Brighton?" Caroline asked.

"Oh, yes, miss." Letty spread her hands to demonstrate the width of the box. "It wasn't big, but it was banded with iron, and had a lock and a padlock. Madam sat with it beneath her feet in the carriage and put it under her bed whenever we stopped for the night."

"Could one person carry it?"

Letty nodded. "Madam said that if she had to leave suddenly, she wanted something she could take with her."

"I assume Sergeant Dawson and his men made a thorough search for the box?" Caroline asked.

"They did, but I don't think they found it."

"Do you have any thoughts about where Madam might have hidden it?" Mrs. Frogerton put a half crown in Letty's hand.

"All I know is that she would've kept it close to her."

"Then it's probably in her bedroom or her study." Mrs. Frogerton nodded. "Would you object if we looked for it ourselves?"

"Not at all, ma'am." Letty smiled. "I'll put the kettle on."

Caroline looked over at her employer as they climbed the stairs together. "Do you really intend to employ Letty?"

"Why not?" Mrs. Frogerton paused on the landing to catch her breath. "I always appreciate a girl with intelligence."

"What if she uses that 'intelligence' against you?"

"She won't because she is also loyal to whoever pays her wages." Mrs. Frogerton continued down the corridor. "And I pay very well."

"I am aware of that," Caroline said as she opened the door into Madam's bedchamber. The now familiar scent of violets washed over her. "And very grateful."

"I don't require gratitude, lass."

Caroline paused to look down at her employer. "But you have mine, anyway, and my loyalty."

"I'm glad to hear it." Mrs. Frogerton winked at her and then surveyed the room. "Now, what did we miss the last time we were here?"

Half an hour later they were none the wiser and went back down to the kitchen where Letty had set a pot of tea on the table.

"Thank you." Mrs. Frogerton sat down and wiped her brow with her lace handkerchief. "I'm covered in dust and soot, my throat is sore, and we're still no closer to finding Madam's strongbox. I wonder if Mr. Murphy found it and took it with him?"

"He certainly didn't have it when he left the other day." Letty poured them all some tea. "I would've spotted it."

"Perhaps he'd already opened the box and helped himself to the contents." Caroline took an unladylike gulp of tea.

"Not without the key." Letty paused. "Madam always wore that around her neck."

"Did she now?" Mrs. Frogerton looked at Caroline. "Do we know what happened to Madam's clothing after she died?"

"The coroner's office took the body, ma'am," Letty said. "I don't think they've returned it yet, because they still haven't identified her next of kin."

"Then it's possible that Sergeant Dawson still has her possessions," Mrs. Frogerton said. "It isn't right that Madam has no one to attend to her burial."

Letty nodded. "She did go to church every Sunday. I'm sure she'd want a proper ceremony and all that."

"What is the name of the church she attended?"

"St. Jude's." Letty pointed to the left. "It's on the opposite corner to this street. You can't miss it."

"I think I will go and speak to the vicar," Mrs. Frogerton said as she sipped her tea. "I'm sure he would be willing to hold a service for Madam after this matter is resolved."

She set her cup back down on the table. "Shall we tackle the study next or the parlor?"

Inwardly Caroline sighed. "Whatever you wish, ma'am."

"Then, let's make a start, shall we?" Mrs. Frogerton stood up. "And when we have to leave, I'm sure Letty will keep looking for us, won't you, lass?"

Chapter 11

"May I help you, ma'am? I'm Mr. Smith, the current incumbent of this parish." The young vicar looked hopefully from Mrs. Frogerton to Caroline. "Is your daughter about to marry and you wish the service to be held here?"

"Not quite." Mrs. Frogerton smiled. "I am here about one of your parishioners—a Madam Lavinia."

"Oh, yes, the poor, dear lady who recently died. May her soul rest in peace."

"I understand she was a regular communicant here."

"Indeed, she was." The vicar nodded vigorously. "And very generous with her donations in the collection plate."

After seeing the dilapidated interior of the vicarage that sat beside the soot-covered stones of the church, Caroline had to assume the vicar was desperate for funds. There was no housekeeper, the fire was inadequate to heat the drably furnished room, and the vicar's clothing needed laundering.

"I assume that when Madam's body is released by the authorities you would be willing to hold a funeral for her here?" Mrs. Frogerton asked.

"I would be honored to do so." The vicar bowed. "Without her this vicarage would have no roof and the church no adequate drainage."

"Did Madam confide in you, Mr. Smith?" Mrs. Frogerton asked. "Was she worried about anything that might have anticipated her unfortunate demise?"

The vicar's smile disappeared. "With all due respect, ma'am, I am hardly likely to share the discussions I've had with a parishioner with just anyone."

"I am not asking you to reveal anything Madam said to you in confidence," Mrs. Frogerton reassured him. "I am merely determined to find out why Madam died so suddenly and who was responsible. If that is not something that concerns you, sir, then we will bid you good day and take our leave."

She nodded to Caroline, who turned toward the door.

"Wait."

Mrs. Frogerton raised an eyebrow. "What is it?"

"She was worried about some of her clientele," the vicar said. "She said she'd received threatening letters."

"Were you aware of Madam's profession, Vicar?"

"That she was a spiritualist?" He nodded. "Yes, indeed. I chose to believe that her powers came from the good Lord himself and that she did much good in consoling those who had lost loved ones."

"How . . . very forward-thinking of you."

The vicar shrugged. "Jesus Christ performed miracles, did he not? How can I not believe that others might have special powers from God as well?"

"I quite agree with you." Mrs. Frogerton nodded. "Why not indeed?"

Caroline decided to take control of the conversation before her employer became too interested in the logistics of spiritualism within the church and forgot their original purpose. "Did Madam mention anyone she was concerned about by name?"

"Not that I recall." The vicar frowned. "But I do keep a daily journal. I can consult my notes if you wish."

"That would be most helpful." Mrs. Frogerton handed over her card. "You may write or visit me at this address."

The vicar tucked it into the pocket of his waistcoat. "Madam did say she thought herself likely to die before the year was out. She said that the forces against her were gathering and that coming back to London had been a mistake." He hesitated. "I have to say that I thought she was being overly dramatic, but perhaps I should have listened more carefully."

"Hindsight is a wonderful thing," Mrs. Frogerton agreed.

The vicar nodded. "I shall say a special prayer for her soul tonight."

"I think she would appreciate that." Mrs. Frogerton handed the vicar a folded bill from her purse. "For your church fund."

"Thank you, ma'am." The vicar's eyes widened as he saw the size of the bill. "That is most generous of you."

"Consider it a gift in Madam Lavinia's name." Mrs. Frogerton hesitated. "I must admit that I thought Madam would be of the Roman Catholic persuasion, being French."

The vicar smoothed his fingers over the bank note and didn't quite meet Mrs. Frogerton's gaze. "I do not think Madam would be offended by me telling you that she wasn't born in France."

Caroline had suspected as much.

"Then where did she come from?" Mrs. Frogerton asked.

"I only know that she spent the majority of her adult life here in London but before that I couldn't say."

"Did she always worship here on her own?"

The vicar crinkled his brow. "She was occasionally joined by a gentleman, but she never spoke of him directly to me, and I didn't feel it was my place to ask."

"I assume she never mentioned if she was married?"

"No, ma'am." The clock in the hallway chimed and he looked toward the open door. "I apologize, but I am due at the children's orphanage in less than half an hour."

"Then we won't detain you further. You have my card."

Mrs. Frogerton nodded and turned to the door. "Come along, Caroline."

It wasn't until they were seated in the carriage and on their way back to Half Moon Street that Mrs. Frogerton spoke again.

"I don't know about you, lass, but this matter is like a ball of wool that becomes more tangled every time I poke at it."

"I have to agree, ma'am."

"I wonder if the gentleman who accompanied Madam to church was her husband? We'll have to ask Letty if he ever appeared at the house."

"I hardly think Madam's marital affairs have much to do with her death."

"Then you'd be surprised how often a spouse is involved in a partner's murder," Mrs. Frogerton said.

"There are so many other candidates that I still think her husband—if she even had one—and Letty wasn't convinced—is unlikely to be the murderer," Caroline replied.

"Sir Alfred, for one." Mrs. Frogerton carried on talking as if Caroline hadn't disagreed with her. "I cannot for the life of me understand why Sergeant Dawson hasn't arrested him yet."

"Perhaps he provided an unshakable alibi?" Caroline suggested.

Mrs. Frogerton snorted. "I'd be surprised if he's even spoken to the sergeant. The authorities have decided they don't want to waste time and resources on this matter and have settled on poor Dr. Harris."

Caroline couldn't argue with Mrs. Frogerton's logic, and silence settled over them until they arrived at the house. The butler let them in and bowed to Caroline.

"You have a visitor, Miss Morton. Mr. DeBloom arrived about five minutes ago and awaits you in the front parlor."

"With all that has occurred in the last few hours I had quite forgotten he was coming today," Caroline confessed as she removed her bonnet and cloak. She turned to Mrs. Frogerton. "Please excuse me for a moment, ma'am. I promise I will come and tell you everything after he's gone."

"Good. I will order us some tea." With a brisk nod, Mrs. Frogerton continued up the stairs. "Don't allow him any liberties, mind."

"I promise you I will not," Caroline called after her.

She made her way to the small parlor where the butler tended to put visitors of uncertain social status and found Mr. DeBloom pacing the room, his expression troubled.

"I do apologize for my late arrival, sir," Caroline said as she came into the room, leaving the door slightly ajar for propriety's sake.

"It is of no matter. You are here now." He took her gloved hand in his and kissed it. "And looking your usual beautiful, composed self."

Caroline went to sit in one of the chairs beside the fire, gesturing for Mr. DeBloom to join her. It would be far easier to keep her composure and her distance if he wasn't towering over her.

He took the seat on the opposite side of the fire and sat forward, his hands linked together between his knees.

"Clarissa said she saw you and Mrs. Frogerton at Madam Lavinia's house and thought that you recognized her."

"In truth, I didn't know it was Miss DeBloom until she told me so herself," Caroline corrected him. "If it is of any consolation, I doubt anyone else would have recognized her either. She concealed her identity very well."

"That's good to know." Mr. DeBloom hesitated. "You might wonder why she was there."

"It is hardly my business, sir."

"I believe she made it your business when she confided in you," he said. "And, as I have complete confidence in your ability to keep a secret, I will try and explain why my sister felt compelled to visit Madam in the first place."

Caroline waited as he visibly gathered his thoughts.

"Clarissa . . . believes that both my uncle's and my father's death were suspicious. She heard about Madam Lavinia and decided to visit her in the hopes that Madam would contact our father in the afterlife." His mouth twisted. "I know it sounds quite bizarre, but maybe as you were at the gathering yourself, you have some belief in such things."

"Oh no, sir. I only went because Mrs. Frogerton wanted to speak to her deceased husband."

"And did she succeed?"

"Mrs. Frogerton was convinced that Madam spoke of him." Caroline hesitated. "She has a marked tendency toward believing such things, and I would assume that the vast majority of those who seek Madam's help are the same."

Mr. DeBloom nodded. "Clarissa thought that she was the only member of our family who had doubts about the circumstances of our father's death and that she had no other recourse than to turn to such an absurd course of action." He paused. "In truth, if she had just spoken to me first, I could have shared my own concerns."

"You believe your father was murdered?"

He sat back. "I wouldn't go quite that far, but I do think that the investigation into his death and the events leading up to it weren't handled correctly."

"Did you tell Clarissa that?"

"I certainly did. I think she was quite relieved to have my support."

"Has your sister been contacted by the Metropolitan Police Force yet?" Caroline asked. "I understand that they have all Madam's records and if Miss DeBloom's name is in the ledgers as a client she will probably be interviewed."

"I don't know if she used her real name." Mr. DeBloom frowned. "I will have to ask her. Mother would not appreciate the police turning up at her front door." He stood up, surprising Caroline with his abruptness. "I just wanted to make sure you knew the extent of my sister's involvement in this matter and that I will take care of her from now on."

Caroline also rose to her feet and faced him. "Did Madam offer Miss DeBloom any answers to her questions?"

Mr. DeBloom smiled. "Do you know, I didn't think to ask Clarissa that. I assume there was nothing, or else she would've told me straightaway." He bowed. "I don't think she wasted too much money on Madam so nothing to worry about."

"Except that Madam is dead and someone who didn't like her speaking up for the dead murdered her."

"That sounds exactly like something Mrs. Frogerton would say." He winked at her. "Well done." He headed for the door. "Please give Mrs. and Miss Frogerton my regards, Miss Morton, and thank you for listening to me."

Caroline waited until she heard the front door slam before she went back into the hall and up the stairs to the drawing room where her employer awaited her.

"Well?" Mrs. Frogerton asked. "What did he have to say for himself?"

"He said that his sister had some doubts about their father's death, and that thinking she was alone in her suspicions she chose to seek out Madam to contact him from the beyond."

"And what did Madam tell her?"

"According to Mr. DeBloom, he forgot to ask her about that."

"How convenient." Mrs. Frogerton set down her cup. "Did you believe him?"

"No." Caroline walked over to the window that overlooked the street where Mr. DeBloom was just departing in a hackney cab. "I think he decided to give me as little information as possible so that I would believe his sister had nothing to do with anything that subsequently happened at Madam's."

"One has to wonder why."

"Because he thinks that behind my pretty face I am a dullard?" Caroline looked over her shoulder at her employer. "Or does he hope that if the police do come calling on his mother, he can try that story out on them, and I will back him up?"

"You seem rather upset, lass."

"Because Mr. DeBloom thinks he can charm his way out of anything, and that as long as his sister is protected, the murder of another woman isn't his concern."

"Come and sit down."

Reluctantly Caroline did as she was asked, her hands clenched into fists.

"Mr. DeBloom would probably say that he's just doing his best to protect his family," Mrs. Frogerton said gently.

"I know that."

"Then why do you care?"

"Because some women have no one to protect them and Madam is one of them."

"We are doing our best for her, lass."

"We're trying to stop Dr. Harris being prosecuted for something he didn't do," Caroline pointed out. "Protecting Madam certainly wasn't our original intent."

Mrs. Frogerton looked at her. "You seem to have forgotten that Madam wrote to you personally and asked for your help."

Caroline took a slow breath. "You're right. I had almost forgotten about that."

"I'm not surprised what with everything that's been going on the last few days." Mrs. Frogerton poured her some tea.

"I can only apologize for my rudeness, ma'am."

"There's no need. I am as flummoxed by all this as you are, lass."

"But you didn't employ me to argue with you."

"Did I not?" Mrs. Frogerton smiled. "If we agreed about everything, life would be very dull indeed."

The butler came into the room and bowed to Mrs. Frogerton.

"Professor Brown wishes to speak to you, if it is convenient, ma'am."

"Then send him up." Mrs. Frogerton looked over at Caroline. "Now what?"

Professor Brown hadn't bothered to remove his hat or cloak and appeared rather agitated.

"Mrs. Frogerton, Miss Morton. I came as soon as I heard. Dr. Harris has been arrested for the murder of Madam Lavinia."

Mrs. Frogerton gasped. "That is ridiculous!"

"I'm glad you agree." He cleared his throat. "He told me that if this happened, I was to come and speak to you because you are the only person he knows with any influence or money."

"And he was quite right to tell you that." Mrs. Frogerton nodded. "Where is he being held? We will go and speak to the authorities immediately."

"Thank you, ma'am." The professor bowed. "I have the details here." He handed her a note. "I wish I could accompany you, but I have to get back to the hospital."

"We will manage perfectly well by ourselves," Mrs. Frogerton assured him. "It's not the first time I've had to bail a man out from jail."

"For murder?" Professor Brown was momentarily diverted.

"Death by misadventure is what they settled on in the end I believe, but it cost me a fair amount to get to that." Mrs. Frogerton was already heading through the door when she spoke again. "Caroline, send a quick note off to my solicitor and ask him to meet us at Bow Street."

"Yes, ma'am."

Caroline was just about to sit down at Mrs. Frogerton's desk when Professor Brown cleared his throat.

"Dr. Harris said that he trusted you and Mrs. Frogerton completely and I can see why."

"Mrs. Frogerton has a generous and caring nature." Caroline looked for a pen and opened the inkwell. "And she considers Dr. Harris a valued friend."

"He is lucky, then."

"Surely not that lucky when he has been accused of a crime he didn't commit."

"You also think he is innocent?"

Caroline raised her gaze to meet Professor Brown's. "Of course."

"I'm glad that we are all in agreement, then." He bowed to her. "I wish to offer my services toward making sure my esteemed colleague is released with all speed and the true culprit is apprehended."

"I'm sure Dr. Harris would appreciate that."

"He'd do the same for me." He paused. "I have already passed copies of my notes on Madam's séances to the police and would be delighted to share the originals with you and Mrs. Frogerton's solicitor."

"That would be most welcome." Caroline finished writing her note, blotted the ink, and folded the paper to secure the contents within. She stood up to ring the bell for the butler and turned to Professor Brown.

"Thank you for coming to let us know what happened to Dr. Harris."

"I'd like to say it was my pleasure, but in this case, I suspect it was more of a necessity." He grimaced and glanced at the clock on the mantelpiece. "I apologize but I must go, but do not hesitate to call on me if you need my assistance. I will send a boy around with my notes this very afternoon."

"Thank you." Caroline followed him to the door. "I have great confidence in Mrs. Frogerton's ability to extricate Dr. Harris from this unfortunate situation, but I know she will appreciate your support."

The butler was coming up the stairs in answer to her

summons. She gave him the note with instructions as to its urgent delivery and handed Professor Brown over to him before heading up to her bedchamber to put on her bonnet and walking boots. She doubted Dr. Harris was in immediate danger, but knowing his acerbic tongue, the sooner they could liberate him from the loving embrace of the Metropolitan Police, the better.

Chapter 12

"I wish to speak to your superior," Mrs. Frogerton repeated firmly. "If you will not give me the courtesy of an answer, I will find out the truth from someone else."

Sergeant Dawson's harried gaze briefly met Caroline's and she returned it with full force. They'd been at Great Scotland Yard for well over an hour after waiting for the sergeant to return from his patrol. His reluctance to speak about the case had ignited Mrs. Frogerton's rare ire.

"My solicitor, Mr. Lewis, will be here at any moment to organize Dr. Harris's release. I do not have all day to linger here waiting for your cooperation." Mrs. Frogerton raised her chin. "What is the name of your superior?"

Mrs. Frogerton hadn't raised her voice, but her tone was that of a woman used to being obeyed.

Sergeant Dawson was just opening his mouth to reply when two gentlemen came through an interior door bringing with them a whirl of cigar smoke and roast beef–scented air.

"Inspector Ross." The sergeant shot to attention.

"Sergeant." The man's gaze swept over Mrs. Frogerton, lingered on Caroline, and then returned to his companion. "I assume these are your clients, old chap?"

"Yes, indeed." Mr. Lewis bowed. "Good afternoon, Mrs.

Frogerton. I'm sure you'll be delighted to hear that my old friend Ross, here, is highly amenable to allowing Dr. Harris out on bail with your surety."

"I'm very glad to hear it." Mrs. Frogerton nodded. "I'd still like to know what convinced them to arrest him in the first place." She directed her attention to the inspector. "Perhaps you could ask your subordinate to share the grounds for Dr. Harris's arrest?"

"Dawson?"

"Yes, sir?"

"Why don't you sit down with Mr. Lewis, Mrs. Frogerton, and this charming young lady and tell them what you know?"

"Surely that will prejudice the case in court, sir?" Sergeant Dawson protested somewhat weakly.

"I doubt Mr. Lewis and his client will share this information with anyone."

"Of course we won't," Mrs. Frogerton agreed. "We are simply interested in protecting our friend Dr. Harris."

"Lucky man." Inspector Ross shook Mr. Lewis's hand. "I'll see you at the club later for a drink."

"Which will be on me," Mr. Lewis replied. "I appreciate your assistance in this matter."

After the inspector left, Mr. Lewis turned to Mrs. Frogerton. "I have already begun the process of securing bail for Dr. Harris, ma'am."

"Thank you." Mrs. Frogerton looked pointedly at the sergeant, whose ears had gone red. "Perhaps you could now persuade this gentleman to tell us why he arrested the doctor in the first place."

Mr. Lewis, who was obviously well used to his client's tenacity and plain speaking, concealed a smile, and indicated a small room to their left. "Shall we go in here and let the sergeant explain?"

Caroline followed Mrs. Frogerton inside and waited as Mr. Lewis shut the door behind them all.

"Go ahead, Sergeant." The solicitor gestured to the policeman. "We're all ears."

Sergeant Dawson produced his notebook and leafed through the pages.

"Dr. Harris had the means and ability to procure the arsenic that killed Madam Lavinia. He was seen at the house on the day of her death. Two witnesses said he attended one of her meetings and was annoyed when Madam singled him out as having 'blood on his hands.' " He looked up. "That was enough for my superiors to agree to his arrest."

Caroline looked over at the solicitor.

"May I ask a question?"

"Please go ahead, Miss Morton."

"I was with Dr. Harris when he visited Madam's house on the day of her death. I have already told Sergeant Dawson that Madam was dead when we arrived."

"Sergeant?"

"We concluded Dr. Harris might have visited the house earlier that day and deliberately brought you back with him as a witness, my lady, to keep his appointment."

"Did anyone see Dr. Harris at the house earlier?"

Sergeant Dawson flicked through his notes. "Not as such, but the butler and maid did say that several people visited the house."

"None of whom they identified as Dr. Harris, or you would've have said so," Mrs. Frogerton spoke. "Even though they saw him that very afternoon."

Mr. Lewis raised his eyebrows as Mrs. Frogerton continued.

"And the hospital accounted for Dr. Harris's time that morning. He was on the wards."

Sergeant Dawson cleared his throat. "We still felt that he was the most likely candidate, and he refused to cooperate with our investigation, which was suspicious in itself."

"As well he might refuse when you had other people

like Sir Alfred Fielding literally threatening Madam in front of a dozen people." Mrs. Frogerton shook her head and tutted. "And where is your investigation into *him*?"

"We have been unsuccessful in our attempts to speak to Sir Alfred so far."

"I wonder why? One might almost think he was avoiding you."

Caroline had never seen her employer so riled up. It was quite a sight. She turned to Mr. Lewis.

"We were at Madam's when Sir Alfred burst in and accused Madam of deceiving his mother. He had to be thrown out by the butler and Dr. Harris. When we called on Lady Fielding a day or so later, we discovered that he had left the house rather abruptly."

Mr. Lewis frowned. "With all due respect, Sergeant, it does rather sound as if you decided to make an arrest before you fully investigated this case."

Sergeant Dawson drew himself up to his full height. "I did what I was ordered to do, sir. Perhaps you might take that up with my superiors."

"Oh, I certainly will be doing that." Suddenly Mr. Lewis looked as formidable as Mrs. Frogerton. "The Metropolitan Police Force doesn't need any more bad press."

Sergeant Dawson stiffened. "We're just doing our jobs, sir."

"Which apparently doesn't include interviewing all the witnesses to a potential crime." Mrs. Frogerton wasn't done. "I do hope you got the butler's address before you allowed him to scuttle off because, by the sound of it, you might need to speak to him again."

"Mr. Murphy is still cooperating with the authorities, ma'am."

"From *Ramsgate*?"

Sergeant Dawson frowned. "He's not been given permission to leave London, Mrs. Frogerton. Where did you hear that he had left?"

"When I interviewed Madam's parlor maid for a posi-

tion at my house, the girl told me the butler had gone."
The certainty of Mrs. Frogerton's tone didn't allow for any
questioning as to her somewhat unorthodox hiring methods. "She said an officer from your force told him he
could go."

Sergeant Dawson frowned down at his notes. "That's . . ."
He looked up. "I need to speak to my constable. Will you
please excuse me?"

"Not until you assure me that you intend to continue
with this investigation?" Mrs. Frogerton asked. "Dr. Harris at least deserves that."

"I'm certain the sergeant will consider his options most
carefully, ma'am, and I will put in a good word for Dr. Harris with Inspector Ross," Mr. Lewis said. "Now, why don't
we let him go about his duties while we wait for further information about Dr. Harris's bail hearing."

"Thank you, sir." Sergeant Dawson nodded stiffly. "I'll
update you, when necessary, Mrs. Frogerton."

Mrs. Frogerton held his gaze. "If you don't, expect to
see me awaiting you here."

Mr. Lewis waited until the sergeant hurried out before
turning to his client.

"You were rather hard on him, ma'am."

"He deserved it. His investigation was shockingly bad."

"I agree with you there." Mr. Lewis paused. "I wonder why?"

"He did imply that there had been some pressure from
his superiors to find the culprit as quickly as possible,"
Caroline commented.

"Yes, I noticed that, too," Mr. Lewis said. "I'll have to
ask Ross."

"Madam did have some rather exalted clients."

"Which might explain a lot." Mr. Lewis lapsed into
thought before turning to address Mrs. Frogerton. "I'll see
what I can find out."

"Ask Inspector Ross if you can see Madam's client list,"

Mrs. Frogerton said helpfully. "I'm sure it will be *most* informative."

Mr. Lewis nodded and rose to his feet. "Now, I must go and advise Dr. Harris as to the legal process he is about to go through."

"And tell him to keep his mouth shut unless absolutely necessary," Mrs. Frogerton advised. "He has a tendency to be far too honest and hotheaded."

"So I noticed." Mr. Lewis shook Mrs. Frogerton's hand. "I'm not sure quite when I'll secure his release, as it depends on the court, but I'll be sure to send a note to your house."

Mrs. Frogerton smiled. "If you would be so good as to send Dr. Harris to me as well, I would be most grateful."

"I'll do my best." Mr. Lewis winked and headed for the door. "Pleasure to meet you, Miss Morton."

"And you, sir." Caroline curtsied and helped Mrs. Frogerton gather her belongings so that they could leave.

It wasn't until they were seated opposite each other in the drawing room in Half Moon Street that Mrs. Frogerton spoke again.

"I think it's time for a bit of plain speaking between us and Dr. Harris, lass."

"It would certainly be useful."

"If he won't be honest, then there's very little more I can do for him."

"Some might say that you have done more than enough already, ma'am," Caroline answered. "He isn't your kin."

"All the more reason to offer him my support." Mrs. Frogerton hitched her shawl higher around her shoulders. "I can't stand by and watch a miscarriage of justice just because the police force can't be bothered to do a proper investigation."

"I am sure Dr. Harris will be grateful for your help."

Mrs. Frogerton snorted. "I doubt it, but that isn't the point."

"I appreciate what you are doing for him even if he doesn't and offer you my gratitude."

"Then all is well." Mrs. Frogerton nodded.

The door opened and Dorothy came in. "Wherever have you been? I came down to breakfast and neither of you were here."

"That's what happens when you sleep your mornings away, dearie." Mrs. Frogerton accepted a kiss from her daughter.

"I was up until four." Dorothy concealed a yawn and sat beside her mother. She wore a plain gown for once and her hair was still in its nighttime braid. "Where did you go?"

"To post bail for Dr. Harris, who has been arrested for murdering Madam Lavinia."

Dorothy gasped. "No!"

"Don't fret, love." Mrs. Frogerton patted her hand. "We succeeded in getting him out on bail."

"I knew you'd manage that," Dorothy said. "I don't particularly like the man, but I don't believe he's a murderer."

"He isn't," Caroline said. "The evidence against him was purely circumstantial."

"Will he have a trial?"

"Not if I have anything to do with it," her mother said briskly. She turned to Caroline. "If Sergeant Dawson refuses to investigate this properly, then I suppose we'll have to do his job for him."

"Not if it impacts me and my Season," Dorothy said. "I don't want to be associated with a murder."

"Have you been associated with it so far?" Mrs. Frogerton asked. "Caroline and I have been involved in this matter for days and you haven't even noticed."

"I've been rather busy trying to secure myself a duke!" Dorothy retorted. "Without much help from either of you."

"There aren't any eligible dukes in London at present,"

Caroline pointed out. "And Viscount Lingard, who is currently dancing attendance on you, is the gentleman with the highest rank available."

"That's what you think." Dorothy paused. "But that is because neither of you have been keeping up."

"What are you on about, Dotty?" Mrs. Frogerton asked as Dorothy smirked.

"One of the royal dukes is attending a garden party at Lady Lincoln's house this very afternoon."

"Do we have an invitation?" Mrs. Frogerton asked Caroline. "I've never seen a royal duke in the flesh before."

"We do." Caroline, who read and replied to all the Frogerton correspondence, considered the day's upcoming events. "It starts at three o'clock. Do you remember which duke it was, Dorothy?"

"Sussex, I think."

Caroline paused. "But he is currently married to the Duchess of Inverness."

Dorothy tossed her head. "Not according to the Royal Marriages Act."

"Then we must all go," Mrs. Frogerton said. "I've always wanted to meet a real duke. If Dr. Harris is released before we return then he will just have to wait."

Several hours later after attending the garden party, a musical evening, and a ball, Caroline and Mrs. Frogerton were sitting in the drawing room together. Mrs. Frogerton had taken off her slippers and set her stockinged feet up on a footstool.

"I am more than ready for my bed," Mrs. Frogerton announced.

Caroline, whose feet were aching just as much, went to ring the bell. "I'll ask the butler to send your maid up to your room."

"Thank you, dear." Mrs. Frogerton regarded her fondly. "What did you think of the Duke of Sussex?"

"He was very pleasant, ma'am."

"And quite forward-thinking for his age I gather."

"I understand that he is passionate about the arts and sciences and a firm supporter of the abolition of slavery."

"All admirable qualities." Mrs. Frogerton paused. "I didn't expect him to be old enough to be Dotty's grandfather."

"He's at least sixty-five."

"Far too old for her, then."

"And he has a wife who might object to being ousted," Caroline added.

"Not that any of that would put Dotty off." Mrs. Frogerton lowered her feet to the floor and grimaced. "I suspect I'll need a much quieter day tomorrow."

"There is nothing that we have to attend until the evening, ma'am," Caroline reassured her as she offered her arm. "And if Dorothy wishes to venture out during the day, we can find her a suitable chaperone."

"I'm sure we can."

The door opened to admit the butler, who bowed.

"I apologize for disturbing you so late in the evening, ma'am, but Mr. Lewis delivered Dr. Harris to the house as requested."

With a groan Mrs. Frogerton sat back down again. "Then send Dr. Harris in and bring me some warm milk with brandy in it."

Dr. Harris looked even more disheveled than usual. His hair was on end, his cravat rumpled, and his coattails muddy. He strode over to Mrs. Frogerton, went down on one knee, and took her hand in his.

"I cannot tell you how grateful I am for your kindness and assistance in this matter."

Mrs. Frogerton squeezed his fingers. "You are a friend of the family. How could I not help you?"

"I do not deserve such consideration."

"Sit down, Dr. Harris. Would you like something to

drink?" She looked at Caroline. "Fetch the doctor a nice glass of brandy from the decanter on the sideboard, lass."

Caroline did as she was asked and brought the heavy glass back to Dr. Harris, who took it with alacrity. His fingers shook as he brought the glass to his lips and drank deeply.

"Thank you."

"Were you only just released?" Mrs. Frogerton asked.

"Yes, ma'am. The courts were very busy today." He hesitated. "If I am to continue in my current employment, I will need to be back at the hospital by midnight to start my night shift."

Caroline glanced at the clock, which was just about to strike a quarter past eleven.

Mrs. Frogerton sat forward. "Dr. Harris, if you wish to truly show your gratitude to me, I require something from you."

"What is that, ma'am?"

"Your complete honesty." Mrs. Frogerton fixed him with a calm stare. "Neither Caroline nor I feel as if you have been telling us the truth."

Dr. Harris grimaced. "I admit that I have not been as . . . forthcoming about matters as perhaps I should have been."

"Then I would appreciate it if you were." Mrs. Frogerton held up a finger as he went to speak. "I suspect we will need more time than we have at present, and I appreciate that you have a prior commitment to your patients. Perhaps you might return tomorrow at noon?"

"Yes, Mrs. Frogerton. I would be delighted to do so." Dr. Harris hesitated. "Did Sergeant Dawson tell you *why* he arrested me? Because I still have no idea."

"We can talk about all of that tomorrow," Mrs. Frogerton said firmly. "Why don't you finish your brandy and be on your way."

He nodded and stood up. It was the first time Caroline had seen him so thoroughly exhausted and dispirited.

"Thank you, ma'am." He looked over at Caroline. "And you, Miss Morton."

She refrained from telling him that she'd done nothing and merely smiled and went to open the drawing room door for him.

"I'll return the items you left with me tomorrow, sir," Caroline said as he went past her and continued down the stairs into the hall.

"Thank you." He stifled a yawn as he put on his hat.

"Are you quite certain you are capable of managing a ward full of patients tonight, Dr. Harris?" Caroline asked as she accompanied him to the front door.

"I have no choice." His brief smile was bleak. "I can't afford to lose my job as well as my reputation. Good night, Miss Morton. I'll see you tomorrow."

"Good night, Doctor." She closed the door and made her way up the stairs to the drawing room where Mrs. Frogerton was sipping her milk and brandy.

"Do you think he'll cooperate?" Caroline asked as she helped her employer find her slippers and rise from her chair.

"What other choice does he have, lass?"

"He is remarkably stubborn."

"Aren't we all," Mrs. Frogerton said. "But if he doesn't want our assistance, there's nothing we can do about it."

"That is the truth, ma'am," Caroline said as she ascended the stairs at Mrs. Frogerton's side.

"He did look a bit crestfallen tonight," Mrs. Frogerton said thoughtfully. "Let's hope he still feels that way on the morrow and is willing to tell us the truth."

Chapter 13

"Miss Morton?"

"Yes?" Caroline halted at the bottom of the stairs and waited as the butler came toward her. She hadn't slept well and had risen early, taken her breakfast in the kitchen, and started answering Mrs. Frogerton's correspondence.

"There is a young person here asking to see Mrs. Frogerton, but as she has not come down for breakfast I wondered if you might speak to her instead?"

"Of course." Caroline followed the butler into the parlor where he usually left Sergeant Dawson and discovered Letty, Madam Lavinia's maid.

"Good morning, Miss Morton."

"Letty." Caroline smiled at the girl. "I understand that you wished to speak to Mrs. Frogerton."

"She asked me to let her know if I thought of anywhere Madam might have kept that strongbox," Letty said.

"And?"

"I remembered something when I was dusting today. A few weeks ago, I went into the back parlor where she held the séances to lay the fire and startled her so badly she shouted at me to get out."

"What was she doing?"

"I'm not quite sure because she had her back to me, but

she was fiddling around near the fireplace." Letty frowned. "And something about it looked odd."

"Did you manage to discover what she might have been doing?"

"Not at the time because I was too scared, but I remembered it when I was in there today. I couldn't see anything obvious, but I thought Mrs. Frogerton might want to know."

"I'm sure she will," Caroline said. "If we have time today, she'll probably want to pop round and see for herself."

Letty nodded. "I'll be there, miss. I'm currently packing up Madam's things, although Lord knows what I'm supposed to do with them then."

Caroline found a coin and handed it to Letty.

"Thank you, Miss Morton." Letty pocketed the coin.

"I know you said that Madam never mentioned whether she was married or not, but did anyone call on her regularly?"

"There were several gentlemen who visited her. I could hardly keep them straight in my head." Letty paused. "I never saw any of them kissing her or anything, they was always very respectful."

"Have you heard from Mr. Murphy?"

"No, but I wasn't expecting to." Letty shrugged. "He came with the house. I've only known him a few months and we weren't close."

"Do you know whom Madam rented the house from?"

"No, I'm sorry, miss." Letty's patience for Caroline's questions visibly waned and she glanced at the clock. "I have to go. That Sergeant Dawson said he'd be coming to talk to me at ten."

"He told me that Mr. Murphy was supposed to have stayed in town."

"Oh, blimey," Letty groaned. "Now the peeler will be wanting his address and everything, won't he?"

"I should imagine so." Caroline escorted Letty to the

front door. "Take care now and don't tell anyone else about what you think you have discovered until you've spoken to Mrs. Frogerton."

"Yes, miss." Letty looked to the left and then the right and ran nimbly across the street, one hand holding on to the rim of her bonnet as she dodged a brewery cart.

Caroline went through to the breakfast room and contemplated the day ahead. Dr. Harris was due to arrive at noon, Dorothy had a party to attend in the evening and a dress fitting at three, and Mrs. Frogerton wanted to return to the library to exchange her books.

"The post has been delivered, Miss Morton." The butler came in with a fresh pot of coffee and a pile of correspondence on a tray.

"Then I'll look through it."

"Yes, miss." He set the tray at her elbow and poured her some coffee. "Will you be requiring more toast?"

"No, I think I have had sufficient for my needs, thank you," Caroline said.

Between sips of coffee she sorted out the post. There was the usual stack of invitations for Dorothy and Mrs. Frogerton, two letters from the north probably about business, and one from Lady Fielding.

Caroline contemplated opening it but as it was addressed to her employer, she decided to leave it to one side. There was one more letter beneath Lady Fielding's with Caroline's name on it.

She paused to examine the handwriting, which wasn't familiar. There was a scrawled signature where the letter had been franked but it wasn't clear enough to read. She turned the letter over, used her knife to break the seal, and unfolded the single sheet of paper, edged in black.

I regret to inform you that Lady Eleanor Greenwood is deceased. May her soul ascend to the highest heaven and rest in the eternal peace of the Lord.

Beneath this script, her cousin Nick, who had recently and reluctantly inherited his father's title, had scrawled:

Would appreciate it if you and Susan could come to the funeral. Will send a carriage to bring you to Greenwood Hall when the funeral date has been established. Mabel will not be joining us.

Yours, Nick.

Caroline carefully reread the letter, her mind not on the words, but on memories of her aunt in better times when she'd provided a home and shelter for her two nieces while their father had run wild. She swallowed hard, aware that her last conversation with her bedridden aunt had hardly gone well and that she'd never have the chance to reconcile with her.

"Why the long face?" Mrs. Frogerton asked as she came into the dining room.

"I just received word that my aunt Eleanor has died. I assume she had another stroke."

"I'm sorry to hear that, dearie." Mrs. Frogerton laid a comforting hand on Caroline's shoulder as she went past. "I know you had your differences, but from what you told me of your childhood she at least did her duty by you."

"Yes, she did her best." Caroline carefully folded the letter back up and took a steadying breath. "I'll need to write to Susan. Once she knows Mabel won't be at the funeral she probably won't want to go."

Mrs. Frogerton helped herself to the coffee. She tended to have her breakfast in bed but often joined Caroline at the table afterward to discuss their plans for the day. "You haven't corresponded with Mabel, have you?"

"We have never been in the habit of doing so, ma'am."

Mrs. Frogerton pursed her lips. "I wonder if she has contacted Susan?"

"If she has, I doubt my sister would tell me." Caroline sighed. "When I write to tell her about our aunt, I'll have to include a note to Rose Harris to find out exactly who might be corresponding with Susan."

"I think that is wise." Mrs. Frogerton nodded. "From

what you told me, Susan was very attached to Mabel. She might share information with her cousin that should perhaps be kept private."

Eager to lay the painful subject to rest, Caroline put the letter away in her pocket and turned back to her employer. "We have already had an unexpected visitor today, ma'am."

"Who was that?"

"Letty."

"Madam Lavinia's maid? What did she want at this hour of the morning?"

"She thinks she might know where Madam hid her strongbox. I said that if we had time we might come and investigate."

"We have plenty of time this morning." Mrs. Frogerton scanned the contents of her two letters from the north and set them aside before turning to the one from Lady Fielding. "Now, I wonder what her ladyship wants?"

She read the note and passed it over to Caroline. "It appears that Sir Alfred has gone missing."

"What a surprise." Caroline read the letter. "Lady Fielding is very concerned as to his whereabouts."

"As she should be, especially if Sergeant Dawson's been sent around with a flea in his ear from his superiors to speak to her again."

"It certainly makes Sir Alfred look guilty," Caroline agreed. "But whether that is enough to interest the police is another matter."

"Especially when they've already decided Dr. Harris is the murderer." Mrs. Frogerton tapped the letter with her fingertip. "Perhaps we should visit Lady Fielding after Madam Lavinia's."

Caroline nodded. "And don't forget your library books, ma'am. We will be passing the circulating library on our way to the Fielding home."

"An excellent suggestion. What would I do without you?"

Mrs. Frogerton finished her coffee and gathered up her correspondence, leaving the invitations for Dorothy and Caroline to look over. "Come along then, lass. We've got a lot to do."

With the absence of the butler and the lack of a constant stream of clients, Madam's house was slowly retreating into shoddy rented anonymity. Caroline rarely thought about how the constant presence of staff and family made a home feel alive, but she was aware of it now as sunlight shone onto the accumulating dust.

"Did you find someone to take Madam's belongings?" Caroline asked Letty as she accompanied them along the corridor to the back parlor.

"Not yet, ma'am."

"Perhaps you should put an announcement of Madam's death in the newspapers?" Mrs. Frogerton suggested. "That might bring her relatives around."

"Can't afford it, ma'am," Letty said.

"Then I will do it and I'll send a man around to pick up Madam's belongings and put them in my cellar where they will be kept safe for whoever comes forward."

"Thank you." Letty paused. "And you'll take me on, too?"

Mrs. Frogerton nodded. "As soon as you can leave this house."

"Thank you, ma'am." Letty broke into a relieved smile. "Me dad will be right pleased to hear that." She opened the door into the parlor. "I've taken out all the things that belonged to Madam. There wasn't much—just the candelabra and bowl, and a couple of ornaments on the mantelpiece."

"And what exactly was Madam doing when you surprised her in here?" Mrs. Frogerton inquired.

"She was standing with her back to the door and was fiddling with something in the fireplace. At first, I thought she was adding coal to the fire, but she wasn't bending down."

"Thank you, Letty."

"I'll go and finish packing Madam's belongings and I'll put everything together in the front hall." Letty curtsied and skipped away.

Without the concealing darkness the room looked even more threadbare than Caroline remembered. She turned her attention to the mantelpiece and discovered it was built of blocks of honey-colored stone that was quite soft to the touch and badly discolored by the smoke from the fire. There was no fire laid in the blackened grate now and a draft swirled down the chimney.

"Reminds me of Bath," Mrs. Frogerton said. "I did enjoy taking the waters there. Have you tried it, Caroline?"

"My aunt was a great believer in the powers of the mineral springs, but I didn't accompany her into the actual bath." Caroline suddenly remembered Eleanor's lace-capped head bobbing in the water above her modest muslin bathing gown and swallowed hard.

"I didn't bathe—" Mrs. Frogerton, who was carefully running her fingers over the surface of the stones, shuddered. "I simply drank a glass of the vile-tasting liquid in the pump room every morning and promenaded around the town. Ah."

"What is it, ma'am?"

"There is a slight indentation here on the inside edge of the second slab down. Can you see it?"

Caroline leaned in to look over her employer's shoulder. "Yes, there is definitely a triangular-shaped notch in the stone."

"Is there anything corresponding on the other side?"

"Not that I can see." Caroline paused. "Wait. There is a worn mark as if the stone has been rubbed against something."

"I wonder if this particular stone simply pulls out, or if there is some mechanism behind it?" Mrs. Frogerton murmured. "There must be a trick to it." She took off her gloves and felt carefully around where the stone met the tiled fire surround. "I think . . ."

There was a soft click and the piece of Bath stone, hinged on the right, swung slowly forward to reveal a large hollowed-out space that was currently occupied by a sturdy-looking strongbox.

Mrs. Frogerton clapped her hands. "Success! Now, do you think you could help me remove it, Caroline? It appears to be something of a tight fit."

It took both their efforts to extract the strongbox and place it on the table. Mrs. Frogerton closed the hiding place, replaced her gloves, and dusted off a few cobwebs from the exterior.

"I suppose we should take this to Sergeant Dawson."

"I should imagine so, ma'am."

"But it would be remiss of us not to at least attempt to open it before we did that," Mrs. Frogerton said. "We wouldn't want him getting any unpleasant surprises."

"And we do have a key."

"We do?" Mrs. Frogerton raised her eyebrows.

"Dr. Harris left some items in my possession the night before he was arrested, and he mentioned that he had Madam's key."

"Then we won't even need to break into the strongbox." Mrs. Frogerton looked pleased. "Sergeant Dawson will never even know we looked."

"Especially if we put it back in its hiding place when we are finished," Caroline added.

She'd always thought of herself as the most law-abiding of people—that is until the unfortunate Sergeant Dawson had decided to arrest Dr. Harris on very questionable evidence.

"Exactly." Mrs. Frogerton nodded. "Letty has the keys to the house so we can return here at will."

"I'll carry the box back to the carriage when we leave, ma'am," Caroline said.

"Excellent." Mrs. Frogerton paused. "Why don't you go and do that right now while I speak to Letty. Ask Giles to keep an eye on it."

"Yes, ma'am."

Caroline waited until Mrs. Frogerton opened the door and checked that Letty wasn't in the hall before she picked up the box and took it out to the waiting carriage. It was heavier than expected and she had to ask the coachman to lift it onto the step so that he could put it under his seat.

By the time she returned to the house Letty and Mrs. Frogerton were chatting in the kitchen as they waited for the kettle to boil.

"What did Sergeant Dawson have to say for himself?" Mrs. Frogerton asked.

Letty made a face. "He wanted to know the name of the policeman who came around and told Mr. Murphy he could leave—as if I'd know."

"It is odd that Sergeant Dawson was unaware of this development," Caroline said as she took the milk jug from the cold pantry and set it on the scrubbed table. "I thought he was in charge of the case."

"He wasn't happy about it, miss, but he tried to make it my fault of course. He asked me to describe the man. I told him he looked the same as he did."

"He wore the same uniform?" Mrs. Frogerton moved out of Letty's way as she transferred the boiling hot water from the kettle to the teapot.

"Yes, ma'am."

"How strange. Did the sergeant ask you anything else?"

"He wanted Mr. Murphy's new address. I told him it was in Ramsgate and that his daughter's married name was Smith, which probably won't help a lot." Letty smirked. "If they want Mr. Murphy, they'll have to move their arses and find him themselves. I told him that, too."

*   *   *

Twenty minutes later, with the strongbox secure under the coachman's bench, they stopped off at the lending library, and then made their way to Lady Fielding's house. Mrs. Frogerton was remarkably quiet on the journey, her brow creased as she stared out of the window. Caroline was reluctant to disturb her and contented herself with quick glances at the contents of the next gothic novel Mrs. Frogerton had borrowed from the library.

The butler admitted them without delay and took them up to the drawing room where Lady Fielding awaited them. She rushed toward Mrs. Frogerton and grabbed for her hands.

"Alfred has disappeared!"

"I'm sorry to hear that, my lady," Mrs. Frogerton said. "He wasn't at your country property after all?"

"The police went there!" Lady Fielding sank down onto the couch, obliging Mrs. Frogerton to follow as she was still holding her hands. "No one had seen him at Hawthorn Hall for months!"

"That must be very worrying for you," Mrs. Frogerton said. "Does he have friends or other family members he might have visited instead?"

"I don't know. I'm trying to think of their names and I'm writing to everyone I know but what if he's left the country? What can I do then? I can't pay my bills without his authorization, and I dread to think what the bank account looks like."

"Did Sir Alfred have a secretary who might help with these matters?" Caroline asked.

"No, he decided he didn't need one." Lady Fielding finally released Mrs. Frogerton's hands but only because she needed to dab at her tears.

"Then a family solicitor?"

"Yes, we do have one of those." She nodded vigorously. "Do you think I should ask for his help?"

"I would," Mrs. Frogerton said. "He can ascertain whether Sir Alfred took a large sum of money out of his bank account recently, and deal with any upcoming legal complications appertaining to the estate. Do you have other children, my lady?"

"No, Alfred is the only one." Lady Fielding's lip quivered. "My pride and joy. Madam told me something like this might happen."

"That your son would disappear?" Caroline asked.

"That all the men in my life would betray me." Lady Fielding shivered. "My husband died too young, and now my son . . ."

"There's no need for despair," Mrs. Frogerton said. "Now that the police are aware that he is missing, I'm sure they'll do everything in their power to find him."

"But . . ." Lady Fielding swallowed hard. "I haven't told them that."

Mrs. Frogerton frowned. "Surely, they must have worked it out for themselves?"

"I told them I must have been mistaken about where he intended to go and gave them the address of my parents, who live in Northamptonshire"

"With all due respect, my lady, why would you do such a thing?"

"To buy myself more time." Lady Fielding spoke rapidly. "Because if he is guilty of . . . something . . . then I need to find him first."

"You believe he killed Madam Lavinia?" Caroline asked.

"No! I mean even if he did, it was probably an accident because he has such a terrible temper, and he's so young, and he panicked, and rather than facing up to his responsibilities and admitting a fault he ran away."

Caroline and Mrs. Frogerton stared at the widow, who refused to meet their gazes and took refuge in her handkerchief.

"You won't mention any of this to the police, will you?" Lady Fielding asked eventually.

"I won't lie to them." Mrs. Frogerton sat forward. "In the unlikely event that they ask me a direct question about your son I'll tell them what I know."

"Which is nothing—" Lady Fielding said sharply. "Everything I've said is pure conjecture."

"You suggested that Sir Alfred might have harmed Madam and run away," Mrs. Frogerton pointed out. She was no longer smiling. "That might be considered an admission of guilt."

"Not by him. And I might simply be worrying about nothing." Lady Fielding tried to laugh. "I do get quite hysterical at times; my husband often remarked on it and took no notice of anything I said."

It was obvious to Caroline that having underestimated Mrs. Frogerton and not receiving the support she had anticipated, Lady Fielding was desperately attempting to retract her confidences.

"I must ask you to leave." Lady Fielding abruptly stood up. "I have letters to write."

"Of course." Mrs. Frogerton stood, too. "I wish you a good day."

When they got back into the carriage, Mrs. Frogerton turned to Caroline. "What did you make of that performance?"

"I think she expected us to go along with her lies," Caroline said. "And was highly indignant when we refused."

"Agreed. But why bother asking me to attend her in the first place?"

"Because she considered you an ally?"

"Her mistake," Mrs. Frogerton said. "I cannot abide liars." She took a deep breath. "I think we need to speak to Sergeant Dawson, lass."

"And tell him what Lady Fielding is up to?"

"No, he's a clever lad, he'll work that one out for himself. I was thinking more of offering him our help."

Caroline sat back. "He won't accept it."

Mrs. Frogerton smiled. "It depends how we present the offer and how attractive we make it for him."

"You'd know all about that, ma'am."

"Indeed, I would." She rapped on the ceiling and stuck her head out of the window. "Take us to Great Scotland Yard, Giles"

Chapter 14

"I think you might be missing my point, Sergeant." Mrs. Frogerton smiled serenely. "You are a very busy man, and we are simply trying to support your efforts by offering our assistance."

"By bailing out my main suspect, ma'am?"

"I believe a judge made the decision on that matter, Sergeant. I simply provided the funds," Mrs. Frogerton said. "Miss Morton and I are willing to assist you in any capacity you think fit."

Sergeant Dawson raised his eyebrows. "With all due respect, I cannot think of a single capacity in which I might require your help."

"That seems remarkably harsh. One might think that an ambitious man such as yourself would prefer to solve as many murders as possible." Mrs. Frogerton shook her head. "Perhaps I'll take this matter up with Inspector Ross."

"There's no need to do that, ma'am," Sergeant Dawson said. "He has complete confidence in me."

"That isn't what he said to my solicitor when they discussed the 'evidence' against Dr. Harris. Quite frankly he apologized profusely, but if you truly believe you are infallible, Sergeant, then . . ." Mrs. Frogerton went as if to rise and Caroline followed suit.

"If I ever think of a situation where I might need your help, ma'am, rest assured I will call on you." Sergeant Dawson stood too and offered a patently false smile before walking toward the door and holding it open for them. "Now, please excuse me. I'm sure you ladies have a luncheon to attend, and I must get back to work."

"Well." Mrs. Frogerton settled herself in the carriage and folded her gloved hands on her lap. "You were right about Sergeant Dawson repudiating our help."

Caroline sat opposite her employer. "He's the one who will regret that choice."

"I suppose I was being naïve believing he might listen to me. I forget that most men prefer women to be seen and not heard."

"We will solve this matter by ourselves and make sure to take all the credit," Caroline said. She didn't like seeing her employer so crestfallen. "He will look like a fool."

"He already is a fool." Mrs. Frogerton raised her chin. "I almost look forward to him asking for our help simply so I can deny it."

"Perhaps things will become clearer when we speak to Dr. Harris," Caroline said. "He is due to visit us at twelve."

"I'd almost forgotten—what with all the comings and goings this morning." Mrs. Frogerton looked out of the window as the carriage slowed to a halt outside their door. "I think I see him coming along the street."

She accepted the coachman's help to descend the steps and waved at Dr. Harris, who touched the brim of his hat in return.

"Good afternoon, Doctor."

"Mrs. Frogerton, Miss Morton."

He looked rather tired. Caroline wondered whether he had gotten any sleep since his shift at the hospital.

"I'll order some refreshments, ma'am," Caroline murmured to Mrs. Frogerton as they went through the front door. "And I'll ask Giles to bring Madam's strongbox straight up to the drawing room."

She made sure to request a substantial amount of food for Dr. Harris's benefit and then went to her bedchamber to retrieve the parcel he'd left with her.

By the time she entered the drawing room, Mrs. Frogerton was already in full flow telling Dr. Harris about their morning adventures.

"And Sir Alfred has disappeared! Lady Fielding was most displeased."

"One can't imagine why," Dr. Harris said. "It almost makes him look like he is guilty of something."

He looked up as Caroline approached, the parcel in her hands.

"You didn't open it?"

"Of course not." She set it beside him on the couch. "I was simply keeping it safe for you."

"Ah, good." For some reason he avoided her gaze.

"I think you mentioned that you might have one of Madam's keys in there?"

"Yes, what about it?"

His attention was distracted as the butler came in with the strongbox and set it on the floor in front of Mrs. Frogerton. "Giles brought this in for you, ma'am."

"Thank you."

"What on earth is that?" Dr. Harris asked.

"Madam's strongbox." Caroline allowed herself a small congratulatory smile. "We found it concealed within the chimney breast of her back parlor."

"You found it?"

"With a little help from Letty, Madam's maid," Mrs. Frogerton added.

Dr. Harris looked hard at them both. "But why is it here and not with the Metropolitan Police?"

"We—intend to pass it over to Sergeant Dawson if he inquires as to its whereabouts," Mrs. Frogerton said.

Dr. Harris's eyebrows rose, and he turned to Caroline. "And you accused me of withholding information from the police."

"If Sergeant Dawson was doing his job properly, he'd be asking the right people the right questions and would have discovered it himself," Caroline said tartly. "We did offer him our help and he declined to accept it."

"More fool him," Dr. Harris murmured, his gaze on the strongbox. "I have a key that might fit that box." He patted the parcel next to him.

"Did you take it from Madam's desk?" Caroline asked.

He frowned. "No, she put it in the envelope she left for me."

The butler and parlor maid arrived with trays of refreshments. Dr. Harris spent a few moments piling up his plate and drank an entire cup of coffee before he addressed them again.

"I suppose I should start by telling you what Madam wrote in her letter." Dr. Harris wiped a few cake crumbs from his beard, which fell onto the rug and were quickly eaten by the dogs.

"Or we could attempt to open Madam's strongbox with your key," Mrs. Frogerton suggested.

"I thought you asked me here to give an account of myself."

"We can get to that in a moment," Mrs. Frogerton said briskly. "We have plenty of time."

With a resigned sigh, Dr. Harris set down his cup and plate and undid the string around his brown paper parcel. He took out and opened an envelope that contained a key and a single sheet of paper.

"It does look to be the right size," Mrs. Frogerton said. "Why don't you try it?"

"As you wish, ma'am."

Dr. Harris got down on one knee and fitted the key to the lock. There was an audible click, but despite his best efforts the lid refused to open. He studied the chest and eventually raised his head. "I think we need a second key."

"Oh, good Lord." Mrs. Frogerton threw up her hands. "Where on earth will we find that? I'll have to call a locksmith."

"Wouldn't that be considered breaking and entering, ma'am?" Dr. Harris asked.

"Hardly, when you have a key."

Dr. Harris didn't look convinced. He sat back down, accidentally dislodging the remaining contents of the parcel, which fell to the floor. Caroline went to help him pick things up and they almost banged heads.

"I'm quite capable, Miss Morton."

"And I was just trying to be helpful, Dr. Harris." She went to hand him the note and saw it was addressed to her. "Oh."

He grabbed it from her and crumpled it up in his fist. "That's of no use now."

"If you say so, sir." She could have sworn that he was blushing. "Do you wish to discuss the contents of the letter Madam wrote to you instead?"

He sat back down and drank more coffee before turning to address them.

"Madam told me to keep the key safe until it was needed, not to trust everyone I was close to, and—" He paused to look at Caroline. "To ensure Miss Morton's safety."

"That's remarkably specific," Caroline said.

"I know. I was quite disturbed seeing as I considered her a charlatan."

"Madam was occasionally right about things," Mrs. Frogerton agreed. "Both Caroline and I remarked on it."

"I have reluctantly come to the same conclusion," Dr. Harris said.

"And what was truthful about the comment she made to you about Amelia and having blood on your hands?"

Dr. Harris studied his coffee cup most assiduously. "I assume she was alluding to the untimely death of one of my first patients. I always felt I could've done more to save her, and her husband certainly thought so."

"How did she die?"

"She bled to death." Dr. Harris winced. "She kept insisting she was pregnant, but after several weeks there were no signs of her womb increasing in size and I suspected something else might be wrong. Both she and her husband refused to accept that or consult another doctor as I recommended. Eventually, I was called to her house where I found her unconscious and bleeding internally. There was nothing I could do. Her husband was beside himself with grief and threatened to ruin me for her loss of life."

"How very unfortunate for her," Mrs. Frogerton said. "Did the husband follow through on his threats?"

"He did his best." Dr. Harris hesitated. "One of the reasons I resented Madam bringing the matter up was that I was already worried that my return to London might expose me to this gentleman's ire again. I did wonder if someone had paid Madam to say such a thing, which was why I decided to go and speak to her the following day and ask what the devil she was playing at."

"Why did you not simply tell us this after Madam died?" Caroline had to ask.

"I suspect I was influenced by what Madam said about not trusting those closest to me." Dr. Harris grimaced.

"Madam herself told you to look after Caroline," Mrs. Frogerton objected. "Did you truly think *I* meant you harm?"

"Not after you paid my bail, ma'am." Dr. Harris had the grace to look embarrassed as he rubbed his hand over the back of his neck. "Which is why I decided to tell you everything."

Mrs. Frogerton didn't look impressed by his stark logic and Caroline wasn't surprised.

"Is there anything else you wish to share with us, Dr. Harris?" Mrs. Frogerton asked rather pointedly. "Do you have any suspicions as to who did murder Madam Lavinia?"

"My money's still on Sir Alfred Fielding," Dr. Harris said.

"Wouldn't you consider poison too soft an option for him?" Mrs. Frogerton asked. "One would assume he'd prefer his victim to cower before him in terror."

"Perhaps he decided to do something out of character so that the authorities wouldn't immediately suspect him." Dr. Harris shrugged. "If so, it seems to have succeeded because I'm the one facing a murder charge, not him."

"I wish there was a way to make Sergeant Dawson aware that Sir Alfred has disappeared," Caroline said. "I doubt Lady Fielding is going to tell him."

"We could send him an anonymous note," Mrs. Frogerton suggested. "That's what they always do in my novels."

"Why not?" Dr. Harris ate more cake. "This whole affair can't get any more farcical than it already is."

The butler appeared at the door. "Professor Brown and the DeBloom family are here, ma'am. Mrs. DeBloom wants to inquire as to whether Miss Frogerton will join them for a promenade in the park?"

"Shall I go and see if Dorothy is awake?" Caroline offered. "She made no mention of such plans to me."

Mrs. Frogerton nodded and pushed the strongbox under her chair where it would be hidden behind her skirts. "Why don't you do that, dear, while Dr. Harris and I entertain our guests."

"Professor Brown is here to collect me, ma'am. We have an appointment at the hospital."

Dr. Harris went to stand, and Mrs. Frogerton waved him back to his seat.

"You and Professor Brown are not going anywhere until we have finished our discussion." She held out her hand. "Give me that key or put it in the lock of the strong-box and sit down. The DeBlooms won't be here for more than a quarter hour, you can manage to be polite for that long."

Dr. Harris meekly handed over the key and subsided into his seat as Caroline went up the stairs to Dorothy's room. She knocked on the door and went in to find Dorothy sitting at her dressing table fully dressed while her maid arranged her blond hair.

She met Caroline's gaze in the mirror. "I understand the DeBlooms have come calling."

"Yes, Mr. DeBloom seems to think you agreed to walk in the park with him."

Dorothy wrinkled her nose. "I might have done so."

"As you are already up and dressed you can come and give him your decision yourself," Caroline said.

"I think I'll go with him. It's such a lovely morning and I don't want the Lingards to think they own me quite yet."

"An excellent plan."

Dorothy rose, shook out the skirts of her blue walking dress, and turned toward Caroline. "Viscount Lingard is being remarkably attentive and even his mother smiled at me last night."

"You don't *have* to get married this year, you know."

"And be thought a failure by all those snobby women if I don't?" Dorothy raised her eyebrows.

"Marriages last a lot longer than other people's opinions," Caroline countered. "You need to make sure you choose wisely."

"I am aware of that. My mother constantly reminds me." Dorothy picked up her bonnet, reticule, and matching cloak and headed for the door. "But Viscount Lingard strikes me as an ideal candidate. He is wealthy, handsome, and very biddable."

"But do you love him?"

Dorothy looked pityingly at Caroline. "What does that matter in a society marriage? I will be a viscountess."

"You still have to live with him," Caroline said as they descended the stairs. "For the rest of your life."

"I think it would be a fair bargain." Dorothy smiled. "Unless I can persuade the Duke of Sussex to marry me instead."

Caroline was still smiling as she went into the drawing room and found the entire DeBloom family awaiting Dorothy. Professor Brown was conversing amicably with Mrs. DeBloom while Dr. Harris loitered by the door looking impatient to be off. Miss DeBloom was her usual composed self and was standing quietly by her brother, who came over to bow to her and Dorothy.

"Miss Frogerton, Miss Morton. What a charming picture you present together."

Caroline stepped back as he advanced toward her. "Good morning, sir. Please excuse me. I have to speak to the butler."

She turned back to the open door and immediately heard a commotion in the hall below. Before she could descend the stairs, Lady Fielding, closely followed by the butler, came up to them at some speed, her agitated gaze sweeping past Caroline as she rushed into the drawing room.

"Mrs. Frogerton!"

Caroline followed her in, aware of the startled expressions on everyone's faces.

"Lady Fielding." Mrs. Frogerton shot to her feet. "Whatever is the matter?"

"My Alfred! They've found him." She paused, her voice rising to a shriek. "Robbed and drowned in the Thames!"

Lady Fielding clutched at her chest and slid to the floor as Miss DeBloom screamed. Caroline went down on her knees beside the prone figure and looked over at Dr. Harris, who had remained transfixed by the door.

"Some assistance, Dr. Harris? This is your area of expertise?"

"Yes, of course." He hurriedly rose to his feet and came to join her. He took Lady Fielding's limp wrist in his hand and concentrated for a few moments. "She's still alive. I suspect she just swooned."

"We should put her to bed and call for her own physician," Mrs. Frogerton said. "If you'll excuse me for a moment, Mrs. DeBloom."

"The butler and I can carry her if you lead the way, ma'am," Dr. Harris said.

Caroline held the door open as the two men followed Mrs. Frogerton up the stairs. She glanced back to find Dorothy and beckoned her over.

"Why don't you take the DeBlooms up on their offer of a walk in the park while we deal with this matter?"

Dorothy, who could be as practical as her mother on some occasions, nodded. "Yes, this is hardly their business, is it?"

She turned to the DeBlooms and smiled. "Shall we take advantage of the fine weather and proceed with our plans?"

Mr. DeBloom looked relieved. "Jolly good." He turned to his mother. "Are you ready to leave now?"

"Yes, indeed." Mrs. DeBloom's smile was chilly. "One never quite knows what will go on in this particular household and I for one want no part of it." She glanced over at her daughter. "Come along, Clarissa."

"I am . . . not feeling well," Miss DeBloom whispered. "I have a terrible headache."

"Don't be silly, dear."

Caroline stepped between the two women. "If Miss De-Bloom wishes to stay and keep me company until you return, that would be very pleasant indeed, ma'am."

"She is not here to entertain the staff, Miss Morton," Mrs. DeBloom snapped.

"Mother . . ." Mr. DeBloom's smile disappeared. "You definitely need some air to clear your head." He took hold of her elbow and propelled her toward the door. "Thank you, Miss Morton. We'll return shortly."

Professor Brown nodded to Caroline and headed to the door. "Tell Harris to join me at the meeting as soon as he can. I'll make his excuses."

"Thank you."

Caroline paused for a moment on the landing to make sure everyone had left, and that Mrs. Frogerton and the doctor were still upstairs before returning to the drawing room where Clarissa DeBloom sat on the couch.

"Is there anything I can do to help with your headache, Miss DeBloom? Some herbal tea or a cold compress to apply to your brow?"

"I saw him." Miss DeBloom raised her stricken gaze to meet Caroline's.

"Who?"

"Lady's Fielding's son—the man who interrupted our evening at Madam's."

"Yes, Miss DeBloom, I saw him, too," Caroline said gently. "He behaved very badly but it is still shocking that he has died."

"You misunderstand me." Miss DeBloom swallowed hard. "I . . . tried to see Madam on the day that she was murdered."

Caroline remembered Letty mentioning that a lady and her maid had visited Madam's on that fateful day. Had it been Miss DeBloom?

"And that man was there, too."

Caroline simply nodded, concealing her sudden surge of interest, and waited to hear what else Miss DeBloom had to say.

"I don't think he saw me because I was just leaving from the front door with my maid, and he . . ." She paused. "Was going down the steps into the basement and looking around in a very furtive manner."

Mrs. Frogerton and Caroline had speculated about whether Sir Alfred might have returned to Madam's house after his initial interview with her. If Miss DeBloom was correct, it was possible that he had concealed himself in the lower regions of the house until he was able to speak to her again and perhaps end her life.

"One has to wonder, Miss Morton, whether Sir Alfred's intentions toward Madam were honorable." Miss De-Bloom raised her chin. "I think I should mention this matter to the sergeant who called at our house."

"Will your mother permit you to do so?"

"I'll ask Philip to take me to Scotland Yard. She won't stand against him."

"I think that if I were in your position, I would do the same thing," Caroline said.

"Madam deserves justice," Miss DeBloom said. "If Philip won't accompany me I will write a note to Sergeant Dawson and tell him what I remember."

"Are you concerned about him knowing you were at Madam's on the same day?" Caroline asked.

Miss DeBloom shrugged. "I'll simply tell him that I had no desire to murder Madam Lavinia. In truth I wish she was still alive to help me find out what happened to my father and uncle."

"Your brother mentioned that you were . . . concerned about the manner of your father's death."

"In truth, I suspect my mother had something to do with both of them." Miss DeBloom's gaze was challenging. "She prefers to control our family and our finances."

"Does your brother agree with you?"

"Not yet." Miss DeBloom sighed. "But the more he challenges her the more worried I become as to his continuing health and safety." She pressed a hand to her forehead. "I wonder if I might trouble you for some herbal tea after all, Miss Morton. My headache is getting worse."

"Of course, Miss DeBloom." Caroline rose to her feet. "I'll fetch you some right now. Would you like Dr. Harris to attend you?"

"No, I'll be fine." Miss DeBloom offered Caroline a faint smile. "And thank you for listening to me. Your ability to remain calm is admirable."

Caroline shrugged. "It is a useful quality for a companion, Miss DeBloom. Please excuse me for a moment."

She hurried down to the kitchen and asked one of the kitchen maids to brew the tea and then went up to the second floor where she met Dr. Harris and Mrs. Frogerton in the corridor.

"Lady Fielding is sedated and settled," Dr. Harris said. "And Mrs. Frogerton has the name of her usual physician and will send him a note forthwith."

"Did she say anything else about Sir Alfred?"

"Only that he'd been washed up with the morning tide and that she was supposed to go and identify his body, which is currently being held by the Thames River Police in their morgue." Dr. Harris paused. "I've seen bodies pulled out from the Thames before. They can be quite gruesome."

"Then I'll go with her if she wishes," Mrs. Frogerton said. "I doubt the poor lady has anyone else to accompany her."

"Let's wait to hear what her doctor advises." Dr. Harris started walking toward the stairs. "I'll stay until he gets here if that is acceptable."

"Most acceptable." Mrs. Frogerton looked worried. "Did Dotty go with the DeBlooms? I thought I heard the front door opening earlier."

"Dorothy went with Mr. and Mrs. DeBloom. Miss De-Bloom is still in the drawing room having suffered a headache and Professor Brown will make your excuses to the hospital," Caroline said. "I was just fetching Miss De-Bloom some herbal tea."

"Much good that will do," Dr. Harris muttered. "But I suppose it's better than dosing herself with laudanum." He sighed. "Do I need to speak with her, too?"

"I don't think so." Caroline wasn't convinced that Dr. Harris's brusque manner was suitable for a young lady and didn't want to send their guest into hysterics.

"What a morning." Mrs. Frogerton set off down the stairs. "The next thing we know the police will be turning up."

"I do hope not." Dr. Harris stood back to allow Caroline to go ahead of him and then followed her down. "Although with Sir Alfred dead I'm the only suspect left."

"Not necessarily," Caroline said.

Both her employer and Dr. Harris turned to stare at her.

"What has happened now?" Mrs. Frogerton demanded.

"Miss DeBloom told me that she saw Sir Alfred at Madam's."

"But we suspected that."

"I didn't," Dr. Harris said.

Mrs. Frogerton shushed him to silence. "Go on, lass."

"She saw Sir Alfred creeping down the basement steps when she was leaving the house with her maid."

"He doubled back." Dr. Harris nodded. "Just as we thought."

"Miss DeBloom said she is going to tell Sergeant Dawson what she saw."

"That's interesting." Mrs. Frogerton pursed her lips. "I wonder why she is willing to speak up now?"

"Probably because she believes the matter is now closed and that Sir Alfred was the murderer," Caroline said.

"Or she thinks she is now absolved of any responsibility for what *she* did while she was at Madam's."

"On the contrary, Miss DeBloom confided in me that she very much wished Madam was still alive because she still wants to know if her mother is implicated in the deaths of her father and uncle."

"How very convenient that she chose to confide in you now," Mrs. Frogerton said.

It was Caroline's turn to frown. "How so?"

"Miss DeBloom was there on the day Madam died, lass. She could just as easily have poisoned Madam as Sir Alfred. What if it is the other way around, and Sir Alfred saw *her*, and she had him murdered?"

Dr. Harris cleared his throat. "With all due respect, ma'am, that is complete nonsense."

"We don't know that." Mrs. Frogerton carried on talking. "Just because she is young and has a pretty face doesn't mean that she isn't capable of murder."

"Mrs. Frogerton does have a point," Caroline conceded. "Perhaps we should wait to hear if Miss DeBloom really does contact Sergeant Dawson and whether the coroner considers Sir Alfred's death suspicious."

"He could've fallen in the Thames after a night's revelry," Dr. Harris said. "It happens more often than you'd think."

"I'm sure it does." Mrs. Frogerton carried on down the stairs. "I'll go and sit with Miss DeBloom, Caroline, while you fetch up her tea. Dr. Harris can keep an eye out for Lady Fielding's physician."

Chapter 15

"I informed Lady Fielding that she is in no fit state to visit a morgue. She has agreed that someone else can go in her stead."

Lady Fielding's physician, Dr. Woods, spoke in an undertone to Dr. Harris. He was a pleasant, elderly man with a quiet, confident manner that reflected his obvious experience. He had arrived very promptly after receiving Mrs. Frogerton's note. They'd gathered just outside Lady Fielding's temporary bedchamber to discuss his findings.

Dr. Harris nodded. "I've met Sir Alfred, and I'm more than willing to identify him if necessary."

"Then I shall rely on you to do so." Dr. Woods turned to Mrs. Frogerton. "I also urged her ladyship to stay in bed for the rest of the day, but she is fretting about not being in her own home."

"From what I understand, Lady Fielding has no family to care for her at home," Mrs. Frogerton said. "She would be much more comfortable here where we can keep an eye on her."

Dr. Woods bowed. "That's exactly what I said to her myself, ma'am. I will go back in and tell her to rest easy. I'll return tomorrow and see how she is before I allow her to exert herself too strongly. She isn't the strongest of women."

He went back into Lady Fielding's room, leaving Mrs. Frogerton, Caroline, and Dr. Harris regarding one another.

"We could go to the morgue together?" Mrs. Frogerton suggested as if offering them a thrilling treat.

"Surely you need to be here when Dorothy returns from the park with the DeBlooms, ma'am?" Caroline said. "And there is the small matter of Miss DeBloom still sitting in the drawing room."

"Then I'll stay, and you can accompany Dr. Harris, Caroline." Mrs. Frogerton nodded. "I'll see if I can get any more information from Miss DeBloom while you're out."

"She doesn't know that you are aware of everything, ma'am," Caroline cautioned. "And if I wish to retain her trust it might be better if you could limit your questions to more conventional matters."

"I suppose you are right." Mrs. Frogerton sighed. "I wonder if Sir Alfred was overcome with guilt after murdering Madam and deliberately drowned himself?"

"That is one possibility, ma'am," Dr. Harris said. "The River Police and their coroner are well used to dealing with bodies pulled from the river and are considered experts in identifying the cause of death."

Dr. Harris looked down at Caroline. "Shall we go right away, Miss Morton? I'd rather not have to deal with the DeBlooms again."

Caroline turned to Mrs. Frogerton. "If that is acceptable to you, ma'am?"

"Yes, off you go." Her employer waved them down the stairs. "The quicker you go, the sooner you'll be back."

Dr. Harris hailed a hackney cab and assisted Caroline inside. An awkward silence descended between them as the horse and driver pulled away from the curb, turned out onto the main road, and attempted to merge with the bustling traffic. Eventually, Caroline felt impelled to speak.

"Is St. Thomas's aware of what has happened to you, Dr. Harris?"

"No, and I intend to keep it that way."

"Does your bail require you to report to Great Scotland Yard or the magistrate's court?"

"Quite possibly, but as I work nights, I am available during the day to fulfill any necessary requirements."

"When you should be sleeping."

He offered a quick smile. "I can't say I am enjoying the most restful of nights right now, Miss Morton, anyway."

"I would assume not."

He looked directly at her. "I was sorry to hear from Mrs. Frogerton that your aunt had passed away."

"I think it might have been a blessing," Caroline replied. "She was such a busy, active person that being confined to bed, and unable to talk coherently, must have been unendurable."

"Some might say she deserved it." Dr. Harris's expression hardened. "She caused a great deal of heartache and misery in her life."

"And she tried to do some good."

"Only to a chosen few." He sat back. "I'm surprised to hear you defending her."

"She cared for me and Susan when our father abandoned us and I'll always be grateful for that, but I am aware that she allowed her sense of what was right to become distorted over time."

Silence fell again and this time Caroline didn't intend to be the one to break it.

Dr. Harris cleared his throat. "What do you think of Miss DeBloom?"

"As in what she told me today?" Caroline shrugged. "We all wondered if Sir Alfred had doubled back to murder Madam Lavinia. It struck me as highly likely."

"It didn't strike you as a planned attempt to divert suspicion away from herself?"

"Why would I think that?"

"Because she was there, she had the opportunity, and she has been very quick to rush out and explain herself to you—a woman who had no official part in this investigation—rather than speak to the police."

"Miss DeBloom intends to speak to Sergeant Dawson at the earliest opportunity."

"And say what exactly?" Dr. Harris folded his arms across his chest.

Caroline met his skeptical gaze. "That she saw Sir Alfred sneaking back into the house."

"Unless you accompany her to Scotland Yard you don't know what she will say."

"Why would she say anything different? If she *was* the murderer, it would provide her with an excellent ability to avoid justice. We both know that Sergeant Dawson won't bother to investigate further if he thinks he has an easy catch."

Dr. Harris raised his eyebrows. "You think he'd be willing to say Sir Alfred, a peer of the realm, is a murderer?"

"Hardly that when he is only a hereditary knight."

"Trust you to know the social niceties of such things," Dr. Harris muttered. "I still think he'll want to convict me."

"How very arrogant of you." Caroline was growing rather tired of being doubted. "I'll remind you that Mrs. Frogerton has offered you the services of her solicitor and an excellent barrister. If it comes to a trial, you'll probably get off."

"That is true," he conceded somewhat reluctantly. "I *am* grateful to Mrs. Frogerton."

"Perhaps you might do a better job of remembering that."

The unmistakable aroma of the river Thames permeated

through the windows of the cab and Caroline resisted the urge to press a handkerchief to her nose as they stopped in front of a nondescript building right on the water's edge. Dr. Harris walked around to help her descend from the cab, and the stench grew even worse. If the river smelled this bad, she dreaded to think what awaited her inside.

They entered the redbrick building and Dr. Harris approached a uniformed man sitting at his desk to the right of the door in the small front office.

"Good afternoon, sir. We have been sent to view a body for identification purposes." He handed over a letter to the officer, who started to read it. "Lady Fielding and her physician gave us permission to attend in her stead due to her fragile health."

The man's shrewd gaze swept over them. "You're one of her doctors, I take it?"

Dr. Harris bowed.

"And you're Miss Morton."

Caroline curtsied.

"Not sure you'll want to view the body, miss. If it's the one I'm thinking of, it was in the water for quite a while."

Dr. Harris frowned. "Perhaps I should go in first, Miss Morton? If I think you can cope, I'll get them to bring you in."

Dr. Harris seemed to have forgotten he was still under suspicion of murder, but Caroline hadn't. If she allowed him to make the identification by himself, she might regret it. And she had promised both to represent Mrs. Frogerton and report back to her.

"I'd rather go in with you, Dr. Harris." She met his gaze calmly. "Two sets of eyes are always better than one."

"As you wish, but don't swoon over the body because I won't be responsible for taking you out."

"Don't you worry, miss." The officer winked at her. "I'll save you."

"Thank you, but I have an extremely strong stomach."

Caroline immediately resolved not to faint. The thought of anyone laying their hands on her and dragging out her prostrate body made her shudder. "Shall we proceed?"

"I'll go and speak to the coroner first so that he can prepare the body for viewing."

"Thank you." Dr. Harris nodded.

The man went through the interior door into the rear of the building while Caroline perused the noticeboards, which contained information about missing persons, discovered goods, and stern warnings against river piracy.

"You don't have to do this, Miss Morton." Dr. Harris spoke from behind her.

"I'm here now, and I'd prefer to be useful."

"It might be very unpleasant."

"So I understand." She deliberately kept her tone light.

"I'm perfectly capable of identifying Sir Alfred and as a medical doctor I'll understand what the coroner has to say for himself."

Caroline looked over her shoulder at him. "Consider me an independent witness, then, Doctor."

His brows drew together. "You don't trust me?"

"That's hardly relevant to the situation we find ourselves in. I am here to represent my employer and I intend to do so."

"In case I try and use a man's death to further my own release from suspicion?"

Caroline held his incredulous gaze. "I suspect I might do the same if I was in your position."

"No, you wouldn't."

"Which just goes to show how little you know me, Dr. Harris." Caroline turned away. "I hope this won't take too long. I have a concert to attend at six."

Unfortunately, it was at least ten long minutes before the man returned during which neither Caroline nor Dr. Harris spoke another word.

"This way, miss, Doctor."

Caroline almost recoiled as the interior door shut behind them and the smell of disinfectant, fish guts, and something nauseatingly sweet surrounded her. They were in a long stone-floored corridor that ran the length of the building. There were two doors on the right and several numbered doors on the left.

"We're going into number three, Dr. Harris."

"Thank you."

For once, Caroline was happy to relinquish her place to Dr. Harris, who strode into the room ahead of her. She paused at the doorway to find her handkerchief and take a moment to compose herself. The body lay on a slab of stone and was modestly covered by a sheet from neck to toe.

"Dr. Harris?" At the head of the table there was a gentleman wearing a large, bloodied apron like a butcher over his immaculately cut suit. "I'm Dr. Walsh, the coroner here."

"Good afternoon, sir."

Caroline remained at the foot of the stone slab, her gaze slowly traveling up the body until it reached the ghastly features of a still recognizable Sir Alfred. The slackness and purplish discoloration of his face made him look like a toddler in the middle of a screaming fit. She swallowed hard as a wave of putrid air wafted over her.

"Are you all right, Miss Morton?" Dr. Harris asked.

"I'm fine, thank you." Caroline raised her gaze to meet Dr. Walsh's. "This is definitely Sir Alfred Fielding."

"I agree," Dr. Harris said. "How did you identify him, Dr. Walsh?"

"He still had his pocketbook on him."

"Which is somewhat unusual if this was a robbery." Dr. Harris frowned. "Have you determined a cause of death? I'm sure his mother would like to know."

"It wasn't difficult." Dr. Walsh lowered the sheet a foot. "His throat was cut."

Caroline pressed her gloved fingers to her mouth while her horrified gaze traced the thin line that traversed Sir Alfred's pallid throat.

Dr. Harris leaned in to get a closer look. "Very neatly done. Blade must have been sharp."

"Yes, indeed." Dr. Walsh nodded. "His clothes were stained with blood, which indicates that he didn't sustain this injury after entering the Thames but before he went in."

"Someone slit his throat and then threw him in the river?"

"One assumes so."

"Which means this was done deliberately," Dr Harris added. "Could he have done it to himself?"

"Theoretically, yes, but most people aren't as precise because they begin to panic, and the cut becomes jagged, or they inadvertently stab themselves right through the neck."

Dr. Walsh sounded like he was discussing what kind of tea he preferred with his crumpets whereas Caroline was thinking about vomiting. She was relieved when he drew the sheet up over Sir Alfred's head.

"If you both agree that this is Sir Alfred Fielding, we can continue our investigation into his untimely death and speak to his family about the proper burial rites."

"You might wish to talk to Sergeant Dawson at Great Scotland Yard." Caroline forced herself to speak. "I believe he wanted to speak to Sir Alfred about another matter."

"Then Sergeant Dawson is going to be disappointed." Dr. Walsh held the door open for Caroline. "Unless Sir Alfred's demise helps him build a case against someone else."

After completing the necessary paperwork Caroline and Dr. Harris left the building and stood together on the busy pavement as the sun came out.

"That was unpleasant." Dr. Harris looked around for a hackney cab and waved one down. "You should have left it to me."

"I survived," Caroline said as he handed her into the cab.

Dr. Harris took the seat opposite and the cab moved off. He dropped his face into his hands and groaned.

"Good Lord, I'm tired."

"Then may I suggest you go directly back to your lodgings and sleep before your next shift at the hospital? There is no need for you to come into Mrs. Frogerton's. I can tell her and Lady Fielding what we discovered."

"For once I am tempted to agree with you."

"That will be a first," Caroline said.

He raised his head to look at her. "You do realize this might make things worse for me."

"How so?"

"Sir Alfred is dead and I'm still alive and under suspicion."

"Knowing Sergeant Dawson, he'll probably be delighted to blame Sir Alfred for Madam's murder because he can't argue back, won't require a lawyer or his day in court, and certainly won't embarrass him with his superiors."

"I hope you are right." Dr. Harris concealed a yawn. "But if Dawson could convict me of two murders he'd be delighted."

"The policeman at the morgue said there are no witnesses to Sir Alfred's murder."

"Who have yet come forward. If Lady Fielding starts offering rewards, and you know that she will, then someone will take the bait."

"Which will exonerate you."

"Not if Sergeant Dawson has his way."

"You think he'd attempt to corrupt a witness?"

"Don't be so naïve." Dr. Harris sat back and looked at her. "Of course he bloody well would."

Caroline was still thinking about Dr. Harris's weary face and fatalistic assertions when she entered the house and went up the stairs to her bedchamber. It was slightly preferable to picturing Sir Alfred's face but equally frustrating. She took a moment to remove her bonnet and outdoor things and wash thoroughly before going to find her employer. The lingering smell of the morgue was harder to eradicate than she'd anticipated.

Mrs. Frogerton was in the drawing room, her dogs gathered in a slumbering pile at her feet as she read the daily newspaper. There was no sign of the DeBlooms or Dorothy. Mrs. Frogerton looked up as Caroline came in.

"You look worried, lass."

"I suppose that's because I am." Caroline sat down. "It was Sir Alfred."

"The poor man." Mrs. Frogerton shuddered. "Drowning is a horrible way to go."

"He didn't drown." Caroline took a deep breath. "Someone slit his throat and threw him in the Thames."

"Good Lord." Mrs. Frogerton took her spectacles off.

"He wasn't even robbed."

"Then it sounds like someone wanted him out of the way."

"Dr. Harris thinks Sergeant Dawson will use it as an opportunity to blame him for two murders, whereas I think the opposite."

"I can't tell what Sergeant Dawson will do." Mrs. Frogerton folded the paper up. "I think I'll wait until Lady Fielding's doctor returns on the morrow to break the news to her." She sighed. "Did the coroner have any idea when Sir Alfred died?"

"He didn't say, but from the state of the body I'd imagine that it happened at least a day or so ago."

"While Sir Alfred was unaccounted for in the country and at his town house." Mrs. Frogerton paused. "If Sergeant Dawson does intend to pursue Dr. Harris, it makes it harder for the doctor to prove he couldn't have done it."

"That's exactly what Dr. Harris fears," Caroline said. "I did remind him that he has an excellent solicitor on his side who has the ear of Sergeant Dawson's superior, but he wasn't reassured."

"I wouldn't want to be in his shoes, love, would you?"

Caroline shook her head and Mrs. Frogerton set the paper on the table beside her.

"Miss DeBloom recovered well after drinking her herbal tea and went off with her mother and brother quite happily."

"Dr. Harris still thinks she might be the murderer and that her confidences to me are a deliberate attempt to shield herself from prosecution."

"Perhaps you shouldn't be listening to Dr. Harris," Mrs. Frogerton said gently.

"I can't exactly stop him talking." Caroline sighed. "And he does make me question my assumptions."

"Which isn't necessarily a bad thing. Poison is still considered a woman's weapon and what man in his right mind would think Miss DeBloom capable of harming anyone? Even if she does go and speak directly to Sergeant Dawson, her family are powerful and wealthy enough to protect her."

"I wish I knew exactly what Madam said to Miss De-Bloom and Lady Fielding." Caroline looked over at her employer. "It is very frustrating."

"Didn't Professor Brown leave you his research papers?"

Caroline sat up straight. "I'd completely forgotten that." She rose from her chair. "If you'll excuse me, ma'am, I'll go upstairs and fetch them."

"I love a puzzle." Mrs. Frogerton smiled. "We have an hour before we need to get ready for our evening event. We might as well put it to good use."

Caroline paused on her way to the door and looked back at her employer. "Are you still convinced Dr. Harris didn't do it?"

"Yes. I wouldn't waste my money if I didn't believe he

was innocent." Mrs. Frogerton sounded very confident. "Let's be honest, lass, murdering Sir Alfred would be the worst thing Dr. Harris could've done if he wanted to be perceived as innocent."

"How so?"

"Because whatever Sergeant Dawson said to us, he *was* after Sir Alfred. If he'd actually met the man, he might have changed his mind as to the likelihood of him being a murderer."

"Sir Alfred did have a terrible temper," Caroline admitted.

"And he would've considered Sergeant Dawson's questions as intrusive and intolerable and let him know it." Mrs. Frogerton paused. "You don't think Dr. Harris is guilty, do you?"

"No, but I am worried that he will be unable to prove otherwise."

"Not if I have anything to do with it." Mrs. Frogerton sat up straight. "And Matty Frogerton is never wrong."

Caroline was still smiling as she hurried up the stairs to her bedchamber to retrieve Professor Brown's notes. It was hard to believe that she had almost forgotten about them when the professor had been kind enough to share them to help his friend.

When she returned to the drawing room, Mrs. Frogerton was sipping a glass of sherry and had poured one for Caroline.

"Thank you, ma'am." Caroline set the package on the desk and accepted the glass. "Although I should be performing that service for you." She took a cautious sip. "The morgue was remarkably unpleasant."

"I should imagine."

"There was a very particular smell . . ." Caroline drank more sherry. "I don't think I'll ever forget it."

Mrs. Frogerton sat at her desk, opened the parcel, and split the pile of paper in two. "I suggest we just read through everything and make notes as we go."

"Yes, ma'am." Caroline pulled up a chair and joined her. "I'm not sure how much information Professor Brown has provided to us, but I hope it will only be relevant to the meetings you attended."

Mrs. Frogerton put on her spectacles, pursed her lips, and started to read. After a while she stopped and looked over at Caroline.

"I'll warn you that his style is rather dry."

"He's a medical doctor, ma'am. I assume he approached the subject matter in the spirit of scientific inquiry."

Mrs. Frogerton made a huffing sound. "It does make it both difficult to read *and* slightly dull."

Caroline had to agree but she persevered.

"Oh!" Mrs. Frogerton looked up. "There's something about Lady Fielding." She read the note aloud. " 'Lady F is consumed by the desire to understand her husband's sudden death and persistently questions Madam even when she is obviously inconveniencing others at the table.' "

"And how does Madam answer her?" Caroline asked. "That's the part we want to know."

Mrs. Frogerton had already started reading again and offered no reply, so Caroline returned to her own pile of papers, which were proving much less interesting.

"Ah . . . Madam told Lady Fielding to beware of nourishing a viper to her bosom." Mrs. Frogerton frowned. "Professor Brown thinks Madam was referring to her son and that"—she read from the text—" 'Lady Fielding was struck dumb by the words and then nodded as if they made sense.' "

"I'm surprised she didn't weep into her handkerchief," Caroline said.

"She probably did that as well and Professor Brown didn't think it was important." Mrs. Frogerton tapped her pen against the paper. "So, it is quite likely Lady Fielding realized her son was capable of murder, or even suspected he had already committed one. I have to wonder whether she told Sir Alfred what Madam said and he decided to murder Madam Lavinia to keep her quiet."

"Or Madam tried to blackmail him, and he murdered her," Caroline added.

"It could be either of those things." Mrs. Frogerton sighed. "But it is helpful."

"Only if we can persuade Lady Fielding to tell Sergeant Dawson what she feared, and I doubt she would be willing to incriminate her dead son."

"I have to agree. Have you found anything interesting in Professor Brown's notes yet?"

"Nothing concerning Lady Fielding or Miss DeBloom, but he does mention a very pleasant lady from the north who sat beside him."

"And what else does he say about me?"

"That you appeared to enjoy the evening and were suitably impressed by Madam's prophecies."

"Which is all entirely accurate." Mrs. Frogerton beamed. "I knew Professor Brown was a good man."

The clock on the mantelpiece struck the hour and Caroline set down her pen. "We should probably get ready to go out, ma'am."

"Yes, indeed." Mrs. Frogerton put the papers into one of the desk drawers. "We can continue tomorrow." She stood and shook out her skirts. "I should probably look in on Lady Fielding."

"I can do that, ma'am." Caroline replaced her chair against the wall. "After the amount of laudanum Dr. Woods gave her, I suspect she will still be sleeping. I'll set one of the maids to watch over her while we are out."

Mrs. Frogerton went toward the door. "I sent Vincent with the advertisement to the newspaper earlier. It will run for a week in the personals."

"Let's hope someone responds and comes to collect Madam's belongings," Caroline said. "It might clear up several mysteries."

"I wonder if the other key to the strongbox is there?" Mrs. Frogerton asked.

"I am more than willing to go through everything and check," Caroline offered.

Mrs. Frogerton nodded. "I think that might be wise, don't you? The second key must be *somewhere* and the quicker we can get that strongbox out of this house and into Sergeant Dawson's custody, the better."

Chapter 16

"My poor little boy!" Lady Fielding sobbed. "Drowned in the Thames."

"I am so sorry for your loss, my lady." Mrs. Frogerton patted her guest's hand while her doctor looked on. It was eleven in the morning, and they'd gathered in the best guest bedroom where a heavily sedated Lady Fielding had slept through the night. "You are welcome to stay in my house and recover for as long as you wish."

"But there are arrangements to be made and who will help me with that?" Lady Fielding wailed. "I have no one left. I am all alone!"

"Miss Morton and I will do anything in our power to help you," Mrs. Frogerton said. "Would you like me to write to your family solicitor and your parents?"

Lady Fielding struggled to sit up in a flurry of bedclothes. "I have to see my child."

Caroline met Mrs. Frogerton's eyes and gave a tiny shake of her head.

"I believe the body is still with the coroner, my lady," Caroline said. "I'm sure they can provide you with the name of a suitable establishment to take care of Sir Alfred's funeral rites."

Lady Fielding pressed her hand over her eyes. "I will

have to reopen the family vault and lay him beside his father, who is barely cold in his coffin!"

"There, there, my lady," Mrs. Frogerton said. "God will keep them both in His grace."

"If there is a God, He will be smiling. Don't they say an eye for an eye?" Lady Fielding demanded. "I wanted Alfred to be held responsible for what he did, but not like this." She shuddered. "Not a life for a life."

"What did Sir Alfred do?" Mrs. Frogerton asked curiously.

Lady Fielding dabbed at her eyes with her handkerchief. "He took his father out for a drive in his high perch phaeton and overturned it."

"And your husband was injured as a result of the accident?"

"He *died*, because Alfred staggered away and left him there, pinned beneath a horse, and went home without calling for help." Lady Fielding gripped onto the sheets so hard that her knuckles went white. "He slept in his bed while my beloved husband bled to death."

"What a terrible thing to have happened," Mrs. Frogerton said gently. "I cannot imagine how guilty Sir Alfred felt when he realized what he had done."

"*Guilty*?" Lady Fielding's expression hardened. "He refused to even admit he was there—he tried to blame his groom and dismissed the man to stop me from speaking to him. But I found out the truth eventually." She looked pleadingly at Mrs. Frogerton. "But what was I to do? I had my suspicions, but Alfred is my only son."

"A horrible position to be put in, indeed." Mrs. Frogerton paused. "I suppose that is why you sought clarification from Madam Lavinia."

"Exactly." Lady Fielding nodded, her eyes filling up with tears again. "She confirmed what I already knew in my heart—that Alfred hadn't lifted a finger to save his own father."

"Did you tell your son what Madam said to you?"

Lady Fielding dropped her gaze to her clasped hands. "I must confess that when he accused me of wasting his money, I did mention it—with predictable results."

"Which is why he appeared at Madam's in such a fury and wanted you to leave with him." Mrs. Frogerton nodded.

"Yes, he was enraged by the idea that anyone would question his actions in such a public manner." Lady Fielding sighed and sank back against her pillows. "But none of it matters now, does it? My son is dead, and he'll take his choices and his secrets to the grave."

Dr. Walsh came forward. "I think you should rest now, my lady."

"Yes . . ." Lady Fielding closed her eyes. "If you would be so good as to contact Mr. Peabody, my family solicitor on Blenheim Street, Mrs. Frogerton, I would be most grateful."

"Of course I will," Mrs. Frogerton said warmly. "And you may stay here for as long as you wish, my lady."

She gestured for Caroline to follow her from the room, leaving the doctor with his patient. They went down to the drawing room. Mrs. Frogerton closed the door behind them and started pacing the carpet much to the bewilderment of her dogs.

"Well, that puts the cat amongst the pigeons, doesn't it, lass?"

"In what way, ma'am?" Caroline asked.

"Sir Arthur probably didn't murder Madam after all, did he?"

"I'm not sure what you mean, ma'am."

"Lady Fielding thinks her son deliberately left his father to die after the carriage accident, but there is no evidence to prove that, so why would Sir Alfred care what anyone else thought?"

"Does it matter whether there was evidence or not?" Caroline frowned. "Surely the very idea that his conduct would be discussed in a public forum would be enough for

Sir Alfred to murder the woman he believed had turned his own mother against him?"

"But what power did Madam really have to affect him?" Mrs. Frogerton countered. "She engaged in a disreputable profession, had no reach in society, and would hardly risk her livelihood to expose him."

"But don't forget that Sir Alfred had a high opinion of himself and a terrible temper. Perhaps he feared someone around that table would spread gossip about him." Caroline added, "He might have gone to Madam's house to tell her to leave him alone and become enraged enough to kill her."

"With *poison*?"

"Miss DeBloom saw him doubling back," Caroline said. "Perhaps he withheld his rage and considered other ways to end Madam's existence and returned to the house with the poison."

"How exactly would he have gotten back in to see Madam and fill the glass right at her elbow without her noticing?" Mrs. Frogerton asked.

Caroline raised her eyebrows. "You might as well ask how anyone could have done that. Only Mr. Murphy had the opportunity to doctor all the decanters beforehand."

Mrs. Frogerton gasped and pressed her fingers to her lips. "Maybe he went back into the kitchen *deliberately* and paid Mr. Murphy to take the poisoned decanter up to Madam."

She shook her head. "And now you have talked me back around into believing Sir Alfred might have done it after all!" She sat in her favorite chair and bent to pat the dogs.

"There is another possibility, ma'am." Caroline took the seat opposite her, "He might have been blackmailed directly by Madam herself."

"That would make more sense." Mrs. Frogerton nodded. "We still can't prove any of it."

"I should check the copy of madam's client book." Caroline went over to the desk and searched for Dr. Harris's notes.

While she was occupied, the butler came in with a note on a silver tray.

"Mr. Lewis's clerk brought this for you, ma'am."

"Thank you." The butler left and Mrs. Frogerton opened the letter and read the contents. "While you are looking at Madam's books, I suggest you search for the name Armitage."

"Why is that?" Caroline looked up from her seat at the desk.

"Because according to Mr. Lewis, that's the gentleman who told Sergeant Dawson to hurry up and close any investigation into Madam Lavinia's death."

Caroline returned her attention to the lists and paused at a familiar name. "The honorable William Armitage? The third son of the Earl of Fortman?"

"How do you know such things?"

"Because I remember dancing with *his* son, George, during my first Season."

"How old is the earl, then?" Sometimes Mrs. Frogerton was easily distracted.

"I believe he is in his late seventies."

Mrs. Frogerton tutted. "Not that a third son would get much from him anyway if he died. I've never understood why the eldest son gets everything. I intend to make sure Dotty is just as well provided for as my son, Samuel." She paused briefly to take a breath. "And what happened to your father's title? Who inherited that?"

"That is still a matter of some contention, ma'am. The family solicitor is attempting to work out who has the best claim to be put forward to the college of heralds."

"Good Lord." Mrs. Frogerton shook her head. "One might think it would be a simple matter."

"Apparently not." Caroline attempted to redirect the conversation back to William Armitage. "I wonder why

Mr. Armitage is on Madam's list?" She checked the information next to his name. "He visited her twice, both times in an evening séance."

"Then he should also be mentioned in Professor Brown's notes," Mrs. Frogerton said.

Caroline retrieved a second pile of papers from the desk and studied the closely written pages. "It might take a while to find him."

"Did Madam record the dates of his visits?"

"No, just that he came from an influential and wealthy family—which is true. The earl is very involved in the legislature of the House of Lords."

"Perhaps Mr. Armitage didn't want his family involved in a potential scandal," Mrs. Frogerton said thoughtfully. "But how would he have found out about Madam's death?"

"One has to assume he has some connection to the Metropolitan Police. Perhaps he and Inspector Ross are members of the same club."

"Mr. Lewis will know the answer to that," Mrs. Frogerton said. "Write him a note and ask him."

"Yes, ma'am." Caroline paused. "Would you prefer me to do that now, or should I continue on our quest to discover more information about Sir Alfred?"

"Start with Sir Alfred."

Caroline bent her head and studied Professor Brown's records. "I do have the Fieldings on my potentially being blackmailed list."

"Then I'll wager that's what happened." Mrs. Frogerton nodded. "Madam tried to blackmail Sir Alfred and he murdered her. Now all we have to do is prove it."

Later that afternoon when Mrs. Frogerton was taking a nap, Caroline ventured down to the cellars where the butler had neatly stacked Madam Lavinia's possessions in one corner. To Caroline's relief, Letty had labeled each box, which should help with her task. She set the candelabra

down on the steps and considered where to start. There
were several boxes, four hatboxes, and two trunks all labeled as containing clothing. The keys were attached to
the handles with string.

Caroline decided to start with the smaller of the two
trunks and knelt on the stone floor beside it. The key turned
easily in the lock and the latch snapped back with an audible click. A faint smell of violets rose from the satin lining
along with a scattering of bay leaves and pennyroyal to
guard against moths. The trunk contained smaller items
such as shawls, fichus, and delicate chemisettes along with
lace caps and undergarments. Caroline made certain to re-
place each item in the same place after she examined it. A
search through the side pockets found nothing more interesting than hairpins, pomade, and a sewing kit.

Caroline closed the lid, aware of the coldness of the
stone permeating through her skirts and petticoats to her
knees, and studied the second chest. She had no idea how
long she'd been down in the cellar. She'd asked the butler
to come and tell her when Mrs. Frogerton woke up and required her presence. She unlocked the second chest, which
was full of heavier outdoor clothing that took up more
space. It was easier to look through than the first one.

"Miss Morton?"

A voice echoed down the stairs making her jump. She
rose to her feet, her knees resisting her at every turn.

"Yes?"

Dr. Harris poked his head through the door and looked
down at her.

"What are you doing?"

Caroline gathered her skirts in her hand and started up
the stairs, her candelabra raised high. Dr. Harris took it off
her as she came through the door.

"Careful or you'll singe my eyebrows off." He blew the
candles out.

"Were we expecting you?" Caroline asked. "Mrs. Frogerton didn't mention it."

"I thought you'd like to know that the coroner is ready to release Sir Alfred's body to his family and that Sergeant Dawson went to view the corpse."

"I suppose that is progress. I'll let Dr. Woods know." Caroline walked toward to the kitchen, and Dr. Harris followed her. "How do you know this?"

"Because Sergeant Dawson came to see me." For once, Dr. Harris was looking quite pleased with himself. "He said that they'd had additional information about Sir Alfred's actions on the day of the murder."

"Then one has to assume that Miss DeBloom followed through on her desire to make a clean breast of it." Caroline offered Dr. Harris a cup of tea from the pot that always sat on the kitchen table.

"I can't say that's what happened, but it seems likely." He paused and scanned her face. "What?"

"I'm waiting for my apology."

"For what?"

"You doubting me." Caroline raised her eyebrows. "I have very good instincts, Dr. Harris."

He made a face as he sipped his tea.

"Mrs. Frogerton received a note from Mr. Lewis suggesting that the Honorable William Armitage was influential in trying to hurry the investigation along." Caroline had to raise her voice above the cheerful bustle in the busy kitchen.

"He obviously didn't care if an innocent man was convicted in the process." Dr. Harris grumbled. "I'll have to ask Brown whether he remembers this man and where he resides."

"I wouldn't recommend getting into an argument with another gentleman of standing in London, Dr. Harris."

"I suppose you're right." Dr. Harris sipped his tea. "Any idea why he tried to stop the investigation?"

"He probably didn't want it to reflect badly on his family if it became known he had attended Madam's sessions."

"Of course, because him saving face is far more important than solving a crime." Dr. Harris finished his tea. "Is Mrs. Frogerton available?"

"I believe she is still sleeping," Caroline said. "Which is surely what you should be doing?"

As usual he ignored her question and asked one of his own.

"I wanted to find out if she'd made any progress with Lady Fielding?"

"Lady Fielding suggested that her son left his father to die after a carriage accident and that Sir Alfred hadn't appreciated her seeking the advice of a spiritualist to confirm her suspicions that he'd done it deliberately." Caroline paused. "In truth, I was quite surprised she said anything so damning to us, but she was remarkably emotional."

"It was probably due to the laudanum. Do you think she'll tell the sergeant?" Dr. Harris asked.

"Of course she won't, but Mrs. Frogerton, Dr. Woods, and I all heard her, and we can certainly report that to the police."

"Will you ask Mrs. Frogerton if she can write her letter today?" Dr. Harris asked.

Caroline nodded. "As I take care of most of her London correspondence, I will draft it for her consideration when you've gone. If we can persuade Sergeant Dawson that Sir Alfred was the murderer then you will be free of suspicion."

"Thank you." He set his cup back on the table and started for the door. "What *were* you doing in the cellar?"

"I was going through Madam Lavinia's belongings trying to find the other key to her strongbox. Letty said she wore a key around her neck."

"Good luck with that." He paused to look down at her in the kitchen doorway. "I suspect that if the key isn't located fairly soon, Mrs. Frogerton will ensure that the strongbox has a terrible accident on the stairs."

"We certainly hope for a resolution soon, Dr. Harris. We need to get the box to Sergeant Dawson, and hopefully someone will come and claim Madam's possessions. We put an advertisement in the papers for a week," Caroline replied.

"Then you'd better make sure you've looked through everything thoroughly before you give anything away." Dr. Harris walked toward the back door. "Give Mrs. Frogerton my best."

"I will, sir."

Caroline watched him leave and turned back to the cellar. There was still no sign of her employer. Even though she was reluctant to follow Dr. Harris's often brusque advice she decided to return to the cellar and continue searching for Madam's missing key.

"Good afternoon, Miss Morton!"

She looked back toward the outer door and discovered Letty coming through, her arms full of bundles.

"They're closing up Madam's house today. I've got my trunk outside in the cart. The man's bringing it down the steps." She grinned at Caroline. "Do you think someone could pay him? I don't have no change."

Caroline smiled back. "The butler is expecting you. Go into the kitchen and ask him to deal with your bags. You can start immediately by helping me go through Madam's belongings in the cellar."

"Right you are, miss." Letty set down her burdens and skipped toward the kitchen. She wore a pretty straw bonnet adorned with cherries and a broad red ribbon that suited her dark coloring. "I'll be as quick as I can."

Caroline reclaimed her candelabra, lit the candles, and took two cushions out of the housekeeper's room. If she had to go through Madam's things on a cold floor, she'd make sure to do it in comfort.

Having Letty, who had packed the bags, helping with Madam's belongings would make the process far easier.

Caroline turned her attention to the first of the hatboxes and was just checking the interior when Letty came down the stairs.

"The butler's a good man, Miss Morton. He paid off the carrier and everything. He said to come back to the kitchen when I've finished here for a bite to eat and to meet the housekeeper." Letty beamed at Caroline. "I even have my own room!"

"I'll let Mrs. Frogerton know you have arrived when she wakes up from her nap," Caroline said.

Letty knelt beside Caroline and looked expectantly at the boxes. "What exactly are we looking for, miss?"

"A key."

"The one Madam wore around her neck?"

"Yes, if it was that important to her it probably opens the strongbox." Caroline pointed at the stack of hatboxes. "Why don't you start with those?"

Half an hour later, the butler came down to tell Caroline that Mrs. Frogerton was awake, and that tea would be served in the drawing room. They had completed their search and come up with nothing but a few loose coins and one of a pair of fake diamond earrings.

"Thank you." Caroline rose to her feet. "I'm sure Mrs. Frogerton would like to see Letty at some point, Duffy. Perhaps you could send her up to the drawing room after Mrs. Jones has done with her."

"Yes, miss."

Letty followed Caroline and the butler up the stairs.

"Miss Morton?" Letty paused before she went off with the butler. "Madam always wore the key. Wouldn't she have been wearing it when she died?"

"Did the coroner's office return her clothing to you?" Caroline asked.

"I don't think so." Letty frowned. "But Mr. Murphy might have thrown everything away without telling me about it."

"Is he returning to London to speak to the police?"

"Not if he can help it—and anyway if he comes back where's he going to go? The house is all shut up now." Letty glanced over at the kitchen door. "I'd better go. Don't want to give a bad impression on me first day."

Caroline went up the stairs to await Mrs. Frogerton in the drawing room. She had several pieces of news to impart to her employer, who would be delighted. They were still no closer to exonerating Dr. Harris, which was remarkably frustrating. If only Sergeant Dawson would do the decent thing and accept that Sir Alfred had murdered Madam and close the case, things would be much better.

She walked over to the desk to compose the letter Dr. Harris had requested for Sergeant Dawson. Despite everything pointing to the fact of Sir Alfred's guilt, Caroline still had a feeling there was more to Madam's murder to discover.

Would it be fair to lay the blame on a man who couldn't defend himself even if such a choice benefited Dr. Harris? Would Dr. Harris even want that? With a sigh, Caroline took out a fresh sheet of paper and opened the inkwell. She hoped Mrs. Frogerton would come down soon. A dose of sound good sense might set matters to rights and calm her fears.

Chapter 17

Lady Fielding had progressed to sitting in a chair in her bedchamber and was more than willing to speak to her family solicitor when he begged for an audience. Letty's timely arrival had allowed Mrs. Frogerton to designate her as Lady Fielding's constant companion, thus allowing the rest of her staff to get on with their work. Caroline wasn't sure how Letty's bright cheerfulness would fare with Lady Fielding, but she took to Letty immediately.

"I will be returning to Northamptonshire at the earliest opportunity," Lady Fielding declared. "My parents will be delighted to offer me a home."

Mr. Peabody bowed. "There are several matters to be decided about the late Sir Alfred's estate, my lady. As he left no will, we will be dealing with the probate court, which is rarely speedy."

"But I don't have to be here for that, do I?" Lady Fielding deployed her handkerchief. "Surely you can take care of everything?"

"I will do my best, my lady." Mr. Peabody hesitated. "But there is still the matter of the investigation into Sir Alfred's death. I understand that a Sergeant Dawson wishes to speak to you quite urgently and you have so far refused to see him."

"Sergeant Dawson is not a gentleman," Lady Fielding snapped. "He lacks compassion, judgment, and understanding of the considerable strain I am under."

"But he still represents the law of the land, my lady, and thus needs to be accommodated."

Lady Fielding positively glared at her solicitor. Mrs. Frogerton, who stood with Caroline near the door, elbowed her in the side and whispered.

"I knew this wouldn't go well."

"She'll have to see him. He's been back three times and is currently in the small parlor threatening to speak to her whether she likes it or not," Caroline murmured back.

Mrs. Frogerton walked over to Lady Fielding. "May I make a suggestion, my lady? Why don't you admit Sergeant Dawson to your presence now while your solicitor, physician, Miss Morton, and I will make sure he conducts himself in a professional manner?"

"You will all stay with me?" Lady Fielding looked around the room.

Everyone nodded.

"Then I will see him." She leaned her head against the back of her chair as if making the decision had exhausted her. "But if it becomes too difficult for me, I hope you will tell him to leave."

"I'll go and fetch him, ma'am," Caroline said, and slipped out of the room. She beckoned Letty, who had been stationed by the door, to follow her.

"Perhaps you might fetch Lady Fielding some of that soothing tea she likes," Caroline asked.

"The kind with the slug of brandy in it?" Letty curtsied. "Yes, miss. I'll get it right now."

Caroline concealed a smile as she went down the stairs to the front parlor. Sergeant Dawson was staring out of the window, his hands linked behind his back. He turned to look at her when she came in.

"Lady Fielding will see you now, Sergeant. Please follow me."

"About bloody time, too," Sergeant Dawson muttered under his breath as she strode toward her. "Wasted half my shift waiting around for her."

"Lady Fielding is mourning the tragic death of her son," Caroline reminded him as he stomped up the stairs at her side.

"I am aware of that, Lady Caroline." He paused on the landing to stare at her. "I'm also wondering how Lady Fielding ended up here."

"Mrs. Frogerton always likes to assist those in need and when she found out Lady Fielding had no family to support her through her ordeal, she stepped in to help."

"I bet she did," Sergeant Dawson was back to muttering while he walked along the corridor. "With all due respect she strikes me as a managing sort of woman."

His gaze fell on Letty, who was just entering Lady Fielding's bedchamber ahead of them. "What's *she* doing here?"

"I believe that after Madam's house was closed up, she needed employment," Caroline said demurely. "She has proved to be very helpful so far."

Sergeant Dawson abruptly stopped walking and looked down at Caroline. "I assume you and Mrs. Frogerton are still meddling in matters that don't concern you?"

"Not at all, Sergeant." Caroline met his gaze. "We are *very* concerned about the fate of Dr. Harris, who has not committed a crime but is currently accused of being a murderer. We will continue to find ways to persuade the authorities that they have been mistaken." She opened the door. "After you, Sergeant."

Lady Fielding uttered a small moan as Sergeant Dawson approached her chair and grabbed hold of Mrs. Frogerton's hand.

"Don't leave me alone with *him*."

As Caroline could count at least six persons present in the room, not including the sergeant, she assumed Lady Fielding was speaking hypothetically.

"Good morning, Lady Fielding. Thank you for agreeing to see me." Sergeant Dawson cleared his throat. "It would have been helpful to know that you were not at your current address before my constable attempted to speak to you there on three separate occasions."

Lady Fielding readied her handkerchief but said nothing.

"I wish to extend my condolences for the loss of your son," Sergeant Dawson said stiffly. "And I want to reassure you that we are doing everything in our power to find out who killed him."

"I am sure you are," Mr. Peabody spoke when Lady Fielding sniffed and remained silent. "We hope you have some better news for us?"

"We are still looking for witnesses to the incident, sir." Sergeant Dawson cleared his throat. "Despite our best efforts, no one has come forward."

"Perhaps you might consider offering a financial incentive for someone to step forward, my lady?" Mr. Peabody inquired.

"If I must." Lady Fielding nodded. "But surely it is the sergeant's job to solve this case?"

Sergeant Dawson's ears went red. "In truth, Mr. Peabody, I wished to speak to Lady Fielding about another matter relating to her son."

"What on earth could that be?" Lady Fielding demanded. "He is *dead*! Isn't that the thing you should be concerned about?"

If she had been able to muster much sympathy for Sergeant Dawson, Caroline would have felt for him then as he stoically faced Lady Fielding, who was visibly trembling with irritation.

"We received new information about your son's activities at Madam Lavinia's house on the day of her death."

"I do not understand," Lady Fielding said.

"Sir Alfred was seen at Madam's on two separate occasions by an independent witness."

Lady Fielding's accusatory gaze slipped to Mrs. Frogerton, who looked as if the news were completely new to her.

"Good Lord!" Mrs. Frogerton gasped. "Who on earth told you that?"

"I am not at liberty to reveal my sources, ma'am, but as they volunteered the information, I trust that they told me the truth," Sergeant Dawson said.

"Are you suggesting that my beloved Alfred had something to do with Madam Lavinia's death?" Lady Fielding's voice rose on each word and Caroline winced.

"It does seem suspicious that he visited Madam Lavinia twice—the second time surreptitiously."

"But he was there on my behalf!" Lady Fielding said.

"I beg your pardon, my lady?"

"I asked him to go and speak to Madam Lavinia because she was . . . threatening me."

"With what?"

Caroline could only appreciate Sergeant Dawson's bewilderment because it mirrored her own.

Lady Fielding glanced wildly at her solicitor. "Alfred told you about this—didn't he? He promised me he would."

Mr. Peabody frowned. "I haven't spoken to Sir Alfred since his father's death when I explained the complexities of his inheritance to him. What exactly did you ask him to discuss with me?"

"How to counter a threat of blackmail."

"If he had spoken to me, I would have suggested writing a letter to the blackmailer threatening them with the full consequences of the law of the land." Mr. Peabody turned to Sergeant Dawson and bowed. "And I would have strongly recommended that you pass any evidence over to the police."

"If I am understanding you correctly, Lady Fielding," Sergeant Dawson said slowly, "you're saying that Sir Alfred's visits to Madam on the day of her murder were on your behalf because she was attempting to blackmail you?"

"Yes!" Lady Fielding nodded emphatically. "So, you must see that he had a perfectly good reason to be there."

There was a slight pause as everyone else in the room looked at Sergeant Dawson.

"With all due respect, my lady, doesn't that make Sir Alfred's behavior even more suspicious?"

"How so?" Lady Fielding demanded. "He was merely trying to protect his mother."

"By murdering Madam Lavinia?" Sergeant Dawson had obviously reached the limits of his patience. "If Sir Alfred believed you were being blackmailed, he had a motive for killing Madam."

Lady Fielding frowned. "That is ridiculous." She looked over at her solicitor. "Tell him I am right, Mr. Peabody."

"I am afraid I cannot do that, my lady," Mr. Peabody said.

"Why ever not?"

"Because whether you meant to or not, my lady, you have given Sir Alfred a motive for murder."

Lady Fielding burst into tears.

Sergeant Dawson nodded. "I would appreciate your cooperation in this matter, sir. If you or your client still have any evidence of this supposed blackmail, I'd like to see it."

"You will never see anything from me if it means you intend to blame my dead son for a murder he didn't commit!" Lady Fielding said between sobs. "I will fight you in every court of the land."

Mr. Peabody went over to Sergeant Dawson. "My client is upset. Perhaps it might be better if we discuss this matter between us at a later date? I fully intend to cooperate with your investigation."

"Traitor!" Lady Fielding cried even harder.

Sergeant Dawson bowed to Mrs. Frogerton. "Before I go, ma'am, I would like to speak to your new maid."

"Letty?" Mrs. Frogerton asked. "Of course. Caroline, will you take the good sergeant down to the kitchen and find her for him?"

"Yes, ma'am." Caroline headed for the door and Sergeant Dawson followed her.

He didn't speak again until they were just outside the kitchen.

"I wasn't expecting Lady Fielding to offer evidence that Sir Alfred had committed a murder."

"That's not exactly what she said, Sergeant. She said he had a *reason* to be there."

"And a great big bloody motive—begging your pardon, my lady." He paused. "I didn't know about the blackmail. Makes you wonder who else Madam was threatening."

"Indeed, it does." Caroline went into the kitchen where Letty was busy pressing one of Lady Fielding's black lace shawls. "Sergeant Dawson wishes to speak to you."

"Then he'll have to wait until I've finished this," Letty called out. "I'm not reheating the irons."

Caroline gestured toward the kitchen table. "Would you care for a cup of tea, Sergeant? I'm sure she'll only be a moment."

Sergeant Dawson sighed. "I'm not supposed to sit down when I'm on duty, but it's been a busy morning."

It was the first time Caroline had seen him look less than assured. "If you wish to remain standing, Sergeant, I'm sure I can pour you a cup and bring it to you. Do you take milk or sugar?"

"Yes, both, my lady." Sergeant Dawson accepted the cup with a gruff thank-you. "I suppose I'll have to review the evidence against Dr. Harris and consult with my superiors."

"That is excellent news," Caroline said warmly.

"What do you want, then?" Letty came over, her cheeks flushed from the heat of the irons.

"Less of your cheek," Sergeant Dawson said. "Do you remember Sir Alfred Fielding visiting Madam's house on the day of her death?"

"Yes. Mr. Murphy let him in, but I saw him in the hallway when I went by."

"Did he and Madam argue?"

Letty shrugged. "I didn't hear nothing from the kitchen, but Mr. Murphy said he warned Madam not to see him because last time he'd been there he'd had to throw the bastard out."

"That is correct, Sergeant," Caroline said. "I was at the meeting when Sir Alfred came in and demanded his mother leave with him immediately. After threatening Madam, he had to be forcibly removed by the butler and other guests."

Predictably, Sergeant Dawson didn't acknowledge her helpful intervention and continued to question Letty.

"Did Mr. Murphy tell you anything more about Sir Alfred's visit?"

"Only that he came out really quickly and looked like he'd seen a ghost," Letty said.

"Were you aware that Sir Alfred returned to the house soon afterward through the basement?"

Letty shrugged. "It wouldn't surprise me if he had, but I didn't see him. Mr. Murphy sent me upstairs to ask Madam what she wanted for lunch." She paused. "But when I came back Mr. Murphy was sitting at the table counting coins and looking very pleased with himself."

Caroline shook her head. "What a shame that Mr. Murphy isn't available to answer your questions, Sergeant."

Sergeant Dawson shot her a very unfriendly look.

"I might send my constable around to take down your statement in writing, Letty." Sergeant Dawson put on his hat and set his cup down on the table. "If you remember anything else, please tell him."

"Yes, Sergeant." Letty curtsied. "Can I go back to work now? I don't want to lose my new place."

"May I ask you a question, Sergeant?" Caroline looked up at the police officer. "Has Madam Lavinia's body been released for burial yet?"

"Not yet. We haven't had anyone claim the body."

"If no one comes forward, Mrs. Frogerton wishes to pay for Madam's burial. She has already spoken to Madam's local vicar at St. Jude's, who is willing to officiate at the funeral."

"That's good of her," Sergeant Dawson said gruffly. "Ask her to put it in writing and I'll forward it to the coroner's office."

"Thank you." Caroline hesitated. "Do you know what happened to Madam's personal items?"

"You mean what she was wearing when she died?" At Caroline's nod he continued. "The morgue will have all her belongings."

"Then I assume they'll come back with her body."

"That's right." He nodded. "Well, I must be off. Pleasure as always, Lady Caroline."

They both watched Sergeant Dawson leave and Letty turned to Caroline.

"Why's he in such a bad mood?"

"Because Lady Fielding told him that Sir Alfred had only been at Madam's house on the day of the murder because she was being blackmailed."

"Oh, dear."

"I think she believed that would exonerate him."

"But it makes it look worse." Letty made a face. "Good news for Dr. Harris, though."

"I hope so, but I suspect Sergeant Dawson isn't going to give up that idea very easily."

Caroline walked back up the stairs and found Mrs. Frogerton in the drawing room. She went in and closed the door behind her.

"How is Lady Fielding?"

"Spitting mad that Sergeant Dawson doesn't seem to realize that a son defending his mother could never be a murderer." Mrs. Frogerton shook her head. "The silly woman. But I suppose it helps Dr. Harris's case."

"But that's the thing," Caroline said slowly. "Does it really change matters or merely complicate them further?"

"How so?" Mrs. Frogerton asked.

"Lady Fielding specifically said that *she* was being blackmailed, not Sir Alfred."

"Why does that make a difference?"

"Because we assumed it was Sir Alfred who was being blackmailed because Madam knew he'd deliberately murdered his father. But if it wasn't that—what was Lady Fielding being blackmailed *for*?"

Mrs. Frogerton sat in her favorite chair. "Ah, I see your point, although I'm not sure such niceties would have occurred to Sir Alfred, who might have murdered Madam anyway. I suppose Madam could have covered her losses and blackmailed them both?"

"It just seems . . . odd," Caroline confessed.

"We can ask Lady Fielding about it when she calms down," Mrs. Frogerton suggested. "Although she has just been sedated."

"And it is good news for Dr. Harris," Caroline concluded, and tried to shake off her unease.

"It will be if Sergeant Dawson decides he can blame the murder on Sir Alfred and close the case down," Mrs. Frogerton said. "But he's a very stubborn man."

She turned to leaf through the post that Caroline had placed on the table beside her chair. "I've had no replies to the newspaper advertisement yet, but it runs for the rest of the week."

"Sergeant Dawson said that no one had come forward to claim her body yet. I mentioned that you were willing to bear the cost of Madam's funeral arrangements and he said he would inform the coroner if you put it in writing," Caroline said. "I can do that for you now, ma'am."

"Please do. I can't bear to think of that poor woman ending up in an unmarked pauper's grave." Mrs. Frogerton shuddered. "Imagine how many people she would come back and haunt for allowing that!"

Caroline went to the desk and took out a fresh piece of paper. "He also said the clothing she was wearing when she died will be returned with the body."

"I should hope so, too!" Mrs. Frogerton said. "Otherwise, she'll be naked!"

"As I've had no success finding the key to the strongbox amongst her possessions, I suspect she was still wearing it around her neck when she died."

"Then we'd better make sure that the vicar at St. Jude's receives her body as soon as possible," Mrs. Frogerton said briskly. "Because the sooner we get into that strongbox the quicker we can return it."

"We could just pass it over to Sergeant Dawson, ma'am," Caroline suggested.

"Without looking inside? Remember, Madam herself asked you to investigate her murder. She'd want you to be the first to see the secrets she's been keeping."

"I'm not sure that I want to know exactly who she's been blackmailing and why," Caroline confessed as she went back to writing her letter.

"You don't mean that, lass."

Caroline looked over her shoulder at her employer. "I assure you that I do, ma'am. I am not enjoying this at all."

"But it is exciting!"

"Perhaps I'd rather a quieter existence."

Mrs. Frogerton looked almost disappointed in her. "Did Sergeant Dawson say anything else of interest?"

"He indicated that he is seriously considering that Sir Alfred might be the murderer after all."

"That is excellent news." Mrs. Frogerton clapped her hands. "We must invite Dr. Harris and Professor Brown over for tea to discuss these latest developments."

"Dr. Harris was here earlier, ma'am, when you were sleeping. He sent his regards."

"What else did he want?"

"To tell you that Sergeant Dawson had been to see him." Caroline blotted her letter. "He seemed far happier about everything than he's been in the past."

"Dr. Harris or Sergeant Dawson?"

"Dr. Harris." Caroline allowed herself a small smile.

"The sergeant was quite overset by Lady Fielding's confession and not amused to see you at the center of everything."

"Why did he wish to speak to Letty?"

"He asked her if she'd seen Sir Alfred at Madam's on the morning of her murder."

"Shame he didn't think to ask that earlier," Mrs. Frogerton said. "It might have saved us all a lot of bother."

Caroline brought the letter over to Mrs. Frogerton to read through. "Will this suffice, ma'am?"

Mrs. Frogerton put on her reading glasses. "Yes, indeed."

"Then I'll seal it up and send it out today." Caroline hesitated. "I truly want Dr. Harris to be vindicated but I still don't think Sir Alfred murdered Madam."

Mrs. Frogerton sighed. "Neither do I, lass. It just doesn't make sense, does it? Sir Alfred didn't throw himself in the Thames deliberately. Someone slit his throat and didn't bother to rob him. And the only person who would have wanted to get rid of him that desperately would be the real murderer."

"One has to assume that the murderer saw Sir Alfred at Madam's house." Caroline set the letter down on the desk and sat opposite her employer.

"Whoever it was must also have feared Sir Alfred could identify him," Mrs. Frogerton said thoughtfully.

"I'm fairly certain Sir Alfred would have had a passing acquaintance with several of the people who attended Madam's meetings," Caroline pointed out. "The DeBlooms, and the Honorable William Armitage spring to mind."

"And Miss DeBloom was there on the fateful day." Mrs. Frogerton's eyes brightened, and she sat up straight. "And she only decided to tell the police that interesting fact when she thought she could incriminate Sir Alfred!"

"I can't quite see Miss DeBloom slitting a man's throat, ma'am."

"Perhaps her brother did it for her or she hired someone?" Mrs. Frogerton suggested. "Miss DeBloom said she saw Sir Alfred doubling back and entering the kitchen. Maybe that's what *she* did, and she paid Mr. Murphy to poison the contents of the decanter or put the poison in there herself when Madam wasn't looking."

"I suppose that could be correct, but why would Miss DeBloom want to murder the woman who was helping her build a case against her mother?" Caroline asked.

"Perhaps Miss DeBloom didn't tell you the truth about what Madam said to her." Mrs. Frogerton sat back. "Did you think of that? She might be an accomplished liar. Maybe Madam told her that her brother was the murderer, and she didn't want to hear that."

Caroline sighed. "I don't know about you, ma'am, but I don't see either of them as murderers."

Mrs. Frogerton nodded. "Neither do I, dear, but if Dr. Harris isn't the culprit, we need to find who is before he is convicted by default." She pointed at the desk. "Write a note to Dr. Harris and tell him to come and see me this very afternoon and don't take no for an answer."

Chapter 18

While Mrs. Frogerton accompanied Dorothy to an afternoon garden party, Caroline stayed behind to finish reading Professor Brown's extensive notes. After three hours of intense study, she had a terrible headache and a far deeper understanding of the people who had attended Madam's sessions and their reasons for doing so. Professor Brown had a useful ability to summarize each supplicant's desires into one of several categories he was using as a basis for his research.

His notes were short, succinct, and clinical, which wasn't surprising considering his profession. His comments on the truthfulness of Madam's prophecies were often dismissive, but he occasionally allowed that she sometimes said something inexplicably correct. On these occasions he often wrote a detailed description of the incident including direct quotes from Madam and her clients.

"I've brought you some tea, miss."

Caroline raised her head to see Letty coming through the door.

"Thank you."

Letty gave her a searching glance as she set the tray down on the desk. "You're looking a bit peaky, You should step outside for a breath of air."

"How is Lady Fielding this morning?" Caroline asked.

"Much better, miss. She's only cried twice and is thinking of coming down to join Mrs. Frogerton for dinner."

"I'm glad to hear she is improving." Caroline gingerly stretched out her neck. "I'll make sure to send Mrs. Frogerton up to see her later."

"She said she wanted to talk to Sergeant Dawson again, but without Mr. Peabody being present." Letty paused. "I wasn't sure what to do about that."

"I'd better mention that to Mrs. Frogerton as well," Caroline said. "It seems unwise."

Letty nodded vigorously. "I know it's not my place to say such things to my betters, but I did tell her that myself. I think she wants to tell him she didn't mean anything about being blackmailed and that she just said it to defend her son."

Caroline pressed two fingers against her aching temple. "I don't think Mr. Peabody would approve of any of that."

"Me neither, miss." Letty turned to the door. "I'd better get back before she has any more funny ideas."

"I think that is an excellent idea, and Letty?"

"Yes, miss?"

"If she does demand to see Sergeant Dawson, please make sure you inform me or Mrs. Frogerton immediately."

Letty nodded and left the room. Lady Fielding was something of a loose cannon firing shots at random even at her own side, but she could still cause chaos. If she recanted all her testimony, would Sergeant Dawson turn his attention back to Dr. Harris? Would it be easier to secure a conviction against a lowly doctor than a recently deceased member of the gentry?

The butler came in with a note on a tray.

"This came from Dr. Harris for Mrs. Frogerton, Miss Morton."

"Thank you." Caroline read the unsealed note.

Dr. Harris would present himself for Mrs. Frogerton's pleasure at three o'clock as requested.

Caroline glanced at the clock on the mantelpiece and rose to her feet. The Frogertons would be back within the hour, and she had yet to eat. Rather than bother the butler to bring up her meal to the dining room she decided to go to the kitchen and share whatever the cook had provided for the rest of the staff. The food would be hotter and more plentiful and although the kitchen staff treated her with respect, they were always welcoming.

As she descended the stairs, she thanked the Fates for finding her such pleasant employment with a woman who valued all those who worked for her. After almost a year of residing with Mrs. Frogerton and speaking to other companions, she was well aware of how she might have ended up and extremely grateful. If Dorothy did decide to marry Viscount Lingard and Mrs. Frogerton chose to return to the north, Caroline would happily accompany her. She paused as she passed through to the servants' quarters. If Mrs. Frogerton wanted her to . . .

She shook that thought away and carried on walking. There was no point in courting trouble and there were still several weeks before the Season officially ended. She would focus her energy on helping her employer's current needs and try not worry about the future.

"It is nice to see you with a smile on your face, Dr. Harris," Mrs. Frogerton commented as Caroline set a cup of tea beside the doctor.

"I'd hardly call that smiling." Professor Brown, who had accompanied Dr. Harris to the Frogerton house, accepted his cup from Caroline with a nod and a wink. "He's regarded as one of the most formidable physicians on the ward."

"I sincerely hope he doesn't treat any children," Caroline said as she resumed her seat. "I suspect they'd all be in tears."

Professor Brown chuckled. "He's kept well away from the little ones, Miss Morton. Don't you worry about that."

"I believe Sergeant Dawson has finally given up his pursuit of me in favor of Sir Alfred, which is cause for celebration," Dr. Harris said.

"But as Caroline and I were discussing earlier that doesn't make much sense, does it?" Mrs. Frogerton looked expectantly at her guests.

"How so, ma'am?" Dr. Harris was back to frowning again.

"Well, Sir Alfred was hardly capable of slitting his own throat and somehow managing to walk to the river and throw himself in, was he?"

"You'd be surprised at what people manage after they suffer a fatal wound, Mrs. Frogerton," Professor Brown said. "Sometimes they don't appear to realize they should be dead."

"Even the coroner didn't think Sir Alfred killed himself." Caroline spoke up in defense of Mrs. Frogerton.

"That's true." Dr. Harris nodded. "He doubted whether Sir Alfred would've had a steady enough hand to execute such a clean cut."

Mrs. Frogerton shuddered and set down her cup. "Good Lord."

"I'm not sure if I care about whether Sir Alfred killed himself as long as Sergeant Dawson believes he murdered Madam Lavinia," Dr. Harris said.

"Even if that can't be true?" Caroline asked. "Surely, if someone wanted Sir Alfred dead, it is because he saw something or someone at Madam's that could convict the real murderer?"

"All I want is to be released from my bond and be allowed to go about my business without the threat of being tried for murder hanging over my head. Is that too much to ask?" Dr. Harris raised his eyebrows. "Sir Alfred is dead and beyond the cares of the mortal world. If he's seen as the culprit, our lives can go on happily without him."

"That seems remarkably callous, Doctor," Caroline said. "What about his mother's right to have her son's murderer brought to justice?"

"That's in Sergeant Dawson's hands." Dr. Harris shrugged. "But just remember if he works out what seems obvious to us, then I'm still his prime suspect."

"Mr. Lewis doesn't believe Sergeant Dawson has a strong enough case to convict you." Mrs. Frogerton rejoined the conversation. "And neither does Inspector Ross."

"With all due respect, having witnessed several miscarriages of justice in my life I know that doesn't matter, ma'am."

Mrs. Frogerton suddenly looked formidable. "It matters to me, Dr. Harris. I can assure you of that."

Professor Brown cleared his throat. "Have there been any other developments in your investigations? Dr. Harris tells me that Miss DeBloom was present in Madam's house on the day of the murder."

"She was, and I believe she was the person who told Sergeant Dawson she saw Sir Alfred sneaking back into the house through the basement." Mrs. Frogerton poured herself more tea. "One has to wonder who else she saw while she waited quietly in the hall with her maid."

"Madam's house was often very busy," Professor Brown said. "I interviewed her a few times for research purposes, and it was never easy to get an appointment."

"Or she simply didn't want to talk to you," Dr. Harris replied. "You were trying to prove she was a fake."

"That's not quite true, my friend." Professor Brown smiled broadly. "I was conducting a scientific study and she was a very interesting subject."

"From what I read in your notes, Professor, you believed she sometimes offered answers that defied scientific logic," Caroline said.

"Yes! Like when she knew the pet name my Septimus called me. No one in London knew that except me," Mrs. Frogerton said.

"Madam did occasionally surprise me," Professor Brown admitted. "And she was always very gracious when I questioned her abilities."

"That's because she knew she had a gift and that nothing anyone said could disprove that." Mrs. Frogerton nodded. "I wish she was here now to help us solve the mystery of her death."

"I'm quite glad she is not," Dr. Harris said flatly. "The last thing we need is a ghostly presence appearing in your drawing room, ma'am. We'd all end up in Bedlam. Have you received any replies to your newspaper advertisement?"

"Not yet, but it still has a few days to run." Mrs. Frogerton sipped her tea. "It would be helpful if we knew what part of the country Madam was from so that we could reach a more local audience. Did you ever ask Madam where she came from, Professor Brown?"

"I did inquire, ma'am, but she insisted she was French, which I didn't believe."

"It would be a shame if no one comes forward to claim her and her possessions before her funeral."

"You have arranged a funeral?" Dr. Harris asked.

"I spoke to the vicar at her local church of St. Jude's. He is very willing to hold the funeral service and find her a burial plot in his graveyard," Mrs. Frogerton said. "I'll hold on to her possessions for as long as I rent this house, but I don't think I'll be taking them back up north with me."

"There are lots of charities who would be grateful for such things," Caroline said.

"I'm sure." Mrs. Frogerton offered her visitors more tea. "Or I'll drop them off at Great Scotland Yard for Sergeant Dawson to deal with."

"If he accepts that Sir Alfred is the murderer and closes the case, he won't want them either," Dr Harris said.

"Then I'll wait until he makes a decision before I decide what to do," Mrs. Frogerton said. "Caroline, do you have Professor Brown's notes for him?"

"I do, ma'am." Caroline indicated the freshly wrapped parcel sitting on Mrs. Frogerton's writing desk and went to fetch it. "Thank you for lending them to us." She handed them back to the professor. "They were very informative."

"You are most welcome." Professor Brown bowed. "The Society for Psychical Research await my findings with great interest."

"I would also be interested in reading your paper, Professor," Caroline said. "Your methodology was very sound."

"Thank you. Sometimes it is hard to find the balance between cynicism and total capitulation, but I hope I can achieve it in this work."

"Whatever will you write about now that Madam Lavinia is dead?" Mrs. Frogerton asked.

"Unfortunately, there are always people willing to deceive others, Mrs. Frogerton," Professor Brown said. "All you have to do is read the local paper and you'll find dozens of fraudsters going about their business of talking good people out of their hard-earned money."

"I suppose that is true and even though Madam did speak some truths, she obviously had other less scrupulous methods of making a profit." Mrs. Frogerton sighed. "I've learned my lesson and will rely on Caroline's good sense before I allow myself to be bamboozled again."

Knowing her employer's insatiable curiosity, Caroline doubted that, but refrained from mentioning it.

"We should go and see the vicar, Caroline," Mrs. Frogerton continued. "The coroner is quite impatient to release Madam's body."

"Yes, ma'am."

"Please let me know the funeral arrangements, Mrs. Frogerton," Professor Brown said. "I'd like to pay my respects."

"Of course, Professor. Now, let's finish our tea and hope that Sergeant Dawson comes to his senses and lets this investigation die along with Sir Alfred."

"Amen." Professor Brown raised his cup in a salute.

Dr. Harris snorted. "And I'll wager you each a shilling that he does no such thing."

"Good afternoon, Mrs. Frogerton, Miss Morton." Mr. Smith, the vicar of St. Jude's, visibly brightened as he recognized his visitors. "Have you come about the funeral?"

"I have indeed," Mrs. Frogerton said. "I wrote to the coroner's office, and they have agreed that as no one has come forward to claim Madam's body I can do so."

"That is very charitable of you, ma'am."

Caroline noted that the vicar still hadn't managed to iron his linen or darn his coat, and that the layer of dust on the surfaces had only increased since their last visit.

As if he was conscious of her unflattering appraisal, the vicar blushed. "I apologize that I can't offer you any refreshments. My cook only comes in the evening."

"You need a housekeeper, Vicar," Mrs. Frogerton said.

He half smiled. "I used to have a wife, ma'am, but she died in childbirth last year."

"I am sorry to hear that." Mrs. Frogerton patted his arm. "But in your profession appearances matter. If your flock think you can't cope with your own problems, how will they have confidence that you can advise them on their own?"

"I hadn't thought of it like that, ma'am." The vicar frowned. "I will try to do better." His gaze went to Caroline, and he looked her up and down. "Perhaps it is time to find another wife."

"That's the spirit, Vicar," Mrs. Frogerton said briskly. "I'm sure there are dozens of young women who would love to be your wife."

"One would hope so."

For the first time a gleam of hope flashed in the vicar's eyes.

"Now, about the funeral arrangements, ma'am."

"I've written to the local funeral directors, Pilkington

and Sons," Mrs. Frogerton said. "They will prepare the body and provide a coffin."

"I received a note from them this morning to say that they have already received Madam's body, ma'am. I was about to call on you and let you know."

"Then we shall proceed to the funeral home and speak to Mr. Pilkington." Mrs. Frogerton smiled.

The vicar bowed. "And I will arrange the funeral when they are ready to proceed. There is little call for my pastoral services at present so I will be able to accommodate you quickly."

"Good." Mrs. Frogerton offered the vicar a firm handshake and Caroline curtsied. "I'll expect to hear from you in the next few days then, Vicar."

Mrs. Frogerton didn't speak again until they were on their way to Pilkington & Sons in the carriage.

"Gentlemen such as Mr. Smith are remarkably incapable when they lose a wife," Mrs. Frogerton mused as the carriage turned the corner onto a more crowded street. "But he is correct that he'll easily find another one. He can at least provide a decent standard of living and there are many women who would consider that a bargain."

Caroline repressed a shudder.

"I noticed him giving you a look-over, lass," Mrs. Frogerton said.

"I can assure you that I have no desire to marry Mr. Smith, ma'am."

"I'm glad to hear it. I suspect he'd make a terrible husband."

"And I have no desire to marry anyone at present." Caroline averted her gaze and looked out of the window.

"You'll change your mind when the right man comes along, lass," Mrs. Frogerton said encouragingly. "And I don't intend to stand in your way when he does."

"I have very little to offer except a passably pretty face," Caroline replied stiffly. "Thanks to my father I have no dowry and a sister who is financially dependent on me."

"I think you underestimate yourself, my dear, and we both know that many gentlemen *are* swayed by a pretty face."

"I always hoped someone would see beyond that." Caroline kept her attention on the scenery.

"And they will." Mrs. Frogerton paused. "Not all marriages are based on financial considerations."

"They usually were in the society I grew up in, but as I'm no longer a part of that world I can only hope you are right."

The carriage drew up in front of a square redbrick building with a large sculpture of a weeping woman over the door. The door was painted black as were the shutters that covered the front windows. A large sign embellished with touches of gold proclaimed PILKINGTON & SONS, FUNERALS OF DISTINCTION.

Caroline stepped out of the carriage and waited to assist Mrs. Frogerton.

"Thank you, lass." Mrs. Frogerton met her gaze. "And you are valued, Caroline. By me, so don't you forget it."

"Thank you, ma'am." Caroline tried to smile. "I appreciate that."

"Then come along and let's see if we can discover what might have happened to Madam Lavinia's clothing."

Mrs. Frogerton linked arms with Caroline, and they walked up to the front door, which opened immediately to reveal a small brown-haired woman wearing a plain black dress and a very sympathetic expression.

"Good afternoon, ladies. I am Mrs. Pilkington. How may I assist you in your time of grief?"

Mrs. Frogerton swept in through the front door and Caroline followed her into a surprisingly spacious front office.

"Good afternoon, Mrs. Pilkington," Mrs. Frogerton said. "We are here to arrange the funeral for Madam Lavinia."

"Oh, yes. The unclaimed body from the coroner's office by the Thames." Mrs. Pilkington's calm expression didn't alter. "We were told to expect you."

"I have just been speaking to Mr. Smith, the vicar of St. Jude's, who will be conducting the funeral," Mrs. Frogerton continued. "He said he had received a note from you."

"We've laid out several loved ones for burial at his church—including his late wife." Mrs. Pilkington shook her head. "Such a lovely woman and such a tragedy to die so young." She gestured to a door at the rear of the office. "Would you care to come through to the parlor where we can discuss your requirements more privately?"

"Yes, please."

Caroline hoped that the décor in the parlor was slightly less depressing than in the main office, which was festooned with samples of gravestones, wall plaques, ghostly sculptures, and miniature coffins. She rarely reflected on her own mortality but was forcibly reminded of her own father's funeral. Despite the evidence that he'd killed himself Aunt Eleanor had bullied her local vicar into burying her brother in consecrated ground. But even she had balked at inviting anyone to attend except Caroline and Susan. Between the vicar's unease and the rain, it had been a hurried and furtive burial in an unmarked grave.

"Which do you think Madam would prefer?" Caroline started as Mrs. Frogerton asked a question. "White or black for her coffin lining?"

"White, ma'am." Caroline turned to Mrs. Pilkington, who was writing notes. "Did Madam arrive with any clothing or jewelry, or do we need to fetch something to dress her in?"

"She was accompanied by a parcel of clothing," Mrs. Pilkington said. "I will go and find it." She hesitated. "Although might I say that in my experience the clothing worn at the time of death is often . . . unsuitable."

"Then we will simply take the parcel home and bring her favorite dress instead," Mrs. Frogerton said. "Letty will know which one to choose."

After completing her long list of questions, including how many horses to draw the hearse, whether they should be black or white, have feather plumes, and how many cushions to place under Madam's head, Mrs. Pilkington went off to write up a bill of sale and fetch the parcel. Mrs. Frogerton leafed through the book containing engravings of the available coffins and pointed out those she would like for her own burial while Caroline nodded, her mind still back at her father's lonely graveside.

"Here we are, Mrs. Frogerton." Mrs. Pilkington came in with a large parcel wrapped in brown paper and string. "And I will have Mr. Pilkington send you the bill when he and the vicar have arranged a suitable date for the funeral."

"Thank you." Caroline took the parcel. "I'll take it out to the carriage."

"And thank you for your business." As Caroline went by, Mrs. Pilkington winked and pressed a coin into her hand.

"Thank you, ma'am." Caroline pocketed the coin and went on her way. A year ago, she might have dropped it to the floor, but she'd learned to accept that sometimes she was rewarded for delivering her employer's business to an establishment whether she'd intended to or not.

The coachman got down from his box to open the carriage door and she placed the parcel on the floor inside. Mrs. Frogerton said her goodbyes and they started back to Half Moon Street.

They had barely entered the house when Dorothy came running down the stairs.

"Where on earth have you been?"

"Arranging a funeral, Dotty." Mrs. Frogerton took off her bonnet and stripped off her gloves. "Whatever is the matter?"

"Mr. and Miss DeBloom are here, and they want to take a walk in the park with me."

"Where is their mother?"

"How should I know?" Dorothy scowled. "You're here and you can chaperone me."

Mrs. Frogerton raised her chin. "I don't appreciate being spoken to in that tone of voice, miss."

"Then tell Caroline to accompany us." Dorothy seemed unaware of her mother's rising ire and looked inquiringly at Caroline. "I'll be perfectly safe with her."

"That's not the point and you know it." Mrs. Frogerton went up the stairs toward Dotty. "You are fast becoming a spoiled brat and I don't like it."

Caroline remained in the hall as the mother and daughter confronted each other.

"I have patiently sat in all morning while you and the person you employ have been out attending to someone else's business. I have a perfect right to feel slighted."

"Slighted? I've spent a fortune bringing you down here to enjoy a London Season that you don't need if you'd simply marry Simon Briggs as God intended!"

"I will *never* marry him," Dorothy snapped. "I am trying to marry up!"

"And much good it will do you. Have you seen how they treat us, Dotty? How they sneer behind our backs at our lack of class while they smirk and curtsy to our faces because they desperately need our money?"

"The DeBlooms don't."

"And you don't want to marry Mr. DeBloom, either." Mrs. Frogerton walked past her daughter. "Please excuse me. I have a letter to write."

"You can't just walk away in the middle of our discussion, Mother!" Dorothy was now speaking to Mrs. Frogerton's back. "What am I supposed to do about the DeBlooms?"

There was no answer and Dorothy spun around to look down at Caroline in the hall.

"What put her in such a bad mood?"

"I have no idea." Caroline met Dorothy's infuriated gaze calmly. "But if you wish me to accompany you to the park, I am more than willing to do so."

Dorothy's nod was all the thanks she received. "I'll go and fetch the DeBlooms then."

"I'll wait here."

After a year of witnessing the heated arguments between Dorothy and her mother Caroline had learned that they needed time apart to regain their tempers. Taking Dorothy out to the park seemed the easiest way of allowing Mrs. Frogerton some peace while her daughter got what she wanted, which usually guaranteed the return of her good humor.

"Miss Morton!" Mr. DeBloom came down the stairs accompanied by his sister. He wore a new blue coat that contrasted favorably with Miss DeBloom's yellow gown. "A pleasure to have your company on our excursion!"

Caroline curtsied. "Miss DeBloom, Mr. DeBloom."

Dorothy was still tying the ribbons of her bonnet under her chin as she followed her guests out of the front door. "We'll take the DeBloom carriage and ask them to set us down in the park so that we can stroll by the Serpentine."

"An excellent idea." Mr. DeBloom helped all the ladies into the open carriage and took the seat next to Caroline. "I've been cooped up all week with my man of business and need to stretch my legs."

Caroline smiled but concentrated her attention on the scenery around her. Having come from a family who never expressed their emotions with quite as much force as the Frogertons, she still found their encounters somewhat unnerving. To her dismay, the fashionable crowd in Hyde Park was larger than usual as people enjoyed the first sunny day in a while.

"I do hope it is less busy by the lake," Miss DeBloom murmured as she stared at the crowds. "I hate being jostled."

"Don't we all," Dorothy agreed. She linked arms with Miss DeBloom and started toward the lake. "Don't worry. I'll keep an eye on you."

Caroline reluctantly accepted Mr. DeBloom's proffered arm and followed Dorothy.

"How have you been, Miss Morton?"

"Quite well, sir."

Silence fell as they negotiated their way down the grassy slope to the shores of the lake. Mr. DeBloom was the first to speak again.

"Clarissa insisted on talking to Sergeant Dawson. She seemed much happier after she'd seen him."

"Confessing to one's sins does seem to have that effect on people." Caroline had to edge closer to Mr. DeBloom as a large group of raucous young boys ran past.

"And are you a sinner, Miss Morton?"

"Aren't we all?" She looked ahead where Dorothy and Miss DeBloom had vanished into the crowd. "Should we attempt to find our companions? I am supposed to be chaperoning Miss Frogerton."

"They'll be all right." Mr. DeBloom patted her gloved hand. "Miss Frogerton has a shrewd head on her shoulders."

The graceful curve of the Long Water that ran southeast toward the Serpentine Bridge came into view. Caroline caught a glimpse of Dorothy's outlandish bonnet feathers and headed toward it.

"Isn't that your doctor friend over there?" Mr. DeBloom suddenly asked.

Caroline had just turned to look where he was pointing when there was a loud shriek and a pair of swans rose from the water and flapped noisily away.

"She's fallen in! Somebody help her!"

Caroline immediately recognized Dorothy's voice and ran toward her. Dorothy was pointing at the water where two men had already jumped in and were retrieving a soaking wet Miss DeBloom.

"Clarissa!" Mr. DeBloom ran straight into the water and helped them haul her out. "Are you all right? Speak to me!"

Caroline spent several moments persuading the curious crowd to ease back as the men laid Miss DeBloom on the grass. She was gasping for air and attempting to cry at the same time.

"Someone pushed me!"

Dorothy, who was kneeling beside her, raised her eyebrows. "Are you sure? It looked as if you slipped."

"No! Someone grabbed my arm and shoved me hard in the back."

Miss DeBloom came out on one elbow and was violently sick, making the crowd recoil and thankfully start to disperse.

"Where's that doctor fellow when you need him?" Mr. DeBloom patted his sister's back as she burst into tears. "And how are we going to get my sister back to the carriage in such a state?"

"Dorothy and I will wrap her in our cloaks, and you can carry her, sir," Caroline said as she handed Miss DeBloom her handkerchief to mop her face. "I will go ahead and alert the coachman to your impending arrival."

"I've only worn this cloak once!" Dorothy complained in Caroline's ear.

"I'm sure your mother will buy you another one," Caroline said as she ruthlessly untied Dorothy's cloak strings. "Use yours for the first layer. It is already outmoded."

"And one of only two I possess," Caroline murmured as she wrapped a shivering Miss DeBloom in it anyway. "Please step aside, Dorothy. Mr. DeBloom needs room to lift his sister from the ground."

After making sure that Dorothy would stay with the DeBlooms, she hurried back up to where they'd left the carriage to prepare the coachman for a speedy departure. Moments later, Mr. DeBloom followed by a large crowd of gawkers arrived with his sister in his arms with Dorothy bringing up the rear.

"Would you prefer us to take Miss DeBloom straight home or to Mrs. Frogerton's?" Caroline asked as Mr. De-Bloom laid his sister gently on the seat.

"To Mrs. Frogerton. My mother will have hysterics." He grimaced.

Caroline spoke to the coachman, and they were soon on their way. She held on to Miss DeBloom, who was shivering violently, while Dorothy and Mr. DeBloom looked on anxiously from the opposite side of the carriage.

Dorothy got out of the carriage first, ran up the steps, and banged hard on the knocker. When the startled butler opened the door, Mr. DeBloom carried his sister into the hall and looked inquiringly at Caroline.

"Follow me, sir." Caroline ascended the stairs calling out to the butler as she went by him. "Please tell Mrs. Frogerton that we have an unexpected guest and that we might need to call her physician."

"Yes, Miss Morton."

She went past Mr. DeBloom and opened the door into the second-best guest bedroom, which was beside the one Lady Fielding currently occupied.

"You may put Miss DeBloom here, sir." She plumped up the pillows of the bed. "I will stay with her until Mrs. Frogerton arrives."

"Thank you, Miss Morton." He smoothed his sister's fair hair away from her forehead. "Don't fret, love. I'll wait in the drawing room."

Caroline persuaded a still weeping Miss DeBloom to remove most of her soiled clothing and get between the sheets in her shift.

"I was pushed." Miss DeBloom grabbed Caroline's wrist. "I *felt* it."

"I'm sure you did. It was extremely crowded, Miss De-Bloom, and not everyone was behaving in a considerate and respectful manner," Caroline attempted to reassure her.

The door opened and Mrs. Frogerton came in. She looked quite recovered from her argument with Dorothy.

"You poor dear!" She rushed over to the bed to pat Miss DeBloom's hand. "What a horrible accident."

"It wasn't an accident." Miss DeBloom's eyes filled with tears. "Someone is trying to kill me."

Mrs. Frogerton's startled gaze met Caroline's, who raised her eyebrows. "Miss DeBloom believes someone deliberately pushed her in the Serpentine."

"They did!" Miss DeBloom declared.

Mrs. Frogerton nodded. "I'm sure you are right, my dear. I've called my physician to attend to you. Would you like me to send a message to your mother?"

"No!" Miss DeBloom sat bolt upright. "She's the one who's trying to kill me!"

Chapter 19

It had taken a considerable amount of time to calm Miss DeBloom down, and only the arrival of the doctor and a hefty dose of laudanum had finally persuaded her to sleep. Caroline left one of the maids sitting beside Miss DeBloom's bed and went down with Mrs. Frogerton to the drawing room where Dorothy and Mr. DeBloom awaited them.

"How is she?" Mr. DeBloom immediately asked.

"Sleeping and apparently unharmed by her soaking." Mrs. Frogerton took her favorite seat by the fire. "She is still quite distraught."

"Should I go up and see her?"

"You may certainly do so, but she isn't in any state to talk to you. The physician prescribed a dose of laudanum to calm her nerves."

"Then perhaps I should go home." Mr. DeBloom made a face. "I'm still not sure what to tell my mother."

"Tell her that Clarissa is having dinner with us and that she will be safely returned to her mother's care in the morning," Mrs. Frogerton advised. "There is no point in alarming her about an accidental soaking."

"Very true." Mr. DeBloom hesitated. "Is she still insisting she was pushed? Miss Frogerton says she didn't see anyone approach her deliberately, but they weren't beside each other when it happened."

"I stopped to observe a duck and Clarissa walked a few steps past me," Dorothy confirmed. "The first I knew of it was when I heard a splash and she toppled sideways into the water."

"As Miss Morton already knows, my sister has this strange obsession that people are intent on murdering members of our family." Mr. DeBloom sounded both slightly apologetic and embarrassed. "I have yet to convince her that it isn't true."

"She is safe now," Mrs. Frogerton reassured him. "And you are most welcome to come back and join us for dinner if you wish."

"Thank you." Mr. DeBloom walked over and raised Mrs. Frogerton's hand to his lips. "You are a remarkable woman."

He bowed to Dorothy and Caroline and half turned to the door.

"I will try and return later this evening, but that will depend on my mother's plans. If you have need of me, send me a note."

Dorothy rose to her feet and looked over at her mother. "I'm beginning to wish I'd heeded your advice and stayed home. Caroline *insisted* on using our cloaks to wrap Miss DeBloom in and mine is ruined."

"It was for a good cause," Caroline reminded her. "And mine took the brunt of the damage."

"Yours was already past praying for," Dorothy said. "Mine was brand-new!"

"And if you stop complaining right now, Dotty, I'll buy you both another one." Mrs. Frogerton looked from Caroline to her daughter. "I don't hear Caroline complaining."

Dorothy rolled her eyes. "We all know she is a better person than I will ever be." She headed for the door. "I think I'll take a nap. This day has been exhausting."

"You do that, dear, and perhaps you'll wake up in a better mood." Mrs. Frogerton's advice appeared likely to be ignored as Dorothy left the drawing room and slammed the door behind her.

"You don't need to buy me anything, ma'am. I have another cloak."

"Blue would be a good color for you," Mrs. Frogerton mused. "I'll ask my modiste."

Knowing it was pointless to argue with her employer, Caroline smiled her thanks.

"Now tell me what happened when you were out with the DeBlooms," Mrs. Frogerton asked.

"It was unusually crowded in the park and Dorothy and Miss DeBloom went on ahead of us. Suddenly I heard Dorothy shouting that Miss DeBloom had fallen in. By the time we reached them two men had already rescued her from the water and were bringing her to safety. Mr. De-Bloom waded in to help."

"How shocking!" Mrs. Frogerton shuddered. "There's nothing worse than being doused with water when you aren't expecting it. Did Miss DeBloom lose consciousness?"

"No, ma'am. She was too busy insisting that someone had deliberately pushed her in."

"And what did you think of that claim?"

Caroline shrugged. "It was extremely busy, there were children and young boys running freely through the crowds. It would have been a simple matter for someone to accidentally shove her in the back and send her into the water."

"Then you think she is imagining things?" Mrs. Frogerton asked with great interest. "Because I was thinking that she might be right."

"On what grounds, ma'am?"

"That Miss DeBloom was there in Madam's house the day she died, and she might have seen the murderer." Mrs. Frogerton sat back as if that was all she needed to say, and Caroline frowned.

"I don't quite follow your reasoning."

"The murderer might have taken the opportunity to get rid of an inconvenient witness to his crimes. One quick push and Miss DeBloom could have drowned."

"It seems unlikely that the murderer would just happen to be by the Serpentine at that very moment."

"Mayhap he has been following her!" Mrs. Frogerton said eagerly. "Just waiting for such a moment to rid himself of a potential witness against him."

"I suppose that might be true," Caroline said slowly. "Mr. DeBloom thinks her claims are all nonsense."

"Of course he does." Mrs. Frogerton waved away Mr. DeBloom's far greater knowledge of his sister. "He simply doesn't want to believe that his own mother is trying to murder him."

"And his whole family," Caroline added. "One can quite see why he might be skeptical about such claims."

"At least that means it is unlikely that Miss DeBloom is the murderer," Mrs. Frogerton continued, and then paused. "Unless she staged the whole thing to draw attention away from herself."

"I . . ."

Mrs. Frogerton chuckled. "Yes, I am letting my imagination run away with me, lass. Even I can see that it would be very farfetched for the murderer to have followed Miss DeBloom to Hyde Park simply to push her into the Serpentine."

Caroline stared at her employer.

"What is it, dear?"

"Mr. DeBloom."

"I hardly think he would push his own sister in the lake, Caroline. I thought you said he was with you?"

"He was." Caroline attempted to collect her thoughts. "But just before Dorothy shrieked, Mr. DeBloom said he'd seen Dr. Harris."

"*Our* Dr. Harris?"

"Yes. In fact, I had turned to look at where Mr. DeBloom was pointing and missed seeing Miss DeBloom fall."

"Did you see Dr. Harris yourself?"

"No, because by that point I was rushing to Miss De-Bloom's side."

"Why would Dr. Harris be in Hyde Park at that time of day?" Mrs. Frogerton wondered. "It isn't exactly close to St. Thomas's."

"I'd guess it's at least two or three miles away," Caroline said.

"Perhaps he was out enjoying the fine weather like the rest of us," Mrs. Frogerton said.

"Or if he is the murderer, he was doing exactly what you suggested and trying to get rid of Miss DeBloom."

Mrs. Frogerton raised her eyebrows. "You don't really think that's true, do you, lass?"

"I don't know." Caroline stared at her employer. "But I wouldn't have felt right if I hadn't shared exactly what happened."

"Dr. Harris does have a terrible habit of turning up in the most incriminating places." Mrs. Frogerton sighed. "I suppose I could write him a note and ask him where he was this afternoon, which would either annoy him, or make him aware that we think he's been up to no good."

"I think it would be better to say nothing," Caroline said. "Mr. DeBloom might have been mistaken."

"He *might* have been trying to distract you while his sister was pushed into the pond!" Mrs. Frogerton gasped. "Think of that!"

"I suppose Mr. DeBloom could have wanted Madam dead," Caroline said dubiously. "But the whole idea is rather farfetched."

"What if *he* is the one murdering his family members? Perhaps this was his way of making sure his sister keeps quiet from now on."

"By making her feel afraid?" Caroline considered that.

"I still don't think he's the murderer. No one saw him at Madam's."

"Has anyone asked Letty or Mr. Murphy about that?" Mrs. Frogerton demanded. "I'll wager Sergeant Dawson hasn't. There *were* others who visited on that fateful day."

Caroline pressed her fingers to her temple and Mrs. Frogerton frowned.

"Are you feeling quite well, dear?"

"It's been an eventful day, ma'am. I appear to have a headache."

"Then perhaps you should follow Dorothy's example and take to your bed. I have no plans to go out today. I am quite content to sit here and read my latest novel."

"I have a few matters to attend to first, ma'am, including the post."

"They can wait."

Caroline summoned a smile. "I'd feel better if I had completed all my tasks before I indulged in a nap, ma'am."

"Then you'd better get on, then, hadn't you?" Mrs. Frogerton smiled.

Caroline escaped from the drawing room and went down to the hall where the butler had left the morning's post. She took it through into the library to sort and was soon back on her way upstairs to Mrs. Frogerton's side.

"There are invitations to look through, ma'am. I have sorted them into those I think you might like to attend and those that you can safely ignore without offending anyone." She set them on the small table beside Mrs. Frogerton. "There is a letter from your business manager, one from your son, and one from an unknown person."

"Give me the last one." Mrs. Frogerton held out her hand. "I do like a mystery."

Caroline waited as her employer put on her spectacles, opened the letter, and read it through.

"How exciting! It's about our advertisement. A Mrs. O'Leary claims to be a relative of Madam's and wishes to claim her possessions." Mrs. Frogerton looked at Caroline over the top of her glasses. "O'Leary doesn't sound very French."

"Perhaps a connection by marriage?" Caroline suggested. "I can write back to her and ask for more information before we invite her to the house."

"Please do so." Mrs. Frogerton handed over the letter. "I am slightly suspicious of her claim."

"Rightly so." Caroline nodded. "There are a lot of opportunists in this world."

She returned to the library, leaving Mrs. Frogerton to peruse the invitations, and composed a short note to Mrs. O'Leary, which she placed in the hall for the butler to post.

There had also been a letter from her cousin Nick containing more details of her aunt Eleanor's funeral, which would take place at Greenwood Hall at the end of the month. Caroline hadn't received a reply from her sister since she'd written about Eleanor's death and wondered whether she should write again. Susan had been very fond of Eleanor and her cousin Mabel and had deeply resented Caroline moving her from Greenwood Hall to boarding school.

Rather than worry about matters that she couldn't control, Caroline remembered that she had yet to deal with Madam Lavinia's clothing from the coroner's office. She'd left the parcel in the scullery and went to the kitchen to deal with it. There was no sign of Letty in the kitchen, but she was probably busy attending Lady Fielding, who had declared her intentions of returning home to prepare for her son's funeral, pack up her house, and await the arrival of her parents to take her back to Northamptonshire.

As far as Caroline knew she hadn't followed through with her threats to contact Sergeant Dawson and attempt to upend the whole investigation. She had mentioned hiring a barrister to defend her beloved son from all charges but seemed halfway to accepting that Sir Alfred was dead and that nothing worse could happen to her than that. In

Caroline's opinion, Lady Fielding appeared to be embracing her role as grieving mother with some relish.

The scullery was deserted, but two sinks full of linen soaking in strong-smelling lye indicated that the maids had already been busy. Caroline cut the string around the parcel and unwrapped the neatly folded garments releasing the faint scent of disinfectant overlaid by violets. She immediately pictured walking into Madam's parlor and the horrible sight of her hostess staring blankly at the beyond. There were the usual petticoats and undergarments, and a lace fichu still pinned together at the ends with a cameo brooch depicting a goddess of some kind.

Madam's dress was of blue muslin with ruffles around the sleeves and edge of the bodice. Caroline picked it up but there was nothing underneath it. She unfolded the dress, gave it an experimental shake, and heard the clink of something metallic. It took only a moment to investigate further and discover Madam had a pocket sewn into the lining of her dress and that the coroner's office had placed her remaining personal effects in there.

She unwrapped the package and discovered Madam's rings and a long chain with a very functional-looking key on the end of it. Caroline couldn't help but smile as she pocketed the key and rings.

"Morning, Miss Morton!" Letty came into the scullery. "Cook said you was looking for me."

"Yes, indeed. Madam's body has been taken to the undertaker's and Madam will need to be dressed for her casket."

"I can do that, ma'am." Letty nodded. "Her gowns are all here in the cellar." She indicated the clothing Caroline had already gone through. "That's hers too, isn't it?"

"Yes, I'll ask one of the maids to launder everything and place it with the rest of her belongings."

"I think the dress will be fine if I just brush it and hang it out to air," Letty said. "I'll wash and iron the lace fichu myself because Mary has a very heavy hand. She can deal with the linens."

Caroline nodded. "Good. When you are finished you can place all the items in the cellar with Madam's other possessions."

"What's happening to her things, miss?" Letty asked. "Because my sister said that sometimes if no one claims anything the clothes can be given to the person's maid."

"We are currently hoping that a relative of Madam's might still come forward, but I'm sure Mrs. Frogerton would be willing to discuss the matter with you if nothing comes of it."

"If that's the case, she'll give them to you to sell off instead." Letty sighed.

"I wouldn't know how to do that," Caroline said. "And I wouldn't object if you were offered the items in my stead. I wasn't employed by Madam Lavinia and have no claim on her."

Letty grinned. "The butler's right about you. He says you're too high in the instep for this household and should be knocking shoulders with royalty."

"Hardly." Caroline smiled. "I need to earn my living just as you do."

"I don't think Madam's brother would want ladies' clothing, would he?" Letty pursed her lips. "Unless he has a wife."

"Madam had a brother? You didn't mention that before."

Letty shrugged as she separated the gown from the lace and the linens. "I don't think you asked me about him, miss, just about whether Madam was married."

"But did he visit her at the house?"

"I think so. You'd have to ask Mr. Murphy. As I said, Madam had so many gentlemen callers it was hard to tell them apart and I wasn't the one answering the door."

"I would really like to speak to Mr. Murphy," Caroline

murmured as she folded the brown paper and string for reusing. "It's a shame that we don't know his exact address."

Letty paused at the door. "Well, as to that, miss, he did tell me that if I needed to write, I could send a letter care of the Mermaid Inn, and it would find him."

"In Ramsgate?"

"Yes, miss. It might be where his daughter works, but I can't be certain."

"I thought you didn't know where he was at all?"

"Don't have to tell the peelers everything." Letty winked as she went out of the door. "Specially that stuck up Sergeant Dawson."

Caroline made sure that the jewelry was safely in her pocket, spoke briefly to the housekeeper, and went up the stairs to the drawing room where her employer was reading the newspaper.

"Any luck?" Mrs. Frogerton inquired as she lowered the paper.

"Yes, indeed." Caroline took out the key and Madam's rings. "And Letty not only told me that she thought Madam had a brother, but that he might have visited her at home."

"Why on earth didn't she mention that earlier?"

"Because apparently I didn't ask her for that specific piece of information."

Mrs. Frogerton sighed.

"She also says that the best person to ask about Madam's supposed brother would be Mr. Murphy," Caroline continued.

"Who is currently living at an unknown address in Ramsgate."

"Not quite so unknown." Caroline allowed herself a small smile. "Letty also forgot to mention to Sergeant Dawson that Mr. Murphy said she could write to him care of the Mermaid Inn."

"Then we must do so immediately!" Mrs. Frogerton

clapped her hands. "In fact, I might simply send my carriage down to Ramsgate to collect the dratted man and bring him back here to answer a few questions."

"He might not wish to be found, ma'am. He could still be the murderer," Caroline reminded her employer.

"You think we should send Sergeant Dawson?" Mrs. Frogerton snorted. "It would be better to go ourselves. We could go right now and be back tomorrow afternoon."

"We are supposed to be attending the Lingard ball tomorrow evening, ma'am. Dorothy thinks Viscount Lingard might propose to her at the event."

"I still don't think she'll accept him."

"If he publicly proposes and she turns him down at his mother's ball, I suspect that would be the end of it."

"Then we really have to be there, don't we?" Mrs. Frogerton said. "I did come to London specifically to give Dotty her Season and I can't go back on that."

"We can always go and fetch Mr. Murphy next week, ma'am," Caroline said encouragingly.

"If Sergeant Dawson hasn't succeeded in placing all the blame on Dr. Harris and sending him to trial."

Mrs. Frogerton looked so downcast that Caroline hastened to lighten her mood.

"We do have the key to Madam's strongbox, ma'am. Perhaps that will make any visit to Mr. Murphy unnecessary."

"I suppose it might." Mrs. Frogerton looked expectantly at Caroline. "Where did you put the strongbox?"

Caroline paused. "The last time I saw it, ma'am, it was pushed under your chair. I assumed you got one of the footmen to put it in a more secure place."

Mrs. Frogerton stood and immediately peered under her chair. "I didn't order anyone to move it anywhere. I thought you had."

"In truth, I'd forgotten all about it," Caroline said as she dropped to her knees and made certain that the box hadn't ended up being pushed to the back wall. Madam's dogs were very interested in her efforts, and she received several unwanted licks to her nose and cheeks as they milled around her.

"I'll ring for the butler." Mrs. Frogerton vigorously pulled the cord and the butler appeared within minutes.

"Yes, ma'am?"

"The strongbox that was under my chair?"

His brows creased. "I was not aware that there was one, ma'am."

"Then you didn't move it or get one of your staff to do so?"

"Not to my knowledge." The butler bowed. "I'll consult with the housekeeper and see if I can find out what became of it."

He exited the room leaving Mrs. Frogerton and Caroline staring at each other.

"How could we have forgotten about it?" Mrs. Frogerton shook her head. "We are a pair of fools!"

"We were distracted by the arrival of Lady Fielding in hysterics," Caroline said. "But I should have been more careful."

"I wonder where it went?" Mrs. Frogerton sank into her chair again. "The house was full of people that day and ever since! Anyone could have taken it."

"Including Dr. Harris, Lady Fielding, and the DeBlooms."

"Both of the DeBlooms were in this room alone," Mrs. Frogerton said. "And Lady Fielding could have sneaked down and removed it at any time during her stay."

"Dr. Harris has been here, too," Caroline said. "And Letty wouldn't be averse to feathering her own nest. She's already got an eye on Madam Lavinia's clothing."

"Then we truly are sunk," Mrs. Frogerton said. "We have Madam's key and no bloody strongbox to unlock!"

Chapter 20

By the next morning it had become clear that the strongbox was missing and that no one had noticed anyone smuggling it out of the house. The original key Madam had given Dr. Harris had also disappeared. Mrs. Frogerton thought it might still have been in the lock when she pushed the box under her chair. She'd begged Caroline to keep the second key safe on her person. Caroline placed the key on its long chain around her neck just as Madam Lavinia had done.

Despite the disappearance of the strongbox there were plenty of other matters to deal with. Dorothy had risen early and was currently driving her mother to distraction with her inability to settle to anything and her refusal to discuss the upcoming Lingard ball. Caroline had left them bickering over the breakfast table and gone down to the library to sort out the morning's post.

There were invitations galore, business letters for Mrs. Frogerton, a parcel of newly published gothic novels from A. K. Newman & Co., and a reply from Mrs. O'Leary. Intrigued as to the connection between the supposedly French Madam Lavinia and an Irish woman, Caroline opened the letter and began to read.

Dear Miss Morton, thank you for your letter and your condolences over the death of my cousin Martha, known to you as Madam Lavinia. We grew up together in Dublin and I have very fond memories of her. I only knew her "other" name because when I was moving to London, I visited her unexpectedly and discovered she had given up on propriety and gone on the stage. She begged me not to tell her parents or mine—a promise I kept for many years. The last time I saw Martha in person was during the Christmas festivities when she came to my house in Kew to enjoy a family dinner. She looked well and seemed happy. It was a shock to find out she had died in a newspaper advertisement rather than through family connections.

If you require proof of the connection between myself and Martha, I can bring a portrait my brother painted of us just before she left Ireland and, as we were of similar age, our baptismal certificate for the same ceremony and day.

Yours sincerely,
Mrs. Mary O'Leary

Caroline read the letter twice and then took it with the other post up to Mrs. Frogerton, who had finished her breakfast and was in the drawing room.

"Dorothy has taken the dogs for a walk."

"That was kind of her." Caroline set the invitations beside her employer.

"I told her to get out of my sight."

"She does seem slightly overwrought."

"*Slightly?*" Mrs. Frogerton raised her eyebrows. "The silly girl can't make up her mind about Viscount Lingard and it's making her extremely difficult to live with."

"I suppose it is the biggest decision of her life," Caroline said.

"And if it's making her that angry, I suspect she knows

she's making a mistake and is refusing to admit it." Mrs. Frogerton sighed. "She's as stubborn as her father. If she truly was in love and he was the right man, one might think she'd be happy!"

Caroline thought back to the magical night when Lord Francis had proposed to her, and she'd imagined her life was complete. After the scandal over her father's death, he'd broken his promises and walked away. It had taken her a long time to come to terms with his betrayal and to finally negotiate a mutually acceptable way to be behave toward each other in society.

"Dorothy is . . ."

"Stubborn and blinded by the idea of being a viscountess," Mrs. Frogerton interrupted Caroline. "And that's all there is to it."

In an effort to distract her employer from Dorothy, Caroline held out the letter.

"Mrs. O'Leary replied to my letter."

"And what did she have to say for herself?" Mrs. Frogerton put on her spectacles and read the missive through. "She sounds remarkably honest."

"That was my thought, too, ma'am." Caroline nodded. "Although I am still quite surprised that Madam was born in Ireland."

"She certainly had no trace of an accent, but Mrs. O'Leary suggests her cousin started her career on the stage. Perhaps she chose to erase that part of herself to get more work and being a French mystic was certainly more financially profitable." She folded up the letter and returned it to Caroline. "I think we should invite her to tea."

"Yes, ma'am."

"I'm very good at picking out the liars of this world and if she is trying to deceive us, I guarantee I'll know it."

Having watched her employer reduce a cheating fishmonger to tears, Caroline didn't doubt it.

"When would you like Mrs. O'Leary to come?" Caroline asked.

"Tomorrow at the earliest. I can only deal with Dotty today."

"Then I'll write to her immediately."

"Thank you, my dear, and be sure to come back quickly." Mrs. Frogerton shuddered. "I don't want to have to face my daughter alone when she's in one of her moods."

Sitting between the two warring Frogerton ladies was the last thing Caroline wanted to do, but she was employed to be useful, and she had to play her part.

"I promise I'll return as quickly as I can."

Several hours later as Caroline and Dorothy made their way up the steps of the Lingard mansion, their skirts carefully raised above the dirt on the street, Dorothy was remarkably quiet.

"I think my headdress needs repinning," Dorothy said abruptly. "Will you come and attend to it, Caroline?"

"Of course." Caroline followed Dorothy up the stairs to the ladies' receiving room while Mrs. Frogerton waited in the hall chatting animatedly to her acquaintances.

As the ball had barely begun, and no other young ladies had ripped their hems or lost their fans or pins, they were alone apart from one of the maids. Dorothy sat at the dressing table while Caroline checked the pearl and diamond hairpins used to secure her elaborate coiffure in place.

"Everything appears to be in place," Caroline said. "But I'll slide a couple of extra pins in to make quite certain everything stays put. We wouldn't want your hair coming down at this particular ball."

"Caroline, when Lord Francis asked you to marry him, how did you feel?"

"I was ecstatic." Caroline put the first pin in place. "I was desperately in love with him, and I feared he didn't feel the same."

Dorothy didn't say anything as Caroline secured the second pin, and she risked a question.

"Are you concerned that you don't feel as excited about a potential marriage proposal from Viscount Lingard as you should?"

Dorothy shrugged. "I certainly don't feel ecstatic at the prospect."

"Does it bother you that you don't?"

"We both know that love has nothing to do with the success of a society marriage. It is all about money and family alliances. I mean, look what happened to you."

"It doesn't change the fact that when Francis asked me, I loved him, and was ready to spend the rest of my life with him," Caroline said simply. "His family interfering because of my loss of social status was unfortunate."

"Yet you survived the loss of your great love." There was an edge to Dorothy's comment that spoke of her internal dilemma.

"Barely." Caroline smiled. "I suspect pride and a determination not to allow society to see me defeated was part of it. It was hard, though."

"The loss of your status or the loss of that particular gentleman?"

Caroline met Dorothy's gaze in the mirror. "Definitely the man because with the right one by your side nothing else matters." She hesitated. "Choose wisely, Dorothy. All the money and titles in the world won't matter if you end up with a gentleman who doesn't love you to distraction."

"Now you are being ridiculous." Dorothy shot to her feet. "And I haven't had a proposal yet."

"But you are expecting one."

Dorothy smoothed down her skirts and put a hand to her head to check that her hair was now secure. She was uncharacteristically nervous.

"There are ways to avoid such a proposal without giving offense until you are ready to hear it," Caroline said gently. "You're a clever woman. The Season hasn't ended yet."

Dorothy tossed her head. "I am well aware of that.

Now, are you ready to go down? My mother will be wondering what has become of us."

Caroline followed Dorothy down the stairs and wondered whether anything she'd said would have an effect. Dorothy was often unwilling to listen to advice, but she had learned to respect Caroline's knowledge and at least give her a hearing.

Mrs. Frogerton waved as she saw them descending. "Look who I bumped into!"

Caroline curtsied to the DeBloom family. Mrs. DeBloom ignored her and spoke to Dorothy, Miss DeBloom barely managed to mumble a greeting, and Mr. DeBloom took her gloved hand and brought it to his lips.

"Miss Morton. Looking beautiful as usual."

"That's because I'm wearing the same gown."

"I wish I could bedeck you in the diamonds and sapphires from my mines."

Caroline raised her eyebrows. "I prefer my mother's pearls, thank you."

"Your beauty would still outshine them."

She eased her hand free and turned to Mrs. Frogerton. "Shall we go through to the ballroom, ma'am? I suspect Viscount Lingard is anxiously awaiting Dorothy's arrival."

To her slight annoyance, Mr. DeBloom stayed at her side as they joined the procession toward the ballroom where the butler would announce their names.

"Any news on Madam Lavinia's murder, Miss Morton?"

"Not that I am aware of, sir." Caroline kept her gaze on her employer.

"Clarissa hasn't heard anything."

"I do hope she has recovered from her fall into the Serpentine."

"It was such a warm day she didn't even catch a chill." Mr. DeBloom chuckled. "She still insists she was pushed."

Caroline instantly resented his casual dismissal of his sister's distress. "Has it occurred to you that she was present on the day of a murder and might have inadvertently seen the killer?"

"You think someone tried to kill her, too?" He laughed out loud, making those around them stare at him curiously. "That's even more ridiculous than Clarissa's imaginings."

Caroline pressed her lips together and decided to ignore him. She didn't like him drawing attention to her in such company and hoped he would take the hint and go away. The line moved forward, and Miss DeBloom came to stand beside her brother, her expression unamused.

"I don't appreciate you laughing at me, Philip, and you are embarrassing Miss Morton."

"There's no need to be upset." Mr. DeBloom patted her shoulder. "I simply find the whole thing farcical."

Caroline took the opportunity to take a step back as brother and sister squared up to each other. She was rather tired of being stuck in the middle of family conflicts and for once yearned for her own family where no one had spoken to anyone except with polite coldness.

"I haven't finished speaking to you yet, Miss Morton." Mr. DeBloom carried on talking despite his sister's efforts. "Perhaps you might allow me to take you into supper?"

"I am busy assisting my employer, sir." Caroline looked past him.

"A dance then."

"I don't dance."

Miss DeBloom elbowed him in the side. "Philip! Leave her *alone*!"

To Caroline's relief, Mr. DeBloom finally took heed of his sister and turned to speak to his mother.

"What on earth is going on?" Dorothy whispered to Caroline. "Have you forgotten that this evening is supposed to be all about *me*?"

"Not at all." Caroline maintained her calm smile. "Mr. DeBloom was being remarkably annoying."

"That's because he likes you."

"Then perhaps he should attempt to behave in a more appropriate manner. Laughing at me and his sister hardly makes him look like an attractive proposition."

Mrs. Frogerton gave their names to the butler, and they were announced and went into the ballroom, which was of a decent size for a London house. Viscount Lingard immediately bounded over to greet them, his gaze on Dorothy.

"At last! I thought you'd never get here." He bowed to Dorothy. "May I have the first dance and the supper dance, Miss Frogerton?"

"Yes, of course." Dorothy smiled at him.

He offered her his arm. "Let me take you to find Mother. I know she's dying to speak to you."

Dorothy placed her gloved hand on his sleeve with a proprietary smile and walked away, leaving Mrs. Frogerton and Caroline watching after her.

"Do you think she'll take him?" Mrs. Frogerton asked.

"I don't know, ma'am." Caroline hesitated. "I suppose it will come down to whether she values status and rank over the possibility of love."

"He's not a bad man." Mrs. Frogerton looked unusually anxious.

"No, he isn't, and he does appear to care for her. I suspect she would soon learn to manage him."

"I'm sure she would, but would she be happy?" Mrs. Frogerton asked. "Septimus and I had a somewhat argumentative relationship, but we did love each other and that's what made the difference in the end."

Caroline had several opinions about that but decided it was not her place to share them with her employer. She'd adored Francis but after he'd broken off their engagement, she'd wondered whether he would ever have truly supported her against his family and what that would have done to her feelings for him if they had married.

The only person she'd ever met who had married for

love was Mrs. Frogerton and she wasn't of the social class Dorothy aspired to, but was she right? Caroline was beginning to hope so, but Dorothy might choose otherwise.

She followed Mrs. Frogerton through the crowded ballroom, avoiding acknowledging past friends and acquaintances who often did not want to be reminded of her existence.

"Miss Morton! Or should I say Lady Caroline."

She turned at the sound of her name to see Inspector Ross bowing to her. He wore a black evening coat over immaculately laundered linen and looked quite unlike his normal self.

"Good evening, Inspector." She curtsied.

"You look surprised to find me in such exulted company, but I have to confess to coming from good stock." He winked. "I understand that my nephew Augustus is an admirer of Miss Frogerton's. She's a beautiful girl."

"She would make him an admirable wife, sir," Caroline agreed.

He lowered his voice and leaned in closer. "I was planning on popping around to see Mrs. Frogerton, but as you're here, can you tell her that I'm advising Sergeant Dawson to drop the charges against Dr. Harris? Far better to attribute the crime to a deceased gentleman who cannot object, eh?"

"I'm not sure Lady Fielding would agree with you, Inspector, but I know Mrs. Frogerton will be pleased to hear that Dr. Harris is no longer a suspect."

"Lady Fielding will be on her way up north shortly to bury her dead and reunite with her parents," Inspector Ross said. "The only evidence of her son's involvement in a case of murder will remain securely in police files and no one needs to be the wiser."

He lowered his voice and leaned in closer. "I was ordered by an acquaintance of the Earl of Fortman to find a culprit quickly so that his son William's name would not come up in the press, but I'm not prepared to convict an innocent man. Sergeant Dawson was a little overzealous in following instructions and Dr. Harris suffered as a result."

"Thank you, sir." Caroline curtsied again. "Mrs. Frogerton is here if you wish to speak to her yourself?"

"I'd much rather speak to you." He cleared his throat. "I've always been an admirer of yours. I thought you and your sister deserved far better from your father and his family."

Caroline met his gaze and he smiled slightly. "Officers of the law are allowed to have opinions on other matters when they are not at work, my lady. And, as the son of a wastrel myself who preferred to make his own way in the world rather than be beholden to others, I admire the way you've come about." He bowed again. "I suspect I've embarrassed you. I do beg your pardon."

"There is nothing to forgive, sir," Caroline said.

He took her hand and kissed it. "I will call on Mrs. Frogerton after I've closed the case to give you both the good news."

"Thank you."

He nodded and walked off leaving Caroline staring after him. Someone bumped into her and apologized, and she moved through the chairs on the side of the ballroom seeking Mrs. Frogerton. The evening wasn't turning out quite how she had expected what with Mr. DeBloom being difficult and Inspector Ross . . .

"Over here, dear!" Mrs. Frogerton energetically waved her fan at Caroline, who hurried to join her. "Dorothy is opening the ball with Viscount Lingard and if that isn't a declaration of intent, I don't know what is!"

The next morning Dorothy didn't appear at the breakfast table and Mrs. Frogerton wasn't pleased.

"The least she could do is explain herself to her mother," she said as she finished her last slice of toast. "Everyone was expecting the ball to end with her accepting Viscount Lingard's proposal!"

"They did appear to be on excellent terms at the end of the evening," Caroline ventured a comment. "Perhaps they agreed to wait for a more private moment?"

"Dorothy? *Private?* She would have insisted on the most lavish and public proposal imaginable!"

Caroline had to concede that Mrs. Frogerton was right.

"I think I will go up to her bedchamber, shake her awake, and demand an explanation." Mrs. Frogerton wiped her fingers on her napkin and stood up. "I believe that after all this expense and disruption I deserve an answer."

"Mrs. O'Leary is expected soon, ma'am. Do you wish to speak to her, or shall I deal with the matter?"

"You can deal with her." Mrs. Frogerton pushed in her chair, her expression purposeful. "I need to speak to my daughter."

Grateful not to be involved in the upcoming argument, Caroline went downstairs to await the arrival of Mrs. O'Leary. She'd already unlocked the door to the cellar and had a lantern ready to carry down the steps into the gloomy darkness below.

The butler met her in the hall. "I have placed Mrs. O'Leary in the small parlor and advised the driver of her cart to drive around to the rear of the house and await her at the mews."

"Thank you."

Mrs. O'Leary was obviously confident that her mission would be successful.

Caroline went into the parlor and Mrs. O'Leary, who was examining the ornaments on the mantelpiece, almost dropped a china shepherdess with a guilty start.

"Good morning, Mrs. O'Leary. How kind of you to call," Caroline said.

"You must be Miss Morton. Pleasure to meet you." Mrs. O'Leary shook hands with a firm grip and great enthusiasm. She was a tall woman with graying hair and a decided twinkle in her eyes.

Caroline indicated that they should sit at the table beside the window.

"I have brought proof." Mrs. O'Leary opened her bag. "Here is the portrait my sister drew of Martha and me and our baptismal certificates." She placed the items on the table in front of Caroline.

Seeing the two faces side by side in the portrait only accentuated the similarities between them. Caroline hadn't really seen Madam Lavinia smile or radiate such happiness, but it was a good likeness of her and the woman sitting opposite.

"We came from a small parish and the priest liked to baptize us in batches like chicks." She smiled fondly. "And, as Martha and I were born two weeks apart, we ended up being baptized together. Her parents acted as godparents to me, and my parents did the same for her."

Caroline kept her gaze on the parchment as she ventured a question. "You mentioned in your letter that you only heard about your cousin's death through our newspaper advertisement and not from your family."

Mrs. O'Leary shifted in her seat and clasped her hands together in her lap before venturing a reply. "Yes, I did say that."

"It seems surprising that no one informed you of her death considering how close you were."

"I expected Douglas to have told me immediately," Mrs. O'Leary said. "I had some strong words to say to him when he finally responded to my messages and came to the house." She rolled up the picture and whisked the baptismal certificates away from Caroline. "But all's well now, and I'm here to set things right."

"Douglas didn't wish to claim Madam's belongings for himself?"

"Why would he want boxes of women's dresses and hats?"

Caroline met her guest's gaze. "Mrs. O'Leary, I don't believe I mentioned what we have of Madam's."

"It was just a guess." Mrs. O'Leary gave an unconvincing shrug. "What else would there be? Douglas assured me . . ."

"Douglas knows the contents of our cellar?"

"That's not what I meant." Mrs. O'Leary rose to her feet. "Oh, good Lord. I told him I was a terrible liar and that I didn't want to get involved in this."

"I assume Douglas asked you to answer the advertisement and collect Madam Lavinia's things?" Caroline asked.

"Yes, miss, although why he couldn't simply do so himself when he was the one in and out of Martha's house all the time and knew what she had, I don't know." Mrs. O'Leary looked suitably chagrined at being found out in a lie.

"And Douglas is your brother?"

"No, he's Martha's brother. He offered to give me all the gowns and hats if I retrieved her strongbox for him. He *said* he was too busy working to afford the time to come here himself."

Caroline stood too and faced an obviously anxious Mrs. O'Leary.

"I think it would be best if you returned with Douglas, don't you?"

"Yes, miss, I'm sorry, miss." Mrs. O'Leary nodded hard. "He should be here to claim what is his."

Chapter 21

After Mrs. O'Leary left, Caroline took a moment to assemble her thoughts before she went upstairs to join Mrs. Frogerton. She was just about to ascend the stairs when there was a knock at the door. The butler admitted Sergeant Dawson and Constable Rice, neither of whom looked happy.

"Good morning, gentlemen." Caroline approached them. "Have you come to see Mrs. Frogerton, or would you rather speak to me?"

"I'd like to speak to you both if you don't mind, my lady." Sergeant Dawson offered a stiff nod. "Is Mrs. Frogerton available?"

As her employer chose that moment to appear on the landing and beckon them enthusiastically from the top of the stairs, Caroline had no choice but to accompany the policemen up to the drawing room. She'd relayed to Mrs. Frogerton what Inspector Ross had told her at the ball on the previous evening and she'd been delighted. If Sergeant Dawson had come to tell them that the charges against Dr. Harris had been dropped, then the inspector had achieved his goals at some speed.

"Good morning, Sergeant Dawson, Constable Rice!" Mrs. Frogerton said. "How delightful to see you again."

"Morning, ma'am, my lady." Sergeant Dawson bowed. "I've come at the behest of Inspector Ross to inform you that the case against Dr. Harris has been closed. Mr. Lewis will be contacted by the court about the bail money."

"Well, thank goodness for that," Mrs. Frogerton said. "I knew you'd do us proud in the end, Sergeant."

"With all due respect, ma'am, I am merely obeying my superior's orders."

"I suspect you are too busy to let that worry you for too much longer," Mrs. Frogerton said briskly. "Perhaps now you'll be able to find the man who murdered Sir Alfred Fielding instead."

The look Sergeant Dawson shot Mrs. Frogerton was remarkably unfriendly.

"I'll do my job, ma'am. Don't ever doubt it."

"As you should, Sergeant, and we are all very grateful for it. Now, do you have time for some tea?"

"No, thank you, ma'am. We don't partake of refreshments during the working hours." Sergeant Dawson inclined his head. "Thank you for your time and I wish you both a good day."

He and Constable Rice left the room and Mrs. Frogerton looked at Caroline.

"Well, that is good news. I wonder whether they've bothered to inform Dr. Harris. He'll probably be the last to know, although I'm sure Mr. Lewis will write and set his mind at ease."

"I could write a note to him, ma'am, and have Vincent take it to his lodgings?"

"That's an excellent idea." Mrs. Frogerton resumed her seat. "I woke Dorothy up and demanded an explanation. She said that Viscount Lingard was going to propose to her last night, but she asked him to wait until the end of the Season so that they could both enjoy the rest of it in peace."

"That sounds like a remarkably sound strategy to me," Caroline said as she bent to pet Max the pug, who had sat on her foot. "If she chooses to accept him, she will have won this Season's marriage mart, and if she doesn't, everyone will have forgotten about it by the time things start up again."

"She said you gave her the idea." Mrs. Frogerton nodded. "Thank you."

"I merely offered the suggestion." Caroline smiled.

"And one never knows whether Dotty will accept the advice." Mrs. Frogerton sighed. "How did your conversation with Mrs. O'Leary go? Was she really Madam's cousin?"

"From the information she provided I'd say it is highly likely."

"You don't sound very convinced."

Caroline set the old pug dog on her knee and continued to stroke him. "Mrs. O'Leary said she and Madam were close both in age and in life, but no one had told her Madam had died."

"That does seem odd."

"She tried to suggest she only found out because of the newspaper advertisement but I suspect it's a little more complicated than that. After I questioned her intentions, she admitted that her cousin Douglas—Madam's brother—had asked her to retrieve Madam's possessions."

"Why couldn't the silly man come himself?"

"Mrs. O'Leary indicated that he was too busy and important to have time for such things. He promised to give her all of Madam's clothing if she secured the strongbox."

Mrs. Frogerton frowned. "How would either of them know exactly what we collected from Madam's and placed in the cellar? I didn't identify anything in the advertisement. Did you mention the specifics in your letter?"

"No, ma'am, that's exactly what I thought. I assume that Douglas was familiar with what Madam had in her house and knew what he wanted to retrieve."

"And used the lure of Madam's other possessions to persuade Mrs. O'Leary to do his dirty work for him,"

Mrs. Frogerton said. "But why go to so much trouble? Why didn't he identify himself to the police and collect her belongings in the normal way?"

They stared at each other for a long moment. Caroline was the first to speak.

"One has to assume that he didn't want anyone to know who he is. . . ."

Mrs. Frogerton nodded vigorously. "I agree."

"Or he fears that we *know* who he is and doesn't want us drawing any unpleasant conclusions."

"Mr. Murphy!" Mrs. Frogerton said in a rush. "He's Irish."

"But he came with the house," Caroline said. "Only Letty traveled with Madam from Brighton."

"That doesn't mean Madam didn't already *know* him. He might have been there to help her carry out her blackmailing schemes all along. In truth, he might have rented the house *for* her."

"But Letty said that Madam's brother came to see her occasionally, which would indicate that he and Mr. Murphy are not the same person." Caroline hastened to dampen the enthusiasm brimming in her employer's eyes. "But perhaps he has some connection with Douglas? That might explain a lot. He did leave in something of a hurry."

"I suppose it would." Mrs. Frogerton subsided in her chair. "But wouldn't it be thrilling if they *were* the same person? It happens quite a lot in my novels." She paused to take a breath. "Or perhaps they are identical twins, and one is evil and the other good?"

Caroline smiled. "Now Dr. Harris has been exonerated, do we need to concern ourselves with this matter any longer? We set out to prove Dr. Harris was innocent, and we have done so."

"I hadn't thought of it like that." Mrs. Frogerton pursed her lips. "I know you are probably right, but I am still desperate to know who *did* kill Madam Lavinia and she did ask for your help."

"She also said I would recover my fortune, and nothing has come of that, either," Caroline reminded her employer.

"That's probably because you haven't discovered the murderer yet."

"The police have decided it was the recently deceased Sir Alfred Fielding who killed Madam Lavinia and as they are the law of the land, I have to respect their decision," Caroline said.

Mrs. Frogerton raised her eyebrows. "That's not like you."

"Maybe it is because I am at a loss about how to proceed further." Caroline gazed at her employer. "Unless we can personally speak to Mr. Murphy—and why would we when this case no longer impacts Dr. Harris—then I suspect Madam's murder will remain unsolved."

"Mr. Murphy was in a prime position to poison Madam's wine. Whether he did it on his own behalf or was paid by someone else is the question." Unlike Caroline, Mrs. Frogerton obviously hadn't given up. "I still think he was in cahoots with this Douglas fellow, and they murdered her together."

"Which is still no concern of ours," Caroline said firmly. "If Mrs. O'Leary returns, I'll hand Madam's possessions over to her without another word."

"Except we don't have the strongbox," Mrs. Frogerton said.

"If she asks, we can say we have no knowledge of its whereabouts, which is the truth, and refer her to Sergeant Dawson." Caroline stood up. "Now, can I get you some tea, ma'am? I think we've had quite enough excitement for one morning."

Caroline went down to the kitchen to ask for a tray to be sent up to Mrs. Frogerton. She spent a few minutes with the housekeeper, who promised to keep the cellar door locked and under her supervision before seeking Letty in the scullery.

"Morning, Miss Morton." Letty was cleaning the silver

cutlery. "I picked out a nice dress and some jewelry for Madam, and Mrs. Jones is going to send it over to the undertaker's today."

"Thank you, Letty." Caroline paused. "I thought you might like to know that Sergeant Dawson has decided not to prosecute Dr. Harris."

"That is good news." Letty rubbed at a stubborn spot on the fork. "I never understood why the peeler went after him in the first place."

"Mrs. Frogerton is very pleased."

"Who do they think did it, then?" Letty asked.

"Sir Alfred Fielding's name has been mentioned."

"But he's dead."

"Which means he can't be prosecuted." Caroline met Letty's gaze. "Which I expect suits everyone rather well."

"Lady Fielding won't like it." Letty frowned as she examined the fork in the light for any further blemishes. "Has anyone told her?"

"I'll leave that up to Sergeant Dawson or Inspector Ross."

Lady Fielding had returned to her home on the previous day with barely a word of thanks to her hostess—her concern all for herself and her upcoming reunion with her parents.

"I'd better write to Mr. Murphy and tell him he can come back to London whenever he wants," Letty said.

"I think Mrs. Frogerton would still like to talk to him."

"Why?" Letty looked up at Caroline. "I thought you said the case was settled."

"Not according to Mrs. Frogerton and I agree with her. Blaming Sir Alfred is far too convenient for everyone."

"She should leave things alone," Letty said forcefully, her attention now on her work. "No point in meddling, if you'll beg my pardon, miss."

Caroline studied Letty's bent head. "Did you ever meet a Mrs. O'Leary at Madam's?"

"What if I did?"

"She came here to claim Madam's possessions. She said she was Madam's cousin and that they were very close."

"I might have seen her." Letty shrugged. "So what?"

"She told me that Madam's brother Douglas visited the house regularly, yet you said you hardly remembered him."

"You asked me about guests, not family," Letty said. "He didn't come in the front door like the rest of them."

"Then I assume he knew Mr. Murphy quite well, too."

Letty picked up another fork from the pile on the table and directed all her attention on cleaning it rather than looking at Caroline.

"Is there a reason why you pretended not to know Madam's brother visited her so frequently?"

There was a long silence before Letty raised her clear gaze to meet Caroline's.

"Doesn't matter now, does it? Your Dr. Harris is free, so why keep harping on?"

"Because someone murdered Madam and I don't think even you believe it was Sir Alfred Fielding," Caroline said. "Did Mr. Murphy pay you to keep quiet about what you saw on that day?"

Letty shrugged. "Mr. Murphy didn't have that kind of money."

"Then was it Douglas?"

"As I said, if we all keep our mouths shut—and that includes you and Mrs. Frogerton—we're all in the clear."

"Is he still paying you?" Caroline asked.

"That's none of your business, miss."

"It is if you are telling him what is going on in this house. Is that why you took the job?"

Letty set the fork down on the table with some force. "That's not fair. Mrs. Frogerton offered me good wages."

Caroline met Letty's defiant gaze. "I will not allow you to place Mrs. Frogerton in any danger."

"Why would I do that?" Letty smiled. "As I said, it's all over now, and there's nothing for anyone to worry about."

"I suppose that depends on whether you trust the word of a murderer," Caroline said. "Personally, I would be very wary if I had information that could implicate a man who has already killed twice."

Letty shot to her feet. "If you'll excuse me, miss. I must go and help Cook prepare lunch."

Caroline remained where she was and considered what she had learned. She had a feeling that having discovered Letty was being paid for her silence she might have blundered into something with unexpected consequences, especially if Letty chose to mention it to the man who was paying her. But even if they all kept quiet, would everything return to normal?

It certainly would make life easier, but was it right?

Caroline rose to her feet and returned to the drawing room where her employer looked up with a smile.

"There you are, Caroline. I have an appointment with my milliner at eleven. Will you order the carriage?"

"I've already done so, ma'am," Caroline said. "But there is another matter I wish to speak to you about before we leave."

"I'm all ears." Mrs. Frogerton set her book to one side.

"It's about what you said earlier about Mr. Murphy being in cahoots with Madam's brother to murder Madam."

"A silly theory perhaps."

"I'm not so sure, ma'am, and I think I know a way to find out if you are right."

Mrs. Frogerton clapped her hands together. "How exciting!"

"Or we could just leave things as they are," Caroline suggested.

"Where's the fun in that?"

"Because we are considering deliberately drawing out a murderer," Caroline reminded her employer. "That might be dangerous."

Mrs. Frogerton waved that notion aside. "If we lay our plans carefully, then what could possibly go wrong?"

After a lengthy discussion over lunch, Caroline went to the kitchen and sought out the housekeeper, who was overseeing the polishing of the silverware in the butler's pantry. Several of the kitchen staff were gathered around the table, including Letty.

"Good morning, Mrs. Jones."

"Morning, Miss Morton."

Caroline made sure to speak as clearly as possible.

"Mrs. Frogerton wanted me to let you know that if she doesn't hear back from Mrs. O'Leary by tomorrow night then she will be donating all Madam's possessions to charity."

"Good, I'd rather they weren't cluttering up my cellar," Mrs. Jones said. "Does she want me to arrange for their disposal if Mrs. O'Leary doesn't turn up?"

"As Mrs. Frogerton is unfamiliar with London's charitable institutions if you can think of an acceptable cause, that would be most welcome."

"I'll sort that out by the end of the week." Mrs. Jones nodded.

Caroline turned her attention to Letty. "If there is anything you wish to have as a keepsake of your former mistress, Letty, please let me know."

"Thank you, miss."

Caroline smiled at the housekeeper and went out to the entrance hall where Mrs. Frogerton awaited her. Dorothy appeared on the stairs and demanded to know why she had been excluded from the excursion. A lively discussion emerged as to why Dorothy needed another hat, which Caroline didn't get involved in.

"Did Letty take the bait?" her employer whispered to Caroline as they exited the house.

"I hope so."

"Then we must make sure we are ready for all eventualities," Mrs. Frogerton said as she followed Dorothy into the carriage.

Caroline wished she had her employer's confidence as she got in, closed the door, and the carriage set off. In her experience things tended to become far more complicated than anticipated and dealing with a murderer who thought they had got away with it was probably the most dangerous risk of all. . . .

Chapter 22

"I had a note from Mrs. O'Leary." Caroline brought the letter to Mrs. Frogerton.

"That was quick." Her employer read the letter. It was the following afternoon and they had just had luncheon. "She will be here with her brother at four this afternoon. How convenient."

"It's almost as if someone alerted her or Madam Lavinia's brother to the possibility of losing all of Madam's possessions, but it does confirm my theory that Letty is still being paid to be useful," Caroline remarked. "Although what they think to find I don't know."

"It is quite perplexing because one has to assume they have the strongbox." Mrs. Frogerton paused. "Oh! I wonder if it was Letty who gave that to them? She was in and out of the drawing room all the time serving tea and tending the fires."

"That's possible—or she might have hidden it somewhere in the house for Douglas to collect at his convenience."

Mrs. Frogerton nodded. "Yes, because Letty could hardly have left the house carrying a strongbox without someone noticing."

"Although we didn't ask whether she had been seen leaving with anything as we didn't think she was involved," Caroline pointed out. "Hindsight is a wonderful thing."

"It might be worth searching for the strongbox in the cellars or in Letty's room," Mrs. Frogerton suggested.

"Mrs. Jones conducts regular inspections of the servants' quarters. I'm fairly certain she would have noticed if Letty had the strongbox in her room," Caroline said. "But I will search the cellars."

Mrs. Frogerton gave a discreet yawn. "And I might take a nap before our visitors are expected to arrive. You will make sure I am awake to meet Mrs. O'Leary and the infamous Douglas, won't you?"

"Of course, ma'am."

After making sure that her employer was settled in for her nap, Caroline went down to the kitchen. The butler was sitting at the table and rose to his feet when she came in. The kitchen was relatively quiet because the Frogertons were attending a supper party at the theater and did not require dinner.

"May I help you, Miss Morton?"

"I was wondering if Letty was here."

"It's her afternoon off, miss, but she did ask permission to go down to the cellar and pick out a memento from Madam's belongings before they departed the premises."

"Then I will check the cellar. Thank you." She paused. "Mrs. Frogerton did ask you to remain here when our visitors arrive?"

"Yes, Miss Morton." The butler squared his shoulders. "I'll keep a close watch on both the front and back doors and be willing to help if necessary."

Caroline went down into the cellar and found Letty sitting with all the trunks open surrounded by Madam's possessions.

"I can't decide what I want," she said when Caroline commented on the mess. "There are lots of things I like."

"I suggest you hurry up and come to a decision," Caroline advised. "Mrs. O'Leary is arriving at four to collect Madam's possessions."

Letty sighed. "Then I'd better pick something." She frowned as Caroline moved deeper into the cellar and her voice sharpened. "What are you looking for, miss?"

"Just something Mrs. Frogerton asked me to find for her."

Caroline allowed the beam of the lantern to sweep over the orderly shelves. The housekeeper was very efficient, and Caroline doubted she would have tolerated something out of place.

"Watch out for rats," Letty called out as Caroline went deeper into the gloom. "There are some big 'uns down here."

Caroline repressed a shudder; her attention focused on the stacked shelves and the large leather trunks Mrs. Frogerton had brought from the north piled on top of each other against the far wall. She set the lantern down and touched the leather straps and facings, which were surprisingly dust free considering how long they had been in the cellar.

Was it possible that Letty or someone else had opened one of the trunks and left the strongbox inside? A sudden draft made her lantern flicker, and she turned to where Letty was sitting to discover she had gone.

She didn't have the strength to lift down the trunks on the far wall. Should she wait until Mrs. Frogerton was awake to ask whether it was worth opening them? In her opinion there was no other place in the cellar where the strongbox could be so easily concealed. But if Letty had been the one to steal the strongbox, how would she have managed to get it into the trunk without some assistance herself?

After repacking the abandoned trunks, Caroline came into the hall and discovered it was well past three o'clock and Mrs. O'Leary was expected at four. After speaking briefly to the butler, she heard the doorbell ring and answered the door in his absence to find Dr. Harris and Professor Brown.

"Good afternoon, Miss Morton." Dr. Harris had a large bouquet of flowers in his hand and a smile on his face. "We brought these for Mrs. Frogerton. Is she available?"

"She was taking a nap, but I will find out if she is awake," Caroline said, pleased to see him looking less careworn. "Come up to the drawing room and I will inquire if she is willing to see you."

She left the men in the drawing room and continued up to Mrs. Frogerton's chambers where she found her employer already awake and ready to greet her guests.

"I'll come down with you now." Mrs. Frogerton paused. "Is everything in place for Mrs. O'Leary's visit at four?"

"Yes, ma'am."

Caroline was just about to follow Mrs. Frogerton when she heard whining and scratching from behind the closed bedroom door. She opened it to discover Max had been left inside. By the time she had consoled him, Mrs. Frogerton had disappeared down the stairs.

As Caroline descended, she could hear her employer chatting animatedly to Dr. Harris in the drawing room.

Professor Brown came out of the door. "Ah! There you are, Miss Morton."

"Good afternoon, Professor."

"I brought you an advanced copy of my first article for the society."

"That's very kind of you."

"I left it on the hall table with my hat. I was just about to go and fetch it for you."

"I can do that," Caroline offered.

"Why don't we go down together, and I can bore you with all my theories before I annoy Mrs. Frogerton, who is having a lovely time with Dr. Harris," Professor Brown suggested.

"Dr. Harris has always been a favorite of hers."

"So I understand," Professor Brown said as they went down the stairs to the hall. "She's certainly stood by him."

"She is very loyal to those she cares about."

"As are you, I suspect." His smile widened. "To a fault, perhaps."

"How so?"

"Both of you are like a dog with a bone—unwilling to let anything go." He turned toward her, and she took an involuntary step back. "I wish you hadn't done that, Miss Morton."

"I wish I knew what you were talking about, sir. Now if you will excuse me—" She gasped as he caught her elbow in a hard grip. "Let me go."

"Not until we've taken a little trip down to the cellar together."

She met his amused gaze. "You're Madam's brother, Douglas."

"Got it in one, Miss Morton." He winked. "You're far too clever for your own good. Now, if you'd just be a good girl and come with me, we can sort everything out and no one will be the wiser."

She opened her mouth to shout for help, but Professor Brown was quicker. He placed his hand over her mouth and pulled her hard against his chest.

"Be quiet." She felt the prick of a knife against her throat and went still, her gaze fixed on the clock in the hall, which was moving far too slowly toward the hour.

"Thank you, Miss Morton. The last thing I want to do is ruin your exquisite face, but needs must," Professor Brown said in her ear. "We will use the servants' stairs and you will promise not to scream or attempt to warn anyone. I truly don't want to hurt you and if you do as I tell you all will be well."

Caroline wasn't sure she believed him, but she nodded, and he removed his hand. Light caught the glint of the scalpel in his right hand as he gestured for her to go ahead of him.

"After you, Miss Morton."

Caroline set off, her skirts held up in her trembling hand to avoid falling down the narrow, carpetless stairs.

"I don't understand why you didn't simply admit your relationship with Madam Lavinia and claim her body when she died." Caroline was proud of how steady her voice sounded.

"And risk being implicated in her murder? Come now, Miss Morton. Neither of us are fools."

"Yet you allowed your friend to be arrested for that murder."

"Only because I knew nothing would come of it and that even if it did, he had rich enough friends to keep him out of prison."

The contempt in his voice was obvious. Caroline reached the bottom of the stairs and turned to face him. She felt curiously calm.

"Why did you murder her?"

He raised an eyebrow. "Did I say I murdered anyone? I wasn't at her house on that fateful day, I was at work and have a ward full of witnesses to prove it."

"Then did you persuade Mrs. O'Leary or the butler to help you achieve your aims?" Caroline refused to be intimidated. "Perhaps I will ask Mrs. O'Leary when she arrives."

"Oh, she's not coming."

Caroline didn't like the way he smiled at her.

"Why not?"

"Let's just say she's been delayed and leave it at that, shall we?" He shook his head. "You have a terrible tendency to overcomplicate things."

"Perhaps that is because I like to see justice delivered to those who deserve it."

"How very admirable of you. Now come along. We don't want Mrs. Frogerton wondering where we are."

He pushed her gently toward the cellar. Caroline caught a glimpse of a startled face in the kitchen as they went past and considered shouting for help, but what good would it do?

"Take the lantern and go down the stairs. I'll be right behind you."

She descended the stairs and set the flickering light beside Madam's belongings. "Here you are, Professor. May I go now?"

"Don't be silly, Miss Morton." His dismissive gaze swept over Madam's possessions. "Where is the strongbox?"

"I don't know."

He considered her, head to one side. "I don't believe you. I know the box is here. In fact, I saw it under Mrs. Frogerton's chair and couldn't think of a way to get it without rousing everyone's suspicions. How did you get hold of it in the first place?"

Caroline decided that keeping him talking was more important than inadvertently saying the wrong thing.

"One of Madam's servants thought they'd seen her with it in her back parlor. We searched the fireplace and found it concealed within the stone."

"That was a clever hiding place. I was in that room hundreds of times and never guessed it was there. Was it Letty who told you where to look?"

"It might have been."

"She's a bright girl." He smiled. "Very helpful, too."

"So I understand, but please believe me that we no longer know where the box is. We thought you and Mrs. O'Leary had it."

"How very convenient for you." He sighed. "I don't want to hurt you, Miss Morton, but you are making everything extremely difficult."

"You can hurt me as much as you want but I still won't be able to tell you, because I assumed you had it." Caroline hesitated. "I am beginning to wonder whether Letty hid it somewhere."

"Letty would've told me that."

Caroline met his gaze. "You did say she was a very clever girl."

For the first time a flicker of doubt crossed his face, swiftly replaced by an approving smile.

"Nice try, but I'm not sure I believe you."

"We could ask Letty," Caroline offered. "It is her afternoon off, but she'll be back at six."

"I have no intention of sitting in this cellar waiting for Letty or letting you leave so that you can betray me."

"Why would I do that?" Caroline tried to look puzzled. "I have no further interest in this matter. Dr. Harris has been exonerated, and the murder has been attributed to the recently deceased Sir Alfred Fielding. If you wish to take your sister's possessions away with you, I'm not going to stop you."

"I don't want her things. I want her strongbox."

"Then I suggest you threaten Letty rather than me." Caroline allowed her gaze to shift to the pile of trunks on the far side of the cellar and linger there. "She has probably hidden the box somewhere."

Professor Brown followed her gaze. "You think she hid it in there?"

"I didn't say that, sir."

"You are a terrible liar, Miss Morton." He had the audacity to smile at her. "But if you're right I don't really care which one of you hid it as long as I get my reward." He strode toward the pile of trunks. "Stay there."

"I have no intention of going anywhere," Caroline said.

She watched as Professor Brown brought down the first trunk with little effort and unlocked it.

"Ah." He lifted out the strongbox. "What a surprise and there's a key in the lock! How kind of you."

"I believe Madam left the key for Dr. Harris."

"Did she now?" He walked over to her with the strongbox and set it beside the lantern. "And where is the other one?"

"I assume it's somewhere in Madam's belongings."

He looked over at the trunks. "Don't try and tell me that you haven't looked through everything. You're not stupid."

"I have looked, but to no avail." She paused. "I am beginning to wonder whether Letty took Madam's other key. What other reason would she have to steal the strongbox?"

She swallowed hard as Professor Brown considered her in the lamplight.

"As I keep repeating, I have no interest in this matter. Mrs. Frogerton wanted Madam's possessions to go to her family. Once I have fulfilled her wishes I am done with it." Caroline held his gaze. "Now, we should return to the drawing room, or my employer will start wondering where we are. You can wait for Letty to return at six and reclaim Madam's key from her yourself."

She held her breath as he stared at her, his expression blank. Her heart was beating so loudly she wondered if he could hear it.

They both jumped when Mrs. Frogerton's voice echoed down the stairs from the hall above.

"Caroline? Professor Brown. Where are you?"

Professor Brown sighed. "I should have known that a lady such as Mrs. Frogerton would be incapable of keeping her nose out of everyone's business."

"Then unless you intend to kill me and leave my lifeless body in the cellar, may I suggest we go to meet her?"

"And you expect me to believe you won't start screeching like a banshee the moment you see her?"

"I am not disposed to having hysterics, Professor, and in my opinion as long as Dr. Harris is cleared of all charges Mrs. Frogerton won't care about anything else."

He rubbed a hand over his bearded jaw. "You're a calm one, aren't you, Miss Morton?"

"It is something of a necessity in my current position." Caroline was glad he didn't know how much her knees were shaking beneath her skirts. "Once you speak to Letty and clear up matters between you, I'm sure things will quickly resolve themselves."

She went toward the stairs, trying not to run, sensing that if she did, Professor Brown's genial exterior would disappear to reveal the murderer within.

"Caroline!" Mrs. Frogerton appeared at the top of the cellar stairs. "What on earth are you doing down there with Professor Brown?"

"I do apologize for being absent for so long, ma'am, but Professor Brown volunteered to take down one of your old trunks from the back wall."

"That was kind of him, but why didn't you ask the butler?"

"He was out on an errand, ma'am." Caroline met Mrs. Frogerton's keen gaze as she reached the top of the stairs and nodded slightly. "Has Mrs. O'Leary arrived yet?"

"She's due any minute now."

Caroline kept walking. "I'll make sure the butler knows she is coming."

Mrs. Frogerton turned her attention to Professor Brown, blocking his view of Caroline.

"Did Caroline tell you that we are about to meet Mrs. O'Leary and her brother?"

"She did mention it, yes."

"Apparently, he is a very busy man and couldn't spare the time to pick up his own sister's effects until now, which is just as well as I was considering giving everything away to charity. . . ."

Mrs. Frogerton's voice faded as Caroline went into the kitchen where the butler was sitting at the table.

"Did you find Letty?"

"Yes, Miss Morton. She's on her way back to the house as we speak."

"And our other guest?"

"Also expected at any moment."

"Then please send them both up to the drawing room as soon as they arrive."

Caroline left the kitchen, her fingers instinctively going to the chain around her neck where the key to Madam's strongbox hung. Part of her wanted to crawl into bed, pull the covers over her head, and shiver, but she had to see the matter through and bring Professor Brown to justice.

Dr. Harris looked up as Caroline came into the drawing room. Mrs. Frogerton and Professor Brown were chatting amicably by the fire.

"You've got blood on your collar."

"Oh!" She pressed a hand to her throat where Professor Brown must have nicked her with his scalpel. "I have no idea how I did that."

Dr. Harris came closer. "It looks quite deep. Would you like me to take a look at it?"

She lowered her voice. "You would be doing me a great favor if you simply stopped talking before you draw attention to it."

His brows lowered. "What's going on?"

"Please . . ."

He sighed. "As you wish."

The clock struck four and the butler appeared with the tea. He gave Caroline a nod as he set the tray in front of Mrs. Frogerton.

"Your guests are here, ma'am."

"Oh good! Please send them up."

Moments later, Inspector Ross came into the room.

"Good afternoon, Mrs. Frogerton, Lady Caroline, Dr. Harris . . ." He paused as he turned to the professor. "I regret that I do not know your name, sir."

"This is Professor Brown. A colleague of Dr. Harris's," Mrs. Frogerton said. "Inspector Ross expressed an interest in meeting Mrs. O'Leary, and I said I was happy to help."

Caroline, who was watching Professor Brown intently, saw a flash of surprise followed by wariness on his face.

"Yes, indeed." Inspector Ross bowed. "I understand that she has evidence regarding Madam Lavinia's murder."

"I thought that was all done with," Dr. Harris said.

"So did I." Inspector Ross smiled. "But a certain young person has been very helpful, very helpful indeed."

"Who is that, Inspector?" Mrs. Frogerton asked.

"Your housemaid Letty."

Professor Brown looked toward the door and took an unobtrusive step toward it and then another one.

Mrs. Frogerton gasped. "Don't tell me she admitted to seeing the real murderer?"

"Yes, indeed. She spent her afternoon at Scotland Yard writing her confession." He turned to Caroline. "I have to give credit to Miss Morton for alerting me to the possibility that Letty held the key to the mystery."

"In truth, I have the key, but Letty had the evidence." Caroline smiled and slowly withdrew the chain hidden within her bodice. "I suspect you'll find some very interesting things within that strongbox, Inspector."

Professor Brown made a sudden lunge for the door, wrenched it open, and found himself confronting the butler and Sergeant Dawson, who immediately stepped forward and grabbed both his arms.

Inspector Ross strolled over. "Professor Douglas Brown, I am arresting you for the murders of Madam Lavinia, Sir Alfred Fielding, and Mrs. Mary O'Leary."

A stream of curses issued from the professor's mouth as he was led away. Inspector Ross turned to the assembled company.

"I must thank you all for your assistance in this matter."

"What the devil is going on?" Dr. Harris demanded. "What on earth does Brown have to do with Madam Lavinia? He was conducting a scientific study, for God's sake."

"A study where he wrote down every detail about Madam's clients and used that information to blackmail them," Caroline said.

"Why would he do that?"

"I suspect it was quite lucrative."

"Then why kill her if she was providing him with a good income?"

"I think he overreached himself," Caroline said thoughtfully. "When he went after the Honorable William Armitage, who was so outraged that he alerted the authorities."

"Which is when I became involved," Inspector Ross said. "I think Lady Caroline is correct that the last thing Madam wanted was anyone paying attention to her, but once her brother got a taste for the money, he refused to stop, and they had a falling-out."

"He certainly wasn't enamored of the English ruling classes," Dr. Harris said.

"That's probably why they argued," Mrs. Frogerton said. "She might have threatened to tell the police what her brother had done, and he decided to poison her rather than face a prison sentence."

"He said there are witnesses to prove he was on the ward all day," Caroline mentioned. "But I suspect that if you brought Mr. Murphy, Madam's butler, in for questioning, he would probably tell you exactly how Professor Brown managed to poison his sister's wine."

Mrs. Frogerton sat down and started pouring the tea. "I don't know about anyone else, but I need a restorative drink."

"I would appreciate a cup of tea, ma'am." Inspector Ross sat opposite her. "I am very curious as to how you and Lady Caroline worked out that Professor Brown was the murderer?"

"That was all Caroline's doing." Mrs. Frogerton smiled fondly at her.

"It was by a process of elimination, sir," Caroline said. "We knew there were only a certain number of people

Madam trusted. When Mrs. O'Leary suddenly appeared and confirmed that Madam's brother had been a frequent visitor to the house—something Letty had denied—things started to fall into place."

"And I suspect Letty became a little overconfident when she heard Dr. Harris had been vindicated and the blame placed on Sir Alfred," Mrs. Frogerton added. "She was the one who stole the strongbox—whether she intended to keep it or hand it over to Professor Brown I do not know."

"In her statement she said that she intended to turn it in to Sergeant Dawson as she'd begun to think Professor Brown meant to murder her, too," Inspector Ross said. "I wonder who put that notion in her head?"

Caroline smiled down at her hands.

"Well, I'm glad we got to the bottom of that." Dr. Harris cleared his throat. "Am I allowed to mention that your throat is still bleeding, Miss Morton? Or will you tell me to go to the devil as you did earlier?"

Epilogue

It was an overcast day and the group around Madam Lavinia's grave was sparse as her brother, her cousin, and her personal maid were all absent for different reasons. Dorothy had refused to attend, but Caroline and Mrs. Frogerton were present. Inspector Ross represented the Metropolitan Police and was accompanied by Madam's butler, Mr. Murphy, who had been brought to town on the inspector's orders.

The vicar had conducted an excellent service on Mrs. Frogerton's behalf and had spoken at length of Madam's kindness and charity to him and his congregation. Caroline moved closer to her employer to make sure she was protected from the light rain with the large black umbrella.

"Thank you, dear," Mrs. Frogerton murmured as the undertakers lowered the coffin into the ground. "The Pilkingtons did very well by Madam indeed."

"Yes, everything has gone off perfectly," Caroline agreed.

The first heavy sods of earth hit the top of the coffin and the vicar began his final prayer. He didn't linger in the graveyard as the rain increased in volume and invited them all back to the vicarage where Mrs. Frogerton had arranged a funeral tea.

Caroline caught Inspector Ross's eye as he waited for them at the entrance to the house.

"Thank you for coming, Inspector."

"I felt it my duty to attend." He bowed and indicated Mr. Murphy standing awkwardly by his side. "I assume you have met before?"

"Yes, indeed," Mrs. Frogerton said warmly. "How do you do, Mr. Murphy?"

"Not too well, ma'am, seeing as I am here under duress." He glowered at the inspector.

"But you will be able to provide valuable information about Madam's murder," Mrs. Frogerton said. "Did that dastardly Professor Brown order you to poison Madam's wine or did he do it himself?"

Mr. Murphy's gaze flicked to the inspector. "I didn't do nothing, ma'am, but Professor Brown did refill the decanter in Madam's study early that morning when she died. I saw him putting it on her desk."

"How convenient." Mrs. Frogerton turned to Inspector Ross. "I knew Mr. Murphy would be useful." She gestured at the door. "Shall we go inside? I would appreciate a hot cup of tea after that rain."

Inspector Ross bowed. "I regret that Mr. Murphy and I need to return to Great Scotland Yard so that we can finish up some paperwork and he can be on his way home."

"I hope you're paying for my ticket, because I don't have the means to do so," Mr. Murphy grumbled as he followed the inspector down the path to the front gate. "I didn't want to be here in the first place."

Inspector Ross winked at Caroline as he opened the gate and she turned to go into the house.

"Miss Morton."

She almost jumped as Mr. DeBloom stepped out of the shadows in the hallway.

"What on earth are you doing here?" She pressed her gloved hand to her chest. "You startled me."

"I wanted to attend the funeral, but I arrived too late

and decided to seek shelter from the rain in the vicarage. I heard that Professor Brown was arrested for Madam's murder, which was quite a surprise. Clarissa immediately claimed that he must have been the one who tried to drown her in the Serpentine."

"You did say at the time that you thought you saw Dr. Harris in the park. Perhaps Professor Brown was with him?" Caroline asked.

Mr. DeBloom smiled. "To be honest, I couldn't tell one gentleman from the other, and might have been mistaken in the first place."

Caroline didn't quite believe him and waited to see what he would say next.

"I also wanted to speak to you."

"About what exactly?" Caroline braced herself.

"Your father and my mother."

She frowned. "I don't understand."

"My mother persuaded your father to invest in a . . . scheme that didn't exist," Mr. DeBloom said.

"My father wasn't the wisest investor."

"But on this occasion, he was deliberately deceived by my mother." He met her gaze. "Despite what Clarissa might think, I am well aware of my mother's dark dealings, and I am attempting to hold her accountable and repay those who were affected by her schemes."

"That is all very well, but I don't understand what relevance it has to me." Caroline looked past his broad shoulders to the house beyond. "And I wish to rejoin Mrs. Frogerton."

"Miss Morton, Lady Caroline if I may. I wish to restore your father's money to you." Mr. DeBloom grabbed hold of her hands, his expression intent. "I cannot give you any more details at present, but I promise I will be in contact as soon as I have the funds available."

Caroline eased her hands free and took a step back. "Mr. DeBloom . . . you are not making any sense."

He grinned at her. "I will be soon." He blew her a kiss.

"Give Miss Frogerton my love and tell her mother I'll be calling on you in the very near future."

He put on his hat and went out of the front door. Caroline closed it behind him with a decided click and decided to put his astounding remarks out of her mind. If she mentioned his outpourings to Mrs. Frogerton, she would want to pursue them, and Caroline wanted none of it. She'd had her expectations raised far too often to care about Mr. De-Bloom's outlandish schemes and couldn't bear to hope again.

"Miss Morton?"

The vicar came out of the kitchen and came toward her.

"Yes?"

"I have something for you." He handed over a sealed note. "Madam gave this into my keeping a week before she died and asked me to give it to you at her funeral."

"Thank you."

The vicar smiled and went back into the drawing room leaving Caroline staring at the note addressed to her in a familiar hand. She opened it and read the scant words.

Thank you and please listen to Mr. DeBloom.

It was signed *Madam L* and dated two months before Caroline had even known Madam existed. . . .

She set the dripping umbrella in the stand, straightened her bonnet in the hall mirror, and went into the drawing room where Mrs. Frogerton was entertaining the vicar. She looked up as Caroline came toward her.

"What did Inspector Ross have to say for himself?"

"Nothing of importance, ma'am." Caroline smiled serenely at her employer. "Now, may I get you another cup of tea?"

Please turn the page for an exciting sneak peek of

the next Miss Morton Mystery,

MISS MORTON AND THE DEADLY INHERITANCE,

coming soon wherever print and ebooks are sold!

Chapter 1

❧❀❧

London 1838

Miss Caroline Morton picked up the morning post from the silver tray placed beside her plate by the butler and began to sort the correspondence. It was a bright, cheerful morning and Caroline was alone in the breakfast parlor of the rented house on Half Moon Street. Her employer, Mrs. Frogerton, and her daughter, Dorothy, slept on after a late night at a society ball where Dorothy had danced the night away.

Having been in attendance but not dancing, Caroline had hardly exerted herself, and had risen at her usual time to start the day. The Season was drawing to a close. Caroline would soon need to decide whether to remain in Mrs. Frogerton's employ or seek another position as a companion in London.

Her employer had strongly indicated that even if Dorothy chose to marry at the end of the season, Caroline would be more than welcome to accompany Mrs. Frogerton back up north. Despite her initial trepidation in taking a paid position after being left penniless by her feckless father, Caroline had come to admire Mrs. Frogerton. She treated Caroline like a daughter and had already supported her through several trying events, including a family murder.

Caroline set the stack of invitations to one side and considered the rest of the post. There were two letters for her, including one from her sister Susan who was now at school in Kent. Susan still hadn't forgiven Caroline for sending her away to school and her letters tended to be stilted, short, and remarkably accusatory. According to Susan every ill in the world, including the weather, the unfairness of her French teacher, and her lack of fashionable new dresses was somehow Caroline's fault.

Caroline put the letter in her pocket. It was a pleasant day, and she was looking forward to visiting Hyde Park and strolling along the paths with Mrs. Frogerton and her dogs. Reading Susan's new list of grievances would depress her spirits, especially when she didn't have the power or necessary finances to change anything. Mrs. Frogerton had generously paid Susan's fees, and Caroline was very careful not to expose her employer to Susan's complaints.

Her hand stilled over her pocket. She'd asked Susan if she wished to accompany her to their recently deceased aunt's funeral at Greenwood Hall. They were supposed to be leaving in two days. She should open the letter to see if Susan wanted to come. With a resigned sigh she took the letter out, unfolded it, and began to read. It did not take long.

> *Dear Caroline,*
> *I do not wish to accompany you anywhere. If you hadn't meddled, I would have stayed with Cousin Mabel, and not been forced to attend this horrible school. Please send my condolences to my cousins.*
> *Susan*

Caroline put the letter away. Susan had spent most of her childhood at Greenwood Hall under the care of Aunt Eleanor. Caroline was disappointed she couldn't bring herself to attend the funeral in person. It was all well and good for Susan to resent Caroline's part in the recent ructions within their family, but to refuse to mourn the dead? Caroline found that hard to accept.

"Whatever is the matter, lass? You look like someone murdered your favorite pet."

Mrs. Frogerton came into the breakfast room. She was already fully dressed in a crimson silk gown with blond lace trimmings and a matching cap. Her dogs milled around her with great enthusiasm as she settled into the chair opposite Caroline, her lively face aglow with interest.

Caroline fought a sigh. "Susan does not wish to accompany me to Aunt Eleanor's funeral."

"Well, there's no surprise in that, surely? Your sister hasn't forgiven you for taking her away from Greenwood Hall and sending her to school." Mrs. Frogerton paused to allow the butler to set a pot of coffee at her elbow. "For what it's worth, my dear, I still think you did the right thing."

"Hopefully one day Susan will realize that for herself." Caroline rose to her feet. "May I get you a plate of food, ma'am? There are some very nice coddled eggs and mushrooms."

"That sounds delightful." Mrs. Frogerton helped herself to some coffee. "And look on the bright side. If Susan doesn't come with us, we'll have more space in the carriage on the journey into Norfolk."

Caroline set the plate in front of her employer. "I don't expect you to accompany me, ma'am. I have enough money saved for the mail coach."

"As if I'd let you go to that place alone." Mrs. Frogerton frowned at her. "As a previous guest of the house I do feel some obligation to honor your aunt's passing. I have already ordered the carriage for tomorrow morning at eight. I must warn you that I have no intention of staying at Greenwood Hall. If we are unable to complete the journey back to London after the ceremony, we will stay at one of the local inns and resume our travels the following morning."

"I have no particular desire to linger there myself, ma'am." Caroline repressed a shudder. "As my aunt was a practical woman, I suspect her funeral arrangements will be relatively straightforward."

"I agree, and your cousin Nicholas doesn't seem the type to go for an elaborate funeral repast," Mrs. Frogerton said. "He doesn't have a wife to organize such things or the staff to carry it off." She ate some of the egg and beamed at Caroline. "This is very good indeed! Do I detect a hint of mustard in there?"

"I'll ask Cook. She'll be delighted that you approve." Caroline passed the two piles of correspondence over to Mrs. Frogerton. "Your business and personal correspondence are on the left, and the invitations on the right."

Mrs. Frogerton gave a theatrical groan. "Perhaps you could consult with Dorothy as to the invitations? I must confess that I am eager to return home and never attend another society ball in my life."

"You don't mean that, ma'am. You are a much-liked guest."

"Only for my money," her employer said. "Don't forget that."

"And for yourself. Many people find you . . . refreshing."

"As in loud-mouthed and too honest?"

"An original," Caroline said firmly and took the pile of invitations back. "I will speak to Dorothy when she comes down. She has developed decided preferences as to which events she wants to attend, which makes my job much easier."

When Dorothy had first entered society, Caroline had guided her as to which balls would be advantageous to attend in her quest to marry into the peerage. As she had recently secured the affections of a viscount, she no longer needed to be seen at all the events and, much to her

mother's relief, had scaled down her social activities considerably.

"I'm looking forward to a much quieter month," Mrs.
Frogerton said as she sipped her coffee. "Between all Dorothy's goings-on and that business with Madam Lavinia I
am quite done in."

"I agree, ma'am." Caroline turned her attention to the
second letter she had received in the post. It was from a
very respectable address near Grays Inn. She opened the
letter and read the contents.

> Dear Lady Caroline,
> Regarding your late father, the Earl of Morton's will.
> Please reply to this missive and let me know when it
> will be convenient for me to call on you.
> Yours sincerely,
> Mr. Jeremy Smith
> Smith, Smith, Potkins and Jones solicitors

Caroline repressed a sigh.

"Don't tell me you have more bad news, lass?" Mrs.
Frogerton asked.

"It's not bad news, ma'am, but it is rather tiresome. My
father's solicitors wish to speak to me about his will and I
cannot imagine why." She paused. "Unless they have discovered more of his debts and expect me to pay them off."

"I don't think that would be legal," Mrs. Frogerton
said. "It is one of the rare instances when being female
protects you from a gentleman's mistakes."

"From his gentlemanly debts of 'honor,'" Caroline murmured. "I can't even imagine how much money he let flow
through his fingers gambling and speculating."

"Enough to bankrupt his own estate and steal his children's inheritance without shame." Mrs. Frogerton rarely
minced words and her disdain for what Caroline's father
had done to his fortune and his family had no bounds.

"One might think he would've stopped there, but apparently not."

'The solicitor didn't specify, but it can't be good news." Caroline ripped the letter in half, took it over to the fireplace, and threw it onto the coals where it burned brightly for a moment before turning to ash. "If it is important, I'm sure he will write to me again."

"That's the spirit, lass," Mrs. Frogerton said. "No need to court trouble." She dropped her toast crusts onto the carpet for her dogs, who gobbled them up in an instant. "If he becomes impertinent let me know, and I'll set my Mr. Lewis on him."

Having witnessed Mr. Lewis deal with the higher-up ranks of the Metropolitan Police and emerge victorious, Caroline was certain Mrs. Frogerton was correct. It was also comforting to know Mrs. Frogerton would use her wealth and power to support her employee.

"Speaking of the Metropolitan Police, have you heard from Inspector Ross?" Mrs. Frogerton asked.

"Why ever would you think he had time to bother with me, ma'am?" Caroline avoided her employer's bright gaze and busied herself resorting the invitations.

"We both know why, miss." Mrs. Frogerton paused. "He is from a very good family."

"Then he certainly wouldn't want to have anything to do with me," Caroline countered. "My father shamed us all."

"Inspector Ross doesn't seem to think so," Mrs. Frogerton said. "And what about Mr. DeBloom? I saw him skulking around at that funeral we attended recently."

Caroline reminded herself that very little escaped her employer's eye.

"I have quite enough to do without concerning myself as to their whereabouts," Caroline said briskly. "If they wish to pay their respects to you, or Dorothy, ma'am, I will of course be in attendance."

"I don't think either of those gentlemen wish to speak to me, dear. Between them and our dear Dr. Harris, you are quite the belle of your own ball."

Caroline met her employer's amused gaze. "I . . . truly do not want any attention. I am quite happy as I am."

"You don't want to be a wife and a mother?"

"I always assumed that would be my destiny, but my circumstances have changed considerably. I try not to think in those terms."

Mrs. Frogerton reached across the table and patted her hand. "You'll come about, lass. I'm sure of it. Some young gentleman will make you forget all about your circumstances, sweep you off your feet, and that will be that."

"I suppose one can always dream, ma'am." Caroline smiled. "But I can assure you that I am fully committed to ensuring that Dorothy marries well, and that you are able to return home in triumph."

"Now that is a worthy goal, indeed," Mrs. Frogerton said. "Shall we finish our breakfast and get ready for our walk? I believe it is going to be a very nice day."

Visit our website at
KensingtonBooks.com
to sign up for our newsletters, read
more from your favorite authors, see
books by series, view reading group
guides, and more!

BOOK **CLUB**
BETWEEN THE **CHAPTERS**

Become a Part of Our
Between the Chapters Book Club
Community and Join the Conversation

Betweenthechapters.net